Captain Gallant's mask was off,

and so was the powdered wig he wore over his own fair hair as part of his disguise. Now the perilous secret was Christina's, whether he would or no. He looked up at her and found that she was gravely regarding him.

"I do not need to tell you that your secret is safe in my keeping," Christina said, as though reading his thoughts.

"It is a secret which could bring you into danger," Adrian said wearily, "and God knows I never wished that. I did not mean for you to know."

"I would never betray you, never! I would sooner die!"

He was silent again for a space, and then he took her hand and lifted it to his lips. "Captain Gallant's life lies here," he said quietly, looking down at the slender fingers, "and Adrian Clare is very content that it should be so."

was Marcus Westlake's eldest brother, and when he died,

Captain Gallant

SYLVIA THORPE

A FAWCETT CREST BOOK

Fawcett Publications, Inc., Greenwich, Connecticut

CAPTAIN GALLANT

THIS BOOK CONTAINS THE COMPLETE TEXT OF THE
ORIGINAL HARDCOVER EDITION

A Fawcett Crest Book reprinted by arrangement with Hurst &
Blackett Limited

Printed in the United States of America

First printing: February 1976

1 2 3 4 5 6 7 8 9 10

1

The Benighted Travellers

The wind had been rising steadily since noon, and now at nightfall had become a gale shrieking out of the east, bringing with it an icy, pitiless rain. Captain Adrian Clare, his gloved fingers clumsy with cold on his horse's bridle, bowed his head against the fury of it and reflected ruefully that five years of soft living had left him ill prepared for conditions such as these. A soldier of his experience should not be so acutely conscious of his own discomfort; nor should he have forsaken a busy and well-marked highway to strike off across unknown country merely to gratify a sentimental whim.

He hunched his shoulders under his sodden cloak, and swore softly as another vicious flurry of raindrops beat against his face. He and his servant, Titus, now following stoically at his heels, were unquestionably lost, and yet to turn back would be futile, for darkness was almost upon them and it was half an hour and more since they had seen any sign of human habitation.

The horses' hoofs sank with a squelching sound into the mud as they plodded wearily along a track, scarcely discernible in the gloom, which was curving now to plunge into the depths of the woodland which it had been skirting for the past half-mile. Beneath the trees the darkness was almost impenetrable, though the yet leafless branches offered little protection from the rain, and it was impossible to guess how far the woods might stretch. From what he had seen of the country-side before the dusk swallowed it up, Captain Clare was inclined to think them extensive, and contemplated with disgust the prospect of a night spent in such inhospitable surroundings.

Suddenly his horse lifted its head and pricked its ears,

and a moment later uttered a piercing whinny. Adrian
drew rein, listening intently, and presently, above the
howling of the wind and the dismal pattering of rain in
the undergrowth, he heard another horse give answer. The
servant edged his mount alongside him on the narrow
track, and they both sat staring into the darkness.

"Somewhere ahead, I think," Adrian said at length.
"What say you?"

"To my mind, sir, 'twas somewhat to our right," Titus
responded doubtfully, "but with this wind blowing 'tis
hard to be certain."

Adrian leaned forward, peering into the gloom ahead.

"The track appears to bear to the right," he said after
a moment. "Forward, then, but have your pistol to hand."

As he spoke he drew and cocked one of his own
weapons, for in an age when every road in England was
the hunting-ground of highwayman and footpad, no
traveller ventured upon even the shortest journey without
being adequately armed. They moved forward again, Titus
following close at his master's heels, and both straining
their eyes in an attempt to pierce the darkness. As Adrian
had said, the track led them to the right, and at length
a shadow moved in the shadows beneath the trees to
betray the presence of the animal they had heard. Adrian
halted again and spoke a sharp challenge.

"Who is there? We are honest travellers and if you are
likewise you have naught to fear, but we are armed and
ready to defend ourselves if need be."

There was no reply. The wind shook the branches and
great drops of water showered down from them, but no
other sound disturbed the silence. Adrian repeated his
challenge, but when there was still no reply, urged his
mount forward again.

"Why, the confounded brute is riderless!" he exclaimed
in astonishment. "Now what the devil does that portend?"

He reached the horse, which was standing patiently by
the side of the track, and leaned over to gather up the
trailing reins. Suddenly Titus gripped him by the arm.

"Captain!" he said urgently. "Did you hear aught?"

Adrian shook his head, and for several endless seconds

they waited for some fresh sound. At last it came, faint but unmistakable from the bushes bordering the path, the groan of a man in pain.

Adrian restored his pistol to its place and dismounted, handing the reins of both horses to Titus. He thrust his way into the undergrowth, and then the ground seemed to give way beneath him as he pitched headlong down the steep bank which it had concealed.

It was a drop of three or four feet. The Captain picked himself up, unhurt, but smothered in mud and swearing emphatically, a sound which reassured the anxious Titus on the path above. The groan sounded again, more distinctly, and Adrian, groping cautiously towards it through the dripping undergrowth, stumbled a moment later upon a recumbent figure.

It was too dark to see anything more than that the man was of medium height and build, but when Adrian tried to raise him he groaned again. The Captain stripped off his gloves and sought to discover by touch the nature of the injury, and on the upper half of the man's body his fingers encountered a wetness not of the rain, a warm and sticky wetness only too familiar to a soldier who had known more than one battlefield. He shouted to Titus, and the servant came scrambling down the bank with the flask of brandy from his master's saddle-bag.

Between them they managed to get a little of the spirit down the man's throat and it seemed to revive him, for he shifted his position, groaned again, and then spoke haltingly.

"Pistol-ball . . . left shoulder. Horse slipped . . . pitched me down the bank."

"Easy, my friend, easy," Adrian said reassuringly. "You need to husband your strength. Be still until we have staunched that wound."

Titus was already busy about that task, working with the brisk efficiency of the veteran soldier he was. With Adrian's help he contrived to get a rough bandage on the injured shoulder, though since they were obliged to work entirely by touch they could not be wholly certain of its efficacy.

"Confound this infernal darkness!" Adrian exclaimed. "That will have to serve for the present, until we can bring him to light and shelter."

"Aye, sir, but how soon may that be?" Titus inquired practically. "We've not seen so much as a barn this half-hour past."

"Perhaps the poor devil himself has some notion of our whereabouts," Adrian replied. "Give him another sup of brandy, and he may be able to tell us where we can find aid for him, and shelter for ourselves."

The servant obeyed, and when the injured man had swallowed another mouthful of the brandy, Adrian, supporting him against his knee, said briskly:

"Listen to me, my friend! We are strangers, and lost in these accursed woods, but if you know of any shelter close at hand, tell us how we may bring you to it."

The man made a feeble movement as though to signify his understanding, and after a moment or two in which he seemed to be gathering his strength, said faintly:

"My home . . . not far. Mount me again on the mare . . . she will make her own way home . . . once I am in the saddle."

This suggestion was with some difficulty carried out, for in the rain and the darkness it was no easy task to get the wounded man on to the path again, and thence to the back of his mount. It was accomplished at last, and at a gasped command from her master the mare moved forward along the track, Adrian on foot beside her to support her rider in the saddle, and Titus riding behind, leading the captain's horse.

How far they travelled in this fashion, or for how long a time, neither Adrian nor Titus could tell. The night had closed in upon them, the rain continued to fall with unabated violence, and nothing could be seen save the wind-lashed trees against the lesser darkness of the sky. The track grew worse, dwindling until they could barely force their way along it, and sloping so steeply downwards that Titus was obliged to dismount and lead the horses. Adrian began to wonder whether the wounded man's faith in the intelligence of his mount was misplaced, and was about to question him again when the mare halted, and the Captain, peering about him, was able to make out the bulk of some small building, the line of its sagging roof looming solidly against a background of tossing branches.

"Key . . . right-hand pocket!" The stranger had fallen forward on to his horse's neck, and the words came in a painful gasp. "Find light . . . within."

Adrian slid his hand into the pocket of his coat and pulled out a cumbersome key. There was a kerchief tangled about it, and this he thrust into his own pocket as he went groping along the side of the cottage in search of the door. He found it at last, and after some further delay succeeded in opening it, and so stepped forward out of the driving rain into warmth and shelter. The glow of embers guided him to the hearth, and showed him a candle and taper set neatly in the ingle-nook. He kindled a light, and setting it on the rough table in the middle of the room, went to help Titus with the wounded man.

They placed him in a big wooden arm-chair beside the fire, and Captain Clare studied him curiously. He appeared to be about forty years of age, with a pleasant, humorous face, now grim with pain, and dark hair somewhat grizzled at the temples. He was dressed in dark, well-worn riding-clothes with a heavy cloak over all, and nothing in his attire indicated his station in life or the trade he followed.

From that brief, comprehensive survey of his host, Adrian turned his attention to his surroundings. The cottage was obviously very old, with tiny, heavily-shuttered windows set deep in thick walls, and a low ceiling black with smoke between the massive beams which supported it. The room was neat and clean, but with an indefinable air of being completely masculine. No woman, Adrian felt sure, dwelt here.

Titus was on his knees before the fire, stirring the embers to life, adding fresh logs from those stacked by the hearth. Adrian threw aside his dripping cloak and hat and bent over the man in the chair. The rough bandages were already stained with blood, and the brown eyes which lifted to meet his bright with pain.

"We will do all we can for you now," Adrian said reassuringly, "and as soon as it is light we will see about fetching a surgeon to tend that wound."

"No!" The denial came quickly, and there seemed to be a flash of alarm in the speaker's eyes. "No surgeon . . . I'll do well enough."

"But you have a pistol-ball in your shoulder, man!" Adrian protested in astonishment. "It will need a surgeon to remove it."

"I want no damned sawbones . . . meddling with me," the other man said obstinately. "I'm grateful for your aid . . . and you're welcome to food, and shelter for the night . . . but you'll bring no surgeon here."

For a moment or two Adrian continued to regard him with a puzzled frown. The effort of argument seemed to have exhausted him, for he lay back in the chair with closed eyes, and beads of sweat on his brow, but a very stubborn expression in his face. Adrian looked at Titus, now standing on the other side of the chair.

"I dare say I could do it, sir," the servant said in answer to the unspoken question. " 'Twould not be the first time, not by a long way, and the sooner 'tis done, the better."

Adrian nodded, and since their host had sunk once more into a swoon, they set about finding for themselves such things as were needed. The only other room of the cottage, which adjoined the kitchen, proved to be a sparsely-furnished bedchamber, and to this they carried the unconscious man. For a while they were too busy to have time for reflection, but even while he assisted Titus with his makeshift surgery, Adrian was plagued by questions arising from the stranger's refusal of competent medical attention. What could be the reason behind it? Poverty, perhaps, if his home were any guide to his circumstances, and yet Captain Clare felt certain that a deeper alarm than that explanation warranted had flashed in the man's eyes at mention of a surgeon.

The thought was still puzzling him when, the wounded man having been made as comfortable as possible in his own bed, Adrian left Titus to find and prepare whatever food the cottage could supply, while he took a lantern from the kitchen and went out again into the streaming darkness to discover what accommodation there might be for the horses. A rough lean-to at the rear of the house appeared to be the only stable, but it was well supplied with fodder and large enough to accept all three animals. The mare belonging to the injured man was an exceptionally fine beast which would have looked more at home in a gentleman's stable than a cottager's shed, and Adrian was conscious once more of a sense of incongruity, and a suspicion too nebulous as yet to be defined.

When he returned to the cottage the fire was blazing merrily and a simple meal of bread and cold meat and ale set out upon the table. Adrian sat down with a sigh of relief and allowed Titus to pull off his muddy boots; his coat, too, was damp and mudstained from his fall, and he stripped that off also and watched the servant hang it carefully by the fire to dry.

"What of our host, Titus?" he said abruptly. "Will your efforts suffice, do you think?"

"I trust so, sir," Titus replied placidly. "Fortunately no vital spot was touched, and now that the bullet is out the wound should heal well enough. There may be some fever, but I don't doubt he has the strength to withstand it. He is one of your tough, wiry fellows, able to stand any number of hard knocks."

"Yes, I have seen the type before." Adrian pulled his chair up to the table and prepared to begin his meal, but paused to wave his servant to a seat. "Oh, sit down, man, sit down! This is no time for ceremony."

Titus bowed, and seated himself with unruffled calm, while Adrian regarded him with affectionate amusement. They had been through a good deal together during the eight years of their acquaintance, for Titus had served him for the last three years of his military career, and by the time Captain Clare left the army he valued the man so highly that he had brought him out also in order that they might not be separated. Nor was the bond between them by any means one-sided. Titus would willingly have laid down his life for his master, who in his eyes could do no wrong.

Such devotion and loyalty were not altogether surprising, for Adrian Clare was a man who by his very nature inspired affection. Reckless, headstrong, and generous to a fault, he was invariably ready to espouse forlorn causes or champion those unable to fend for themselves, and though these traits had won him innumerable friends, they were also partly to blame for the plight in which he now found himself. Captain Adrian Clare was a ruined man.

His fortune had never been large. The younger son of an Oxfordshire squire, he had entered the army at the age of eighteen with a commission purchased for him by his maternal great-uncle, the Marquis of Warham. His lordship had been a soldier himself until the loss of a leg at Blenheim forced him to leave the army, and it was his abiding sorrow that his only son was of too delicate a constitution to follow in his footsteps. Further disappointment awaited him in his two grandsons, who preferred the world of fashion to professional soldiering, and so he turned the more eagerly to the young grandnephew who was willing enough to carry on the family's military tradition.

As a soldier Adrian had prospered, as much by his own ability as Lord Warham's influence, and between the one and the other might well have had a highly successful career had it not been for the waywardness which was his besetting sin. Having acquitted himself well in the fighting in Flanders, he was sent back to England to recover from a wound sustained at Fontenoy, and before rejoining his regiment felt it to be his duty to pay a visit to his kinsman and benefactor, who chanced at that time to be taking the waters at Tunbridge Wells.

The old Marquis received him with pleasure, insisting that he remain for a while as his guest, and thus unwittingly paving the way for the destruction of his own hopes, for it was during that visit to the Wells that Adrian met Miss Helen Thurston. The young lady, a golden-haired, creamy-skinned beauty of nineteen, was visiting the fashionable spa with her godmother, and Adrian no sooner saw her than he fell head-long in love with her. Nor was his passion unrequited. Miss Thurston's suitors were many, but it was not long before Adrian was the most favoured, and they were to be seen everywhere together, walking on the Pantiles, dancing at the assemblies, or exploring the pleasant country around the Wells.

They made a striking couple, that tall, golden girl with the figure and carriage of a goddess, and the handsome young officer in his scarlet regimentals, but disillusion was in store for Captain Clare. Helen was willing enough to have him for her gallant, to grant him more of her company than any other man enjoyed, even to admit that she returned his affection, but marriage was a very different matter. She had extravagant tastes and no fortune to match them, and the prospect of becoming the wife of a young man who had very little besides his army pay appealed to her not at all. Adrian pleaded and demanded in vain, and was obliged at last to return to his regiment with the bitter knowledge that unless a miracle occurred he had no hope of attaining his heart's desire.

He was soon to find in action an antidote for his hurt. It was the summer of 1745, and rebellion blazed suddenly out of the north as the Highland clans raised the banner of an exiled dynasty and sought to sweep the Hanoverian king from the throne. It was an attempt foredoomed to failure, but there was fighting and to spare before all was done, and Adrian, his wound of Fontenoy healed but the other, deeper wound a constant torment, was glad to find himself in the thick of it. Once more he bore himself with credit, and he was still in Scotland when word reached him that his elder brother was suddenly dead, and himself master of the pleasant Oxfordshire estate.

His reaction, once the first shock of the news had passed, was typical of the man. Helen had refused to marry a soldier, but a landowner with a comfortable competence was a different matter, and without pausing to consider either the fact that more than a year had passed since their parting, or that his actions were bound to enrage his uncle the Marquis, Adrian lost no time in selling out of the army and returning to England to claim his inheritance and his bride.

Although every inclination prompted him to ride straight to Helen, he deemed it prudent to restrain his impatience long enough to visit his home, and there he received her answer to the letter he had written to her before leaving Scotland. It was an answer which for the second time, and this time irretrievably, shattered all his hopes. Couched in coldly formal terms which made a mockery of those shared weeks at Tunbridge Wells, it informed him that three months earlier she had become the wife of Mr. Marcus Westlake of Coombe Royal in Wiltshire, and that though she would always remember Captain Clare with kindness, it was not to be thought of that they should ever meet again.

That was five years ago, and in that short period of time Adrian had contrived to run through his entire patrimony. Having abandoned his military career, and with no taste now for the duties of a country squire, he had turned to London in search of distraction. Lord Warham, with an anger born of bitter disappointment, refused to acknowledge his existence, but his lordship's grandchildren hailed their cousin's arrival with delight. Kinship with them opened the doors of polite society to Captain Clare, and his own qualities made him popular wherever he went, so that before long he found himself caught up in the endless, frivolous round of sport and pleasure that filled the days and nights of a man of fashion.

It was an age of great wealth and great extravagance, and though well aware that he was living far beyond his means, Adrian deliberately ignored the fact, and laughed to scorn the dire prophecies of his harassed man of business. Inclined by temperament to live only for the present, he seemed possessed now by a veritable demon of recklessness; no extravagance was too wild for him, no tale of misfortune too improbable, no cause so hopeless that he would refuse it his support. Money flowed through his hands as though he had the revenues of a dukedom at his command.

Inevitably the time came when, with his resources entirely at an end, he found himself in debt on every hand. Many of his so-called friends melted away as soon as his situation became known, and though there were as many more who would gladly have come to his assistance, he resolutely refused all offers of aid. Finally, when he had reached the stage of wondering whether to blow his brains out or to leave the country and try to sell his military training in some foreign land, help came from an unexpected quarter. Lord Warham, urged thereto by his grandchildren, deigned to become aware once more of his young kinsman, and agreed to pay Adrian's debts on condition that he left England for good. A junior branch of the family had settled in Virginia, and thither Captain Clare must go, to make what he chose of a future in which his lordship had no interest whatsoever.

Reluctantly, and because the alternatives to this ultimatum were even more disagreeable, Adrian agreed, and now, in this first week of March, with his affairs once more in order, he was on his way to Bristol to join the ship which was to carry him to America. His baggage had been sent on ahead by the carrier's wagon, for Adrian, with the faithful Titus in attendance, had chosen to make the journey on horseback in preference to the slow, uncomfortable stage-coach, though not even the servant was aware of the true reason behind that decision. Captain Clare would obey his uncle's commands, but first, come what might, he would see his lost love again.

Just what he hoped to achieve by such a meeting even Adrian himself was not certain, and that he was behaving like a fool he knew, but he knew also that it was unthinkable to leave England for ever without seeing her just once more. There had been other women in his life, both before Helen and since; he had loved them lightly and let them go without a pang, and now was hard put to it to remember them. Helen he had never forgotten. Her image was as clear in his memory now as it had been when they said farewell nearly seven years ago.

So at Marlborough he had turned aside from the busy Bath road they had followed from London and plunged into the wooded Wiltshire countryside in search of Marcus Westlake's house of Coombe Royal. Titus, following him with deepening bewilderment, was not in the least surprised when they lost their way, and now that they had so providentially been granted a night's shelter, could only hope that by morning the Captain would have abandoned whatever fool's errand he had set out upon.

When they had appeased their hunger, and the remains of the meal had been cleared away, Titus went quietly into the inner room to see how the injured man was faring. He returned with the information that the sufferer had fallen asleep, and appeared to be as comfortable as any man in his situation could expect to be.

"Though he'll need someone to care for him, sir, when we have gone," he added reflectively. "He'll not be fit to fend for himself for a few days."

"I know," Adrian agreed. "We must see to that before we go on our way. He must have kinsfolk or friends to call upon at need."

Titus pursed his lips.

"To my mind, Captain, there's something plaguey queer about the fellow," he said. "Why was he so set against us fetching a surgeon to him? Downright scared, he seemed to me."

Adrian nodded.

"Nor is that the only strange thing, Titus. Consider, for instance, the style and position of this cottage, for who, save perhaps a gamekeeper, would live in so god-forsaken a spot? And our friend yonder has not the look of a keeper." He got up as he spoke, and thrust his hand into the pocket of his coat in search of his snuff-box. "A gamekeeper, moreover, does not usually own a thoroughbred mare."

He broke off abruptly, for in extracting the snuff-box he had pulled out also a piece of black material which was certainly not his property. For a moment he stared blankly at it, before remembering that it had come, with the key of the cottage, from the stranger's pocket. He shook it out, and stood staring at it in silence for so long that Titus said sharply:

"What is it, Captain? What's amiss?"

Very slowly Adrian turned to face him, holding up the object he had found, which, thus displayed, revealed itself as a black crêpe mask. He was smiling rather grimly.

"The mystery is solved, Titus," he said quietly, "and our host's alarm is explained. I fancy that a highwayman needs to be more than ordinarily careful who he admits to the secret of his hiding-place."

2

Christina

The storm blew itself out during the night, and the following day dawned bright and clear, with only a light wind to stir the budding branches. Captain Clare, stepping out of the cottage while Titus prepared breakfast, found the woodlands transformed, and could scarcely credit that this was the scene of their miserable journey the previous night. The cottage stood in a little hollow, the encircling trees and undergrowth crowding close about it, and broken in one spot only by the narrow path down which they must have come in the darkness. If it had ever possessed a garden, this was now completely overgrown, and the building itself seemed more a natural growth of the forest than the work of men's hands. Its deep thatch was green with moss and a mantle of ivy shrouded its grey stone walls; it crouched there in its hidden glade like the scene of some old fairy-tale, and might well have housed a witch or a captive princess rather than a highway-robber.

It was the problem of that same highwayman which was exercising Adrian's mind as he paced to and fro in the early morning sunlight. He had helped Titus to change the dressings on the injured shoulder, and as far as he could tell the wound was in no worse state than it had been the night before, but the man was undoubtedly a trifle feverish and it was clear that he could not be left to fend for himself. As yet he had exchanged only the merest commonplaces with his rescuers, but Adrian knew that the matter could not be delayed for much longer. He still intended to visit Coombe Royal before continuing his journey to Bristol, and he had not a great deal of time at his disposal.

Finally he decided that only complete frankness would meet the situation, and when he had eaten he bade Titus go with him into the bedchamber. The highwayman was propped up in bed, somewhat flushed of cheek and bright of eye, but apparently in full possession of his senses.

"Well, my friend," Adrian said briskly, "I fancy that we have each been of some use to the other during the past twelve hours, but now it is time for us to part. I have business which admits of no delay, and though it is plain that you need someone to care for you until that wound is healed, I fancy you would not wish us to talk indiscriminately of your plight, or the location of this house."

The other man regarded him warily, a faint frown between his brows.

"That be a queer thing to say, sir," he said at last. "Why should you suppose that?"

"Why?" Adrian's brows lifted. "Because, my friend, I can make a shrewd guess at the trade you follow, so spare yourself the effort of denying it. A lonely cottage, a thoroughbred horse, and a mask in a man's pocket point to one thing only—the High Toby! Unless I am much mistaken, that wound was dealt you by some traveller you sought to rob."

There was a brief silence, broken only by the twittering of birds in the trees outside the window. The challenge of Adrian's words seemed to hang upon the air; the man in the bed had not moved, and his brown face remained inscrutable as he looked from Adrian at the foot of the bed to Titus by the door. At length he sighed deeply and shook his head.

"So you've guessed that, have you?" he said slowly in a tone of some regret. "I was hoping it'd not come to this, but since it has—" he paused, and his sound hand came out from beneath the covers grasping a small pistol. " 'Tis not to my liking to return evil for good, sir, but a man must protect himself."

Titus had made an involuntary movement, hastily checked, but Adrian stood quite still, looking at the levelled weapon with an expression of mild and faintly amused interest.

"Where the devil did that come from?" he inquired lightly. "You did not have it when we dressed your shoulder, that I'll swear."

" 'Twas in the chest yonder, and I fetched it while you were at table," the highwayman replied frankly. "I've no mind to be dragged off to gaol without making some attempt to save myself."

Adrian's glance lifted sharply to his face, and this time there was no amusement in it. His mouth had hardened, and the blue eyes held a cold anger that was almost disdainful.

"You are a fool, my friend, and an insolent one at that!" he said contemptuously. "It is not my custom to accept a man's hospitality and then hand him over to the hangman, but if it were, I should not be rash enough to warn him of my intention. No information will be laid against you by me or by my servant. I give you my word upon that!"

He paused, but the highwayman made no reply, merely staring at him beneath frowning brows while the pistol remained levelled unwaveringly at the Captain's heart. After a moment or two Adrian went on:

"What did you hope to achieve by this? You might kill me, but my servant would overpower you before you had a chance to reload. If you wished to dispose of us both you should first have tried to separate us, so that you could deal with us one at a time. I have given you my word that we mean you no harm. Put up that pistol!"

He had been speaking as a man will when he reasons with another, but with those last few words a subtle change had come into his voice. It was the voice now of authority, accustomed to instant obedience to its commands, and in spite of himself the sick man felt the force of it. The hand that held the pistol wavered a little, and he lay staring up at Adrian with an expression of mingled doubt and obstinacy in his face.

The figure confronting him was certainly one to command respect. Titus, invaluable servant that he was, had somehow contrived to remove from his master's clothes all signs of their rough usage the previous night, and Captain Clare was immaculate in a superbly-cut coat of dark blue cloth, fawn buckskins and shining top-boots. His fair hair, tied back with a broad black ribbon, framed a face at once strong and reckless, the faint haughtiness of the patrician features softened by a humorous mouth, and eyes which seemed always to hold a trace of laughter. He was clearly one of "the Quality", but it was to the man himself rather than to a member of a ruling class that the highwayman finally yielded. He laid his weapon down on the blanket which covered him, and brushed his hand across his eyes.

"You be right, sir! Threats won't help me," he said in a low voice. "I'm in your hands, and well I know it. But for you and your man yonder, I should be lying dead in the woods this morning."

"And we did not save your life in order to see it taken from you again," Adrian replied in a lighter tone, "so set your mind at rest on that score. If the authorities wish to lay you by the heels, they must do it without our help, for neither of us relish the rôle of informer, eh, Titus?"

"No, Captain, that we do not," Titus agreed emphatically. "There's too many such vermin as it is without honest men doing their dirty trade for 'em."

The highwayman looked from one to the other, and shook his head as though he could not quite credit his good fortune.

"I ask your pardon, sir," he said at last. "There's none o' the gentry hereabouts as would treat poor Jerry Brigg so handsome, and I wish there was summat I could do to repay your kindness. By Heaven, that I do!"

"You have repaid us already with food and shelter," Adrian replied with a smile. "Now tell me, is there an estate hereabouts called Coombe Royal?"

"Aye, sir! Squire Westlake's house, that be—and a hard man he is, saving your presence! 'Tis a matter o' five miles or so from here, if 'tis to Coombe Royal you are going."

Adrian nodded.

"It is, and in a moment you shall tell me how to reach it, but first, is there someone you can trust to whom I can carry word of your misfortune?"

"There be my sister, sir, Polly Barnby. Her husband keeps an inn called the Merry Month of May, and I'm sure o' shelter there whenever I need it. Polly and Japhet'll do all as is needful, once they know what's befallen me."

"Then they shall be informed of it without delay. Is their inn far from here?"

"Not more than two miles, sir, through the woods. Take the path out o' the hollow, and turn left-handed when you reach the wider track. Follow that till you come to a road, and the inn's a quarter of a mile to your right. They'll set you on the road for Coombe Royal from there."

"Very well!" Adrian spoke briskly and turned to his servant. "Titus, you will remain here until I can send someone from the inn to relieve you of the charge. I will wait for you there." A thought struck him, and he looked again at Jeremy Brigg. "Will your kinsfolk accept my word for what has happened, or should I carry some proof of my good faith?"

Jeremy frowned.

"Maybe you should, sir, at that. 'Tis perilous work sheltering an outlaw, and Japhet'll be suspicious of a stranger. Now what can I give you as he'll know for mine? I'm no scholar, or I'd give you a writing for him." He fell silent, considering the problem, and finally said triumphantly: "I know, sir! You ride the mare, and your man can bring your own horse after you."

Adrian agreed to this scheme, and Titus went to saddle the mare. This was soon done, and when he returned to say that all was in readiness, Captain Clare held out his hand to the sick man.

"Good-bye, Jeremy Brigg," he said with a smile. "I will wish you a speedy recovery, and better fortune in the future."

"I've no quarrel with my fortune this day, sir," Jeremy assured him fervently, grasping the proffered hand. "If there be aught I can do for you, no matter how or where, I hope you'll do me the honour o' telling me."

"I leave England for good in a few days' time, my friend, so it is not likely that I shall hold you to that," Adrian said with a laugh, "but I thank you for the thought, none the less."

He went out, Titus at his heels, and mounted the chestnut mare. With a word of farewell to the servant, and a last look at the ancient, tree-bowered cottage, he rode away up the steeply-sloping path out of the hollow. The undergrowth brushed the mare's sides as she picked her way along, and at the point where the path gave on to the wider track Adrian was forced to bend low over her neck to avoid the down-sweeping branches above. Looking back as he gained the track, he saw that the screen of evergreens through which he had forced his way had sprung back into place, so that to a casual passer-by there was no indication of the path which lay beyond. Jeremy Brigg's cottage was most admirably concealed.

He was nearing the edge of the woods when suddenly a frightened cry sounded from somewhere just ahead. With an involuntary response to the alarm and distress in the sound he set spur to his mount, and a moment later rounded a bend to see the road before him, a roan horse with trailing reins, and in the mouth of the track a slight, grey-cloaked figure struggling in the arms of a thickset youth in a mulberry-coloured coat.

At the sound of Adrian's approach the girl cried out again, and her tormentor flashed a startled glance over his shoulder. He had no time to do more. The mare was reined in to a rearing, plunging halt, and Captain Clare was out of the saddle almost in the same instant. Seizing the youth by the back of his collar he spun him away from his victim, and his riding-whip cracked vigorously across the shoulders of the mulberry coat half a dozen times before a final hearty push sent the lad sprawling in the mire. The girl had stumbled aside and was leaning against the trunk of a tree, a hand at her throat and her eyes wide and startled as she watched that summarily administered punishment.

The boy staggered to his feet, plastered with mud from head to foot and white with pain and fury. He had a broad, unprepossessing face, heavily freckled, beneath a crown of sandy hair, and eyes of a singularly light and piercing blue. He came to his feet with fists clenched to avenge his humiliation, but a second glance at his assailant made him pause. Captain Clare was poised for instant action, and his tall, vigorous figure, and the heavy whip balanced in his hand, did nothing to suggest that he owed his victory entirely to surprise. Mulberry-coat hesitated, and before he could nerve himself for an attack the Captain spoke, briefly and contemptuously.

"Unless you desire to feel my whip across your back again, you will ask this lady's pardon and then take yourself off. I've a profound dislike of bullies, and an equally profound pleasure in giving them a lesson in manners. Nor is my patience inexhaustible."

For a moment the lad hesitated, but then prudence overcame his anger, and mumbling something which might have been an apology, he turned away and heaved himself on to the back of the roan. From the comparative safety of that eminence he ventured a retort, in a voice thick and shaking with rage.

"You'll be sorry for this, I promise you. My father shall hear of it, and he's not the man to brook insolence from any damned, upstart knave."

He wrenched his horse round and rode away in the opposite direction to that which Captain Clare had been instructed to take. Adrian, watching him go, said quietly to the girl:

"Who is this lout who hopes his father will fight his battles for him?"

"I—I do not know!" Her voice was unsteady, trembling on the verge of tears. "I have never seen him before."

Adrian turned, and for the first time bestowed upon her more than a fleeting glance. She was much younger

than he had supposed, not more, he thought, than four-
teen or fifteen years old, a tall, slim, fine-boned child with
huge, luminous grey eyes in a thin face which narrowed
from broad brow to pointed chin. Her complexion was
transparently clear and pale, in striking contrast to the
masses of dark hair which looked almost too heavy for
the slender column of her neck to support. She was
dressed very plainly in a lilac-coloured gown, and both
it and the grey cloak with its pink-lined hood were
decidedly shabby, and yet she had an unmistakable air
of breeding and refinement. A basket of primroses, half
its contents scattered and trampled in the mud, lay at
her feet to indicate the errand which had brought her to
this lonely spot.

She was staring apprehensively at him, her lower lip
caught between her teeth, and he was conscious of a
swift surge of compassion, a protective tenderness evoked
as much by her extreme youth as by her distress and the
valiant effort she was making to conquer it. He went
across to her and took her hand reassuringly between
his own.

"Don't cry, child," he said gently. "It is all over now,
and if I handled that young scoundrel roughly it was no
more than he deserved for frightening a little maid."

She looked up quickly, her lips parting as though she
were about to speak, but then the long lashes veiled her
eyes again and she remained silent and with bowed head.
Adrian stood looking down at her, and after a moment
went on:

"It is not wise, you see, to roam about by yourself
in so lonely a place. Will you let me take you to your
home?"

"You are very kind, sir," she replied without looking
up. Her voice was soft, and singularly pleasing to the
ear. "I am staying with my mother at an inn a little way
along the road, and I shall be very grateful if you will
go so far with me."

Adrian concealed the surprise which this information
evoked, for the inn to which she referred could be none
other than the Merry Month of May, and he had not

supposed it to be the sort of hostelry which catered for gentlefolk. Wondering, a trifle uneasily, if Japhet Barnby and his wife would be able now to care for their out-lawed relative, he said easily:

"As it happens, I am bound for the inn myself, so nothing could be more fortunate. Shall we go on our way, in case your mother has noticed your absence and become alarmed?"

She nodded, and moved away from him to pick up the basket of primroses. She limped as she walked, and Adrian said sharply:

"Did that young brute hurt you?"

"No!" She gathered up the surviving flowers and rose to face him, and though her voice was calm, the colour had risen painfully in her cheeks. "I am lame, sir, and have been so since I was a baby."

"Forgive me!" He was furious with himself for having unwittingly blundered, and spoke with less than his usual composure. "That was a clumsy thing to ask."

"It does not matter," she replied in a low voice. "You were not to know, and it does not trouble me greatly any more." She turned aside to where Jeremy Brigg's mare was standing, and ran her hand down the glossy chestnut neck. "What a beautiful creature, and how gentle and patient she is."

"Let me set you on her back as far as the inn," he suggested, hoping thus to divert her thoughts from his earlier blunder. "Come, my dear, it will spare you the necessity of tramping through all this mire."

Once again the grey eyes rested upon him with an expression he could not fathom, but she made no protest as he picked her up and set her in the saddle. She thanked him gravely, and settled herself composedly with one hand on the pommel and the other holding the basket of flowers, and Adrian led the mare out of the track and on to the road.

Within a matter of minutes they came in sight of the inn, an old, rambling house standing at a spot where four roads met, trees about it, and between it and the road a pond where ducks were swimming. The situation

was a lonely one, for none of the roads had the appearance of being greatly used, and once again Adrian was
conscious of surprise that gentlefolk should be staying at
such a place.

He led the mare up to the door and halted beneath a
faded sign depicting a maypole with boys and girls dancing
about it. There was no one to be seen, the door of the
house was closed, and only the smoke rising from the
chimneys showed that the place was inhabited.

The girl had not spoken once during their short journey,
and when Adrian lifted her down from the saddle she
merely thanked him politely before turning to go into
the house. Half puzzled, half amused, he twitched at a
fold of the grey cloak to detain her.

"Don't run away so fast, little one," he said lightly.
"At least let me know the name of the fair lady I rescued."

She had already thrust open the door, and now paused
on the threshold to look back at him over her shoulder.
He thought that she was not going to reply, but then a
fleeting smile touched her lips and she turned more fully
to face him.

"It is Christina, sir," she said softly. "Christina Westlake," and sketching a hurried curtsy she limped quickly
into the inn, leaving Adrian to stare after her in the most
profound astonishment.

3

House of Secrets

He was still standing there when a man emerged from the
door which Christina had left open. Although the white
apron girt about his middle suggested that he was the
landlord, he in no way resembled the traditional inn-
keeper, being a tall, powerfully-built fellow with a square
and rather pugnacious face. He came with civil words

of greeting on his lips, but at sight of the chestnut mare his eyes narrowed and he favoured the Captain with a quick glance charged with suspicion.

With an effort Adrian dragged his thoughts away from the wild conjectures provoked by the disclosure of Christina Westlake's name, and met the suspicious eyes frankly.

"Are you Japhet Barnby?" he asked without preamble.

The other man nodded.

"That be my name, sir."

"Then I have no doubt that you recognize this animal." Adrian nodded towards the mare. "It belongs, I believe, to a relative of yours."

The suspicion deepened in Barnby's eyes; he said gruffly:

"Suppose it do, sir. What be that to you, if I may make bold to ask?"

"Your caution is natural, my friend, but unnecessary," Adrian replied with a smile. "Jeremy Brigg is in need of help, and lent me the mare to convince you of my good faith. I mean no harm to him, or to you."

In a discreetly lowered voice he described the events of the previous night, and presently succeeded in overcoming Barnby's instinctive suspicion. At the inn-keeper's request Adrian went with him into the kitchen, where Polly Barnby and her two daughters were at work. Japhet said something in a low voice to his wife, and Adrian noticed with approval that apart from a sudden anxious glance in his direction she did nothing to betray alarm. She spoke sharply to the two girls, who were whispering together and casting covert, curious glances at the elegant stranger, and they went with reluctant obedience out of the room. When the door had closed behind them, she whisked the corner of her apron across an already spotless chair and begged the Captain to be seated.

"You'll forgive us, sir, for asking you to step into the kitchen," she said briskly, "but we've people putting up in the house, and what's to be said is best said here."

Adrian sat down with a smile and a word of thanks. He had taken an immediate liking to this small, dark, quick-spoken woman who formed so marked a contrast to her fair, slow-moving and probably slow-thinking husband, and it crossed his mind that if ever Jeremy Brigg's safety depended upon quick-wittedness, it would be to Polly rather than to Japhet Barnby that he would need to look for his salvation.

Once more he repeated his story, and Mrs. Barnby listened attentively and asked one or two questions concerning the exact nature of her brother's injury. Adrian answered these to the best of his ability, and she nodded her satisfaction.

"I'll send one of the girls to the cottage at once with a few comforts," she announced, "and then your servant will be free to come to you, sir. The mare will be safe enough here. Jerry'll not be riding her again yet awhile."

"Is that not a needless risk to take?" Adrian protested. "If a search were made, and that mare recognized as your brother's mount, it would go hard with you."

Japhet shook his head, and spoke for the first time.

"She'll not be found, sir," he said with a grim smile. " 'Tis not the first time she's been stabled here, and if the redcoats come, they may search wi' my goodwill. There be ways o' hiding what's best not seen, eh, wife?"

Adrian laughed and rose to his feet.

"Then I shall not presume to advise you," he said lightly. "Now if you will show me some room where I may wait for my servant, I will hinder you no longer, but first, tell me one thing. Do either of you know an unprepossessing youth, with blue eyes and sandy-coloured hair, who rides a roan horse? He has the appearance of a gentleman, and manners which would not be out of place on a dung-hill."

The husband and wife exchanged glances.

"That do sound like Mr. Gilbert Tedburn, sir," Japhet volunteered after a moment. "His father be Squire Tedburn o' Mereton Hall."

"And a nasty young varmint he is," Polly added roundly. " 'Tis not a week since I sent him about his business for trying to make free with my Betsy. There's some men as thinks that if a wench works as serving-maid at an inn, she be no better than a trollop."

"He does not confine his attentions to serving-maids, Mrs. Barnby," Adrian replied drily. "Less than half-an-hour ago I caught him molesting the little maid who is staying here, and was obliged to lay my whip about his shoulders. The child was badly frightened, and her mother should have better care of her."

Mrs. Barnby looked startled, but before she could make any comment the door opened, and the elder of the two girls who had been banished came back into the room.

"If you please, sir," she said, bobbing a curtsy to Adrian and obviously repeating the message word for word, "Mrs. Westlake begs you will do her the honour of joining her and Miss in the parlour at your earliest convenience."

Adrian nodded resignedly. He supposed that Christina had hastened to pour an account of her adventure into the maternal ear, and could only hope that she had not unduly magnified the service he had done her. On the other hand, he was exceedingly curious concerning the presence at this lonely inn of a mother and daughter who bore the same name as Helen's husband.

"I will go immediately," he said, and turned again to Mrs. Barnby. Japhet had gone out, presumably to stable the mare. "When my servant arrives, will you be good enough to inform me? I do not wish to delay my departure longer than is needful."

"That I will, sir," she assured him. "Betsy, take the gentleman to the parlour and then come back here. And bring Ruth with you. There's work to be done."

Adrian followed the girl out of the kitchen and along a short passage towards the other end of the house. They mounted a few stairs, turned a sharp corner, and Captain Clare looked about him in astonishment, for here was oak panelling finely carved, and a moulded ceiling to which traces of gilding still clung here and there. He had noticed as he approached the inn that one part of it appeared to be much older than the rest, and now he concluded that the humble dwelling which he had first entered had been added to the remains of an earlier and finer house.

The parlour into which he was ushered a moment later confirmed this opinion. It was a room of no more than medium size, but panelled like the corridor and handsomely proportioned, with a great fireplace of carved stone where logs glowed cheerfully. On one side of this the girl Christina was sitting, playing with a small grey kitten in her lap, and opposite to her, in a high-backed chair, sat the lady who was presumably her mother.

Mrs. Westlake was perhaps five-and-forty years old, a thin, sickly-looking woman with the same delicate build and clear, pale skin as her daughter. There the resemblance ended, for her hair was a faded gold thickly streaked with grey, and she had turned towards the newcomer a pair of mournful dark eyes. Her face was deeply lined, as much, it seemed, by discontent as by suffering, and her black gown and widow's cap, though exquisitely neat, were of a shabbiness which gave an impression of faded gentility.

"Madam, your servant!" Adrian advanced into the room and bowed. "Permit me to present myself. Captain Adrian Clare, at your service."

Mrs. Westlake inclined her head in gracious acknowledgement of the words, and he reflected with a touch of amusement that however reduced her circumstances, her manner would have done credit to a duchess. Apparently her appraisal of him had been satisfactory, for a faint smile lifted the corners of her mouth and she said in a languid, complaining voice:

"We are honoured, Captain Clare. Honoured and deeply grateful. My daughter informs me that you rescued her from a most unpleasant situation."

"I am glad that I was at hand to do so, madam," Adrian replied. "To force unwelcome attentions upon any unprotected woman is, in my opinion, the act of a coward. To force them upon a child of your daughter's age is infinitely worse."

"Your sentiments do you credit, sir," Mrs. Westlake commended him, "and I am in complete agreement with them. In that last respect, however, the young man's conduct was not quite as reprehensible as you suppose. Christina is nineteen years old."

Considerably taken aback by this information, Adrian cast an incredulous glance at Christina, and discovered that though she was still apparently intent upon the kitten, her lips quivered as though she had with difficulty repressed a smile. For the second time in their brief acquaintance he felt himself at a disadvantage, and the sensation was uncommon enough to irritate him. Why the devil, he wondered, had she allowed so absurd a misunderstanding to persist, when a word from her would have made everything plain?

"In that event," he said stiffly, "I can only ask Miss Westlake's pardon, and assure her that any lack of formality in my bearing towards her arose from misapprehension."

"There is no need, Captain Clare. Your conduct was everything it should be," Christina replied composedly, "and indeed, I found it extraordinarily comforting after so unpleasant an experience. Besides, you are by no means the first person to suppose me to be younger than I am. I used to find it mortifying, but now I comfort myself that if it is still happening ten years hence I shall be flattered rather than displeased."

She looked up as she spoke, with such friendly good-humour in her grey eyes that his irritation was dispelled. An answering gleam of amusement woke in his own, and he said with a smile:

"A truly feminine philosophy, Miss Westlake! May I say that I have no doubt it will be so, ten years hence?"

Christina laughed. Like her voice, her laughter was a pleasing sound.

" 'Tis a comforting thought, at all events," she said lightly. "Will you not be seated, sir? You said, I think, that you were bound for this inn, so I trust that we do not detain you unduly?"

"Not in the least, madam," he replied, taking the chair she indicated. "I am waiting for my servant to join me here. I am on my way to Bristol, but we missed the road last night in the rain and the darkness, and were obliged to seek shelter at the first cottage we stumbled upon." That was, he thought, close enough to the truth to sound convincing, yet so vague that it disclosed nothing.

"It was indeed a dreadful night," Mrs. Westlake agreed plaintively. "So you, too, are a stranger in these parts, Captain Clare? We arrived here ourselves only a few days ago, and so have no acquaintance with society hereabouts."

Adrian saw in these words a chance to satisfy his curiosity, and was quick to seize upon it. Turning courteously to the elder lady again, he said pleasantly:

"This is my first visit to Wiltshire, ma'am, for I was born in Oxfordshire and lately have lived in London, but surely Westlake is a local name? It had occurred to me that you might be related to Mr. Marcus Westlake of Coombe Royal."

"Are you a friend of Mr. Westlake's, Captain Clare?" Christina put the question casually, and yet Adrian had the impression that she had spoken with the intention of forestalling anything her mother might say. He shook his head.

"I have never met him, Miss Westlake," he replied, "though I believe I was acquainted with his wife some years ago, when she was a Miss Thurston. I heard of her marriage, but I have not had the privilege of meeting her since."

This masterpiece of understatement was received in silence by Christina, but Mrs. Westlake's reaction was less passive and utterly unexpected. At the first mention of Marcus Westlake a curious change had come over her. She had stiffened in her chair, her thin hands clenching hard upon its arms, and now she said, in a voice which had become almost shrill:

"Does she know, do you suppose, what manner of man she married, or by what cruel injustice he enjoys his wealth? I wonder—"

"Mamma!" Christina spoke sharply, on a note of warning and dismay, but the only effect of her intervention was to provoke her mother's displeasure.

"How often, Christina, must I tell you not to interrupt me?" she demanded querulously. "I will not tolerate this constant impertinence! Captain Clare is a man of honour! I have no hesitation in taking him into my confidence."

She turned again to Adrian, who had risen to his feet in mingled perplexity and embarrassment. Christina opened her lips to make another protest, but her mother rushed on without giving her a chance to speak, and with a gesture of despair she sank back into her chair.

"You are a man of the world, Captain Clare!" Mrs. Westlake's voice was high; two bright spots of colour burned in her cheeks, and her fingers clenched and opened spasmodically. "It is not necessary to describe to you the miserable poverty in which we live—you have only to look at us! Yet if there were any truth or justice in this world, Marcus Westlake would be in our place today, and we in his, for by all the laws of God and man, Coombe Royal belongs to us!"

4

A Tale of Three Brothers

Adrian, still standing by the chair from which he had risen, one hand resting on its back, listened with stupefaction to this amazing statement. He said blankly, "I beg your pardon?" and felt that he had uttered the ultimate extreme of banality, and yet he could not believe that he had heard her correctly. Then Christina's soft voice, a striking contrast to her mother's hysterical tone, spoke in reply, and the unbelievable was suddenly made credible, and fantasy became fact.

"It is quite true, sir!" She spoke resignedly, almost wearily, as though now that her mother had betrayed their secret, frankness alone would serve. "My father was Marcus Westlake's eldest brother, and when he died,

I inherited the estate from him. That is why we have come to England. We hope to claim it."

"We must claim it!" Mrs. Westlake declared hysterically. "I cannot endure this hand-to-mouth existence any longer. Coombe Royal is ours. We have been robbed and cheated by Marcus Westlake long enough." She leaned back in her chair, pressing a handkerchief to her lips, and after a moment or two continued in a calmer voice: "You must forgive me, Captain Clare. I am not well. My health has been undermined by all I have endured. Christina, my smelling-salts!"

Miss Westlake got up, putting the kitten aside, and fetched a vinaigrette which she placed in her parent's feeble grasp.

"Do not distress yourself so, Mamma," she said quietly. "It can do no good, and you exhaust yourself to no purpose."

Her tone was dutiful, even concerned, but Adrian thought he could still detect a trace of resignation in it, as though scenes like this were all too familiar to her. His mind was still bemused by the astonishing revelation which had been made, and when it appeared that the elder lady had somewhat recovered, he said slowly:

"No doubt I am singularly obtuse, but I fear I have not yet properly understood the situation. Do you mean that Mr. Westlake has deliberately deprived you of your inheritance?"

"That is precisely what I mean," Mrs. Westlake replied tearfully. "He has not a shadow of right to the estate. He stole it from my husband, and now he is robbing my child, too, of her rights. Oh, there is no end to his infamy!"

"Mamma, please," Christina spoke firmly now. "You know quite well that my uncle is totally unaware of my existence, and even of Papa's marriage to you. Pray do not put yourself about in this fashion." She turned to Adrian, and he saw that there was a challenging expression in her eyes which belied her apparent composure. "Believe me, Captain Clare, I have no desire to burden a stranger with our troubles, and you are under no obligation to listen to them. Since I am sure, however, that your curiosity has been aroused by what you have already been told, I would prefer to tell you the whole story rather than leave you to guess at the truth."

The words were spoken with admirable calm, but the betraying colour had risen in her face and he realized suddenly how difficult she must feel her position to be. He guessed, too, that, young as she was, she had long been obliged to accept responsibilities which her mother could not or would not bear, and he felt again that compassionate desire to protect her which had come to him the first time he saw her.

"If you wish to tell me, Miss Westlake, I shall be happy to listen," he said gently, "but if you do not, let me assure you that your mother's confidences will always be respected. If I am under no obligation to listen, you are certainly under none to speak."

For several seconds the grey eyes searched his face as though seeking proof of his sincerity. Apparently they found it, for she smiled faintly and gestured to the chair from which he had risen.

"You are very understanding, sir," she said in a low voice—too low, he thought, to reach her mother's ears, "but I should like to tell you. I should like you to know the truth."

So, sitting there before the fire, with her mother interposing fretful remarks from time to time, Christina told Adrian Clare her story. Her father, Godfrey Westlake, had been the eldest of three brothers, of whom Marcus was the second, while the third, Edmund, was some years younger than either.

Godfrey had inherited Coombe Royal when he was barely twenty-two, and for the next ten years had done his best to take his father's place where Edmund was concerned. The bond between them was very close, and strengthened on Godfrey's side by the fact that the lad's health was a constant source of anxiety. Delicate from birth, adored and cosseted by his mother, assured always of his eldest brother's protection, Edmund had grown up with a character as weak as his constitution, and yet so sweet-natured that everyone, with the exception of his brother Marcus, was exceedingly fond of him.

Marcus, however, was at odds with most people. For this he was not, perhaps, entirely to blame, for his position was a difficult one, lacking as he did both the authority of the head of the family and the indulgence bestowed upon the youngest son. Moody, discontented, hiding a sense of inferiority beneath a blustering manner, he desperately courted popularity and found none, while his brothers, making no such effort, had friends everywhere.

Then, when Edmund was just twenty-one, tragedy came to Coombe Royal. For several months Edmund's health had steadily deteriorated, though only Godfrey knew that his days were numbered, and this knowledge he shared with no one save the family physician. At that time there lived in the neighbourhood one Giles Carew, a man of somewhat unsavoury reputation, whom Godfrey had bested in a matter concerning some land. The incident had cost Carew a certain amount of money and considerable loss of prestige, and being of a vindictive disposition he resolved to avenge himself through Edmund. He contrived to worm his way into the boy's confidence and then by veiled hints and subtle innuendo began to sow discord between the two brothers.

The climax came one evening when Godfrey returned from dealing with some business in Marlborough to discover that Edmund, in defiance of warnings against the place, had gone with Carew to a cock-fight at a certain disreputable tavern. Godfrey, knowing only too well where the real blame lay, had cursed Giles Carew very heartily and then set out in pursuit, with Marcus, pressed reluctantly into service, to support him.

By the time they reached the tavern the cock-fight was over, and Edmund and Carew at cards in a private room and drinking heavily. Godfrey, whose temper was as violent as it was slow to rouse, was by this time in a black rage, and no one in the place dared gainsay him as he demanded Giles Carew and thrust his way into the man's presence.

Only Marcus was a witness to what followed. During

the course of a fierce and bitter quarrel, Carew's true nature and villainous purpose became clear even to the ingenuous Edmund; the liquor, to which he was unaccustomed, had done its fatal work; and, beside himself with fury at the ease with which he had been duped, the drunken boy had pulled out a pistol and shot Carew dead.

That pistol-shot was destined to destroy more lives than one. Edmund, sobered by the horror of what he had done, had turned instinctively to the one whose protection had never yet failed him. Nor did it fail him now. Without pausing to consider the consequences, Godfrey had assumed the guilt of the crime and commanded his two juniors to support his story. The three brothers had then forced their way from the tavern, and that same night Godfrey set out for France, leaving Coombe Royal in Marcus's charge.

For eighteen months he had travelled about Europe, living comfortably enough on the money which his brother sent him regularly by the hand of a trusted servant, Reuben Barnby. It was during this time that he met and married Miss Phoebe Lulworth, the daughter of an impoverished Jacobite gentleman with whom he had struck up an acquaintance. Drawn together by the common bonds of exiles in a foreign land, they became close friends, and when her father died it seemed to Miss Phoebe both right and natural that she should accept Godfrey Westlake's offer of marriage.

Scarcely had the wedding taken place when Reuben Barnby arrived with an urgent summons from England. Edmund was dying, and begged his brother to return so that he could make all right before he died. Leaving his bride in the care of friends in France, Godfrey hurried home, but for all his haste he came too late. When, secretly and by night, he reached Coombe Royal, it was Marcus who met him, and told him that Edmund had died the previous day with his guilt still unconfessed.

Godfrey, dazed though he was by weariness and grief, refused to believe this. Edmund's last letter had made so clear his agony of mind, the torments he had suffered in knowing his brother to be bearing the weight of his

sins, and it had mentioned, too, that it was Marcus alone
who had dissuaded him from confessing long ago. With
an awakening suspicion of the truth, Godfrey had accused
his brother of lying to him, but Marcus, who had tasted
the pleasures of wealth and authority and had no intention
of relinquishing them, laughed in his face. Then he issued
an ultimatum. Godfrey could choose between returning
whence he had come, or standing trial for the murder
of Giles Carew.

Knowing that such a trial could end only in one way,
and remembering the responsibilities which his marriage
had brought him, Godfrey left Coombe Royal that same
night, and sought refuge at the Merry Month of May, the
inn kept by Reuben Barnby's twin brother, Japhet. It was
Reuben who discovered that when Edmund Westlake
died there had been present only his brother Marcus and
a young attorney named Walter Kelsby, and Godfrey,
still hoping desperately to uncover the truth, took the risk
of seeking an interview with the lawyer. He gained nothing by it. Kelsby's account corresponded exactly with
Marcus Westlake's; Edmund had died without even men-
tioning his eldest brother's name.

Godfrey had no choice but to return empty-handed to
France, but for the rest of his life he remained unshaken
in the belief that Marcus and Kelsby had conspired to de-
prive him of his birthright. Christina had been told the
story as soon as she was old enough to understand it, and
it had been constantly impressed upon her that she was
the heiress of Coombe Royal, and that it would be her
duty to claim it when the time came. When he lay dying,
worn out by years of poverty and the constant, endless
struggle to keep his family housed and fed, Godfrey Westlake had exacted from her a solemn promise that she
would go to England and challenge her uncle's right to
the possession of estate and fortune.

"But it was easier to promise than to do," Christina
concluded quietly. "My father died in Italy, and it was
more than a year before we could save enough to travel
to England. Nor was our journey a swift one, for my
mother's health is not good, but we arrived at last, and

sought shelter with my father's good friends here. That was three days ago."

Her tone as she spoke of their travels was matter-of-fact, and Adrian marvelled anew. He could imagine what that journey must have been like, with little money, and Mrs. Westlake, fretful and complaining, as a companion, and it seemed incredible that Christina had ever found the courage to embark upon such an undertaking, much less carry it through successfully.

"You made the journey from Italy alone?" he said, and an astonishment he could not altogether conceal sounded in his voice. Christina shook her head.

"No, we were fortunate enough to have an escort," she replied. "An old friend whom we have known for many years."

"Mr. Stephen Ancroft," her mother added to elaborate this somewhat brief reply. "His father was a close friend of my late brother, and Stephen is almost as a son to me. I do not know how we should have contrived since my husband's death, had it not been for him."

"Captain Clare," Christina broke in, "you have been kind enough to listen to our story. Will you add to that kindness by telling me frankly what chance, in your opinion, we have of establishing a claim to Coombe Royal? We are sadly in need of advice."

Adrian's brows lifted.

"Only a lawyer can tell you that, Miss Westlake," he said with a smile. "My advice, for what it is worth, is to discover who handles the affairs of your family, and acquaint him with your presence. You have, I presume, all the necessary proofs of your identity?"

She nodded.

"Oh yes, and Stephen rode into Marlborough yesterday to see Mr. Henry Beauchamp, who was my father's lawyer in the old days. Father told me that Mr. Beauchamp would be the man to help us when the time came, and that we could trust him absolutely."

"Was Mr. Ancroft successful?"

"He has not yet returned," she explained. "He meant to come back last night, but I dare say the bad weather prevented it. I expect he will be here soon."

"Then if he succeeded in finding your father's man of business, you cannot do better than place yourselves in his hands. He will know better than anyone how matters stand." Adrian paused, looking at her with a faint frown between his brows. "One thing puzzles me. You spoke just now of another lawyer, who was present when Edmund Westlake died. What part does he play in this?"

"You mean Walter Kelsby?" Christina replied. "My father said that Kelsby dealt with all my uncle Marcus's private affairs. There had been some sort of disagreement, I believe, because my uncle thought that Mr. Beauchamp was prejudiced against him. That is why Father was convinced that Kelsby was party to the plot to rob him of Coombe Royal."

"It seems very likely," Adrian agreed. "I wonder what has become of Kelsby."

"He still lives in these parts," Christina said drily, "and, according to Mrs. Barnby, he has prospered exceedingly. So greatly, indeed, that he is now partner to Mr. Beauchamp, and has purchased a small estate just outside Marlborough." She paused significantly, and raised her eyes to Adrian's. "I wonder, Captain Clare, if that suggests to you what it suggests to me?"

He met the look frankly, with the thought flashing through his mind that Christina Westlake had more worldly wisdom than might be supposed. Those clear eyes saw straight to the heart of things, and belied the childishness of face and figure.

"I would say, Miss Westlake, that Kelsby has a rich and influential patron who dares deny him nothing because of a secret shared. A secret which Kelsby has turned to good account over the years."

"My uncle, in fact," Christina concluded for him. "Yes, that is what I fear. So I shall have them both against me."

The last words seemed to be spoken half to herself, and something in the way she said them struck him as curious. It was the first time she had said anything to suggest that she was the person primarily concerned in the struggle to regain possession of Coombe Royal; until that moment, she had coupled herself with her mother in that claim. Before he could pursue the train of thought her words evoked, however, his attention was claimed once again by Mrs. Westlake, who, while Adrian and Christina talked, had been lying back in her chair, languidly passing the vinaigrette to and fro beneath her nose. Now she roused herself, and said in a tone of fretful reproof:

"No matter how many are against us, Christina, we have right upon our side. Coombe Royal is ours, and I will not rest until we are in possession of it. Do not imagine, Captain Clare," she added, turning to Adrian, "that it is for myself I am so determined to come by my rights. My life is almost over, and worldly wealth means little to me. No, it is for my child that I am concerned. When I am gone, what will become of her if she is left alone and unprotected?"

She paused to touch her handkerchief to eyes which were perfectly dry, and Adrian, assuming the question to be purely rhetorical, made no attempt to answer it. Christina said, "Mamma, for pity's sake!" in a tone of mingled exasperation and embarrassment, but Mrs. Westlake paid no heed to the interjection.

"It is my dearest hope," she continued tragically, "to see my daughter creditably established before I die, and to know that I leave her safe in the care of a good and honourable man, but what likelihood is there of that if we cannot regain her inheritance? I know the world, Captain Clare! A young girl who lacks both looks and fortune has small hope of contracting a suitable marriage, and Christina, as you can see, is even further handicapped by a sad affliction."

She had made no attempt to lower her voice, and Adrian, aghast at such lack of consideration, looked involuntarily at Christina. At her mother's reference to her lameness, a flame of colour swept up across her throat and face, and she sprang to her feet as though seeking to escape. The kitten, which had been playing in the folds of her skirt, let out a squeal of pain and terror as she inadvertently set a foot on its tail, and she stumbled and would have fallen had not Adrian, who had risen hastily to his feet, flung out a hand to save her. Just for an instant her face was lifted to his, and he saw that her eyes were brimming over with tears. Then she turned away and limped across to the window, where she stood with her back to the room.

"You see!" Mrs. Westlake said with mournful resignation. "It is always so. She was not born lame, of course! It is the result of a fall when she was very young. Believe me, Captain Clare, it is a great affliction to me."

Adrian had been looking towards Christina, who was standing rigidly still with one hand gripped tightly on the curtain, but at that he turned back to Mrs. Westlake. He had already decided that her self-pity was equalled only by her foolishness, but even if her cruelty was unintentional, as he believed it was, it roused him to a white heat of indignation.

"I venture to think, ma'am, that it is a greater affliction to your daughter," he said, and though his manner had abated not one jot of its courtesy, there was ice in the tone of his voice, "and it would be kinder, would it not, to refrain from drawing attention to a misfortune which is no fault of hers?"

He sensed rather than saw Christina's hasty movement as she turned to look at him, for he was still watching her mother. Faint colour had come into her cheeks, and resentment was kindling behind the astonishment in her eyes, but before she could speak again an interruption occurred. Swift footsteps sounded in the passage, the door of the parlour was flung open, and a young man came quickly into the room.

This was, presumably, Mr. Stephen Ancroft. Adrian judged him to be about three- or four-and-twenty years old, a well-built lad nearly as tall as himself, with dark brown hair drawn neatly back from his face. His dress was very plain, lacking ornamentation of any kind, and without being precisely shabby, looked as though it had seen a good deal of hard wear. He entered impetuously, as though he were the bearer of important news, but at sight of Adrian he checked, the hasty words withering on his lips.

"So you have returned at last, Stephen!" Christina had command of herself again, and spoke calmly from her position by the window. "Captain Clare, may I present our good friend, Mr. Stephen Ancroft?"

The gentlemen bowed gravely to each other, though perplexity, suspicion and dawning resentment were struggling with each other in Stephen's eyes. Adrian regarded him thoughtfully. He was not very favourably impressed, for though the boy was good-looking enough in his way there was something lacking in his countenance, and an indefinable hint of weakness or of evil. Captain Clare decided that he would not care to trust Mr. Ancroft very far.

"Well, what news from Marlborough?" Christina asked impatiently, adding, as Stephen hesitated: "You may speak freely before Captain Clare. He is acquainted with our story."

The displeasure in Ancroft's face became more pronounced, and he shot a glance at Mrs. Westlake as though he had no doubt of the source of the Captain's knowledge. He said shortly:

"Bad news, I fear. A week ago Mr. Beauchamp suffered some sort of seizure, and is still too ill to receive anyone. All his business is in the hands of his partner, Walter Kelsby."

There was a dismayed silence. Mrs. Westlake gave a stifled moan and brought the vinaigrette into play again, but no one paid any heed to her. The two young men were watching Christina, but she was still standing with her back to the light and it was difficult to read the expression in her face. At last she said in a low voice:

"Is Mr. Beauchamp expected to recover?"

Stephen made a helpless gesture.

"No one could tell me that. At all events, it is sure to be many weeks, if not months, before he is capable of dealing with any business. Meanwhile, Kelsby controls all. I told him nothing, of course. When I learned that Mr. Beauchamp was not available, I said that my business was not important, and came away."

"What are we to do?" Christina tried to speak calmly, but there was an uncontrollable quiver of despair in her voice. "My father distrusted Walter Kelsby as greatly as he did my uncle. Oh, surely we have not come so far for nothing?" As though scarcely aware of what she did, she turned towards Adrian, putting out her hand to him in an imploring gesture. "Captain Clare, can you not advise me?"

Slowly Adrian shook his head, for though he was both touched and startled by this proof of confidence in his judgement there was little he could say to reassure her. He went forward and took the outstretched hand in his own.

"How I wish I could," he said in a low voice, "for this is a cruel blow for you to meet with at the very outset. All I can suggest is that you do nothing without first carefully considering it, for in an affair such as this, hastiness could spell disaster." He looked away from her, to Ancroft's glowering face, and thence to Mrs. Westlake drooping in her chair by the fire. "You will wish to discuss these matters without the presence of a stranger, so I will leave you now. If you find that there is any way in which I may serve you, I beg that you will tell me of it."

He lifted her hand to his lips and let it go. A bow to Mrs. Westlake, a curt nod to Ancroft, and then he turned and went quietly from the room. It irked him that he had been able to help her so little, but he felt himself to be too intimately involved in the affair to commit himself to any course without some pause in which to analyse his own feelings. Christina's plight aroused his ready compassion, and the courage he sensed in her filled him with admiration, but the man against whom she was pitting herself was Helen's husband. To pledge himself to opposing Marcus Westlake was to range himself also against her, and he could not yet tell in which direction his loyalty lay. That was the issue which must be settled before he plunged any deeper into the affair.

He was not to be granted the leisure to decide it. Emerging from the parlour, he made his way back towards the kitchen, but when he reached the passage on to which this opened he became aware of a buzz of voices from a half-open door further along it. A number of people appeared to be engaged in altercation, and only a word or phrase here and there could be distinguished, but as Adrian paused, the words "a chestnut-coloured mare" came clearly to his ears. With a sudden conviction that he was somehow concerned in this discussion, he walked on down the passage and pushed the door wide.

The room beyond seemed to be full of people. Japhet Barnby was there, and his wife, and another man who resembled Japhet so closely that he could be none other than his brother, Reuben. There were the red coats of soldiers, and in the forefront of the crowd a muddied, mulberry-coloured coat which Captain Clare recognized with no difficulty whatsoever.

His entry caused a sudden hush to fall upon the assembly. For a few seconds he stared at them, and they at him, and then the wearer of the mulberry coat took a pace forward and flung out an accusing arm.

"There he is, curse his impudence!" he cried triumphantly. "The man who rides a chestnut mare! Yes, Corporal, there's your damned highwayman. I knew that we should find him here!"

5

The Military Patrol

For perhaps five seconds Adrian stared at the speaker in blank surprise, and then the humorous aspect of the situation struck him, and he began to laugh. The Corporal regarded him doubtfully, but another man in civilian dress thrust his way belligerently forward. He was middle-aged, stocky and corpulent, with broad features and light blue eyes which proclaimed his kinship to the boy in the mulberry coat.

"Damme, sir, this is no laughing matter!" he declared angrily. "A very serious charge has been made against you, and I demand that you answer it."

"Do you, egad?" The laughter still lingered in Adrian's face, but there was an undertone in his voice which made the Corporal shift uneasily from one foot to the other. "And by what right do you make that demand, which seems to me to exceed even the charge itself in impertinence?"

"By right, sir, of the authority vested in me," the other retorted pompously. "I am George Tedburn of Mereton Hall, and I have the honour to be a Justice of the Peace."

"I congratulate you," Adrian said softly, "but I imagined that it was the duty of a Justice to punish malefactors, not to play the part of catchpoll. This must be a singularly law-abiding community if you are driven to these lengths to find an offender." He strolled past the purple-faced and stuttering magistrate and addressed his next words to the Corporal. "Perhaps you, my friend, will be good enough to tell me what all this nonsense is about."

The Corporal hurriedly effaced the grin which Captain Clare's retort to Mr. Tedburn had provoked, and instinctively came to attention. This superbly elegant gentleman was like no highwayman he had ever seen, and there was a note of authority in his voice which the Corporal recognized.

"We're looking for a highwayman, sir, as held up and robbed a coach on the Bath road at dusk yesterday," he said respectfully. "One o' the gentlemen fired on him as he made off, and 'tis certain the rogue was hit. It seemed he was headed for these parts, and a search was ordered to be made."

"Well?" Adrian prompted impatiently as the man paused. "I have no doubt that the affair happened just as you have described it, but what the devil has that to do with me?"

The Corporal reddened, and looked unlovingly at the Tedburns.

" 'Tis the matter o' the fellow's mount, sir," he explained reluctantly. "Both gentlemen in the coach, and their servants, swear 'twas a chestnut mare. As to the man, there's little they can say beyond the fact that he was on the small side, but to the horse they can all swear. Young Mr. Tedburn said he saw you riding just such a mare not more than an hour ago, and that if a highwayman found shelter anywhere hereabouts, 'twould be at the Merry Month of May."

"Did he, indeed!" That was Polly, leaping into the breach almost before the Corporal had finished speaking. "Let me tell you, young man, that this is a respectable house, and always was! Highwayman, indeed! You can search from attic to cellar, and find no highwayman here. A fine way that is to talk of honest folks!"

"I sympathize with your indignation, Mrs. Barnby," Adrian said calmly, "but it should not be directed at the Corporal. He, after all, is merely doing his duty." From the corner of his eye he observed the Corporal's grateful glance, and knew that he had won at least one ally. Mr. Tedburn opened his mouth as though to protest, but was given no opportunity. Adrian was speaking again.

"Let us leave the question of the mare for a moment. This highwayman, we are told, is a small man, and wounded." He had been half-sitting, half-leaning against the table in the middle of the room, but now he straightened to his full height and looked sardonically from one to the other. "That description fits me to admiration, of course!"

"No, sir, that it don't!" the Corporal replied heartily, and even Mr. Tedburn nodded reluctant agreement. His son, however, was less easily diverted.

"They could have been mistaken," he said scornfully, "for twilight can play queer tricks on a man's sight. But they were not mistaken about your mount, the mare you were riding again this morning. I don't wonder you are so anxious to turn our attention from that."

Adrian's lips tightened, and he shot a steely glance at the speaker.

"Your manner, my lad, is beginning to irritate me,"

he said shortly. "Are chestnut mares so rare a phenomenon in Wiltshire that if a man rides one he must necessarily be a highwayman?" He turned again to the Corporal. "Have you seen this animal, my friend?"

"No, sir, not yet. I sent two o' my men to the stables as soon as we got here, but what's keeping 'em so long I can't say. I'd best send after 'em."

"There is no need!" The softly spoken words drew their attention towards the doorway. Christina was standing there, slim and self-possessed in her lilac gown. "I can describe to you the horse which Captain Clare was riding this morning. It was chestnut-coloured, certainly! A gelding with a white blaze on its forehead and one white forefoot."

"She's lying!" Gilbert Tedburn broke in furiously. "I tell you, they are all in league with each other at this confounded inn. Why, the wench was waiting for him this morning where that track from the woods joins the road!"

Adrian moved swiftly, taking them all by surprise. He took two quick strides forward, and his hand shot out to fasten upon the front of young Tedburn's frilled shirt, jerking him almost off his feet. Holding him thus, he said in a quietly menacing tone:

"You do not profit by your mistakes, do you? I should have thought that the thrashing I gave you a while ago would have taught you prudence if it could not teach you courtesy. Until I had the honour of rescuing her from your mannerless importunities, I had never set eyes on this young lady in my life."

He released his grip as suddenly as he had taken it, and Gilbert, caught off balance, staggered back against his father with a force that nearly knocked him off his feet. Adrian's lip curled scornfully.

"What need to say more?" he demanded of the company in general. "This puppy bears me a grudge for the rough handling he received, and his accusation is no more than a clumsy attempt to settle the score. You will not, I think, venture to doubt this lady's word?"

He was looking at the Corporal as he spoke, and beneath the cold challenge of those blue eyes the soldier reddened and made haste to agree that he would not. The arrival at that moment of the two men detailed to search the stables clinched the matter. The only chestnut horse to be found, they reported, was a gelding with white markings, and though they had searched every outbuilding belonging to the inn, they had found no trace of any other.

The Corporal was profuse in his apologies, which Captain Clare readily accepted, thereafter winning the good opinion of every man in the patrol by commanding Japhet to provide them all with a tankard of ale at his expense before they went on their way. Mr. Tedburn also begged the Captain's pardon, in a curt and grudging fashion, and went away, commanding his son to accompany him in a tone of voice which boded that young man no good at all.

The soldiers had all trooped after Japhet and his brother into the tap-room, while Mrs. Barnby, remarking crossly that with one thing and another the dinner was in a fair way to being spoiled, bustled away to the kitchen, so that Adrian and Christina were left alone. For a moment they regarded each other in silence, and then she said calmly:

"What did become of the mare, sir?"

Adrian laughed.

"I have no idea, Miss Westlake," he admitted frankly. "The only explanation I can offer is that by some witchcraft she was transformed into the gelding which you described."

"No, that is Stephen's horse," Christina replied with a smile. "He bought it when we first arrived in England." She lifted candid eyes to his face. "Are you the highwayman, Captain Clare?"

He shook his head.

"No, Miss Westlake, I am not. As for the mare—well, that is not my secret, and so I must say no more. Forgive me."

"No need to ask forgiveness." Christina limped across to the window-seat and sat down. "This house is full of secrets, I believe, but I did not follow you in order to pry into them. I want to explain something to you."

He looked at her with amused surprise.

"You followed me?"

"Yes," she said simply. "My mother and Stephen are engaged in arguing whether or not you should have been taken into our confidence, which seems to me exceedingly pointless at this stage, so I slipped out and came after you. When I heard what was being discussed in this room, I said the only thing I could think of. I knew that Stephen's horse would be in the stables, and I hoped to convince them that a mistake had been made."

He crossed the room and stood looking quizzically down at her.

"What if I had been the man they were seeking?"

She smiled a little, tilting her head back to look up into his face.

"A small man, I heard the soldier say," she remarked pensively, "and injured also. I think you would have acted less vigorously at our first meeting if you had sustained a wound as recently as last night. Besides, it seemed certain that that objectionable young man was bent upon causing trouble for you, and the least I could do was to try to foil a vindictiveness provoked on my behalf. To be honest, I did not greatly care whether or not you were the man they were looking for."

He laughed and shook his head.

"This is frankness indeed," he said lightly, "but I am none the less deeply in your debt. Now what was it you wished to explain to me?"

"I will tell you, sir, but will you not be seated?" She indicated the place beside her and Adrian sat down, but for several moments longer Christina remained silent, looking down at her hands tightly clasped in her lap. He waited patiently, and at length she said in a low voice:

"It is not easy to find the right words, for I would not have you think me lacking in respect towards my mother. It is simply that I do not share her reasons for wishing to regain possession of Coombe Royal. To me, that is but a means to an end."

"Which is?" he prompted quietly, though already he could guess whither this was leading.

"To clear my father's name," she replied, "for that I have sworn to do if it is humanly possible. I made that promise to him and to myself the day he died." She was still speaking quietly, but a deep and powerful emotion throbbed in her voice. "You do not know how he suffered under the unjust stigma of murder. He assumed the guilt of that crime willingly for his brother Edmund's sake, and he bore it willingly as long as Edmund lived, but he was convinced that the truth would be made known in time, when the real culprit was beyond the reach of justice. But then he found that burden fastened upon him for all time by another man's greed, and that man his only surviving brother. It was a bitter sorrow which never left him for the rest of his life. I will make his innocence known! It is the only thing I can do for him now!"

Adrian's glance rested thoughtfully on her face. She was not looking at him, but staring straight before her as though she had forgotten his presence and was merely expressing her thoughts aloud. He felt himself strangely moved by her words, and by the realization that she had dedicated herself to this well-nigh impossible task undeterred by the fact that she was poor and almost friendless, and pitting herself against a man of wealth and influence. This was the sort of sublime folly which woke an instant response in his own heart.

"If faith and courage can achieve it," he said quietly, "then you will fulfil that promise."

The look of high purpose faded from her face as she turned towards him again, and her next words showed that her dreams were built upon a foundation of practical common-sense.

"Faith and courage alone are not enough," she replied, "and that is why I must first get possession of my inheritance. Wealth spells power, Captain Clare! This is a lesson I have learned only too well, and I will spend every penny of mine, if need be, to establish my father's innocence before all the world."

"You have a plan, then?" Adrian asked with a hint of

surprise in his voice, and she shrugged, spreading out her hands in a gesture more French than English.

"Scarcely that, but I have given the matter much thought. If my uncle Edmund did confess the truth before he died, then two men know of it—Marcus Westlake and Walter Kelsby. My claim to Coombe Royal is just! If it succeeds, I will pay Kelsby as well to reveal his knowledge as my uncle has paid him to keep silent, and unless he is less shrewd than I suppose, he will see the wisdom of giving his support to the lawful heir."

Adrian frowned.

"To achieve that, it will be necessary to inform Kelsby of your presence in England and the claim you have come to make."

"Well, why not?" There was a gleam in the grey eyes as they met his. "You said yourself that only a lawyer could deal with this matter, and does not boldness often fare better than timidity?"

He smiled, but said warningly:

"True, but rashness often leads to a disaster which prudence could have averted. Go to Kelsby if you must, but leave all the papers which prove your claim in some safe hiding-place meanwhile. Copies will tell him all he needs to know, and if you place the originals in his hands, you put it in his power to sell you to Marcus Westlake if he chooses."

"Yes, that is very true, and I thank you for the warning," she agreed. "Such a possibility, I confess, had not occurred to me." She sighed, setting an elbow on the window-sill and cupping her pointed chin in her hand. "There are so many pitfalls to be avoided, and I feel that I am groping all the time in the dark. If only I knew for certain what my uncle is like! I would not even know him if we met, for I have been told that he does not resemble my father in the least." A sudden thought seemed to strike her, and she added eagerly: "Did you not say, Captain Clare, that you were acquainted with his wife at one time? What is she like? She is much younger than my uncle, is she not?"

"Yes, she was about your own age when I knew her."

Adrian paused to take out his snuff-box, seeking a respite, however brief, in which to consider a question for which he had been totally unprepared. What was Helen like? Had he ever really known that, even in those enchanted days so long ago? He had been dazzled by her beauty, and had bitter experience of her wilfulness, but beyond that his knowledge did not go. "She was one of the most beautiful women I have ever seen," he said quietly at last, "and her character was imperious rather than gentle, but that was close upon seven years ago. She may have changed since then."

Christina had been watching the ducks disporting themselves on and about the pond before the inn, but now her gaze returned to the man beside her. He was looking down at the snuff-box which he still held, but in a manner which suggested that he did not really see it, and he was unaware of her grave, searching regard. After a moment or two he appeared to dismiss whatever thought or memory had possessed him. He returned the box to his pocket and looked at her with a smile.

"It was already my intention, since I find myself in this neighbourhood, to pay my respects to Mrs. Westlake," he said briskly. "Probably I shall make the acquaintance of her husband, also, and though it is not always possible to form an accurate judgement from such a meeting, I shall be happy to return here and describe him to you."

"You are very kind, sir, and I am most truly grateful." She paused, smoothing a fold of her skirt with slender fingers, and after a moment added carefully: "Mamma does not yet know the purpose I have in mind. As you have seen, she is not strong, and I do not wish to worry her more than is needful."

"I understand, Miss Westlake, and you may trust to my discretion," Adrian assured her at once, but though Christina cast him a grateful glance, it seemed that she had not yet completed all that she desired to say.

"You must not think, either, that she means to be unkind," she pursued, not looking at him. "I know I am a sad disappointment to her, for all that she says is true.

I am plain, and a cripple, but I have learned to accept it, so I do not know why I behaved so absurdly when she spoke of it just now. I am not usually so foolish, I assure you."

Compassion shook him again as he looked down at the dark, bowed head, and the long, slender hands whose nervous restlessness belied the calm words; he wished fervently that he could tell her, with truth, that she was beautiful, but she would despise any such compliments for the empty flattery they were. Christina Westlake would never be a beauty, and she had the honesty and the courage to admit it. Yet she was by no means as plain as she had apparently been led to believe, for those luminous, expressive grey eyes would have redeemed the meanest countenance.

When he did not reply, she looked up almost defiantly, but it was not until the colour swept across her face again that he realized how intently he had been studying her. To cover both her embarrassment and his own, he said lightly:

"If it is foolish to wish for beauty, then every woman who ever lived is guilty of folly. Believe me, when you are able to take your rightful place in the world you will find that you have admirers in plenty."

"To be sure I shall!" The rallying tone had served its purpose, and she spoke drily. "They will come wooing my fortune, and see in the estate of Coombe Royal beauty enough to make up for my lack of it. Stephen is only the first of them."

"Stephen?" Constantly she was surprising him with her perception and her frankness. "Stephen Ancroft?"

"Who else?" She was smiling now almost mischievously, and yet there was a trace of sadness in her voice. "Did you suppose it is concern for Mamma or for me which makes him so anxious to serve us? His father was a Jacobite, as Mamma's family were, and lost everything after the rebellion in 'fifteen. Stephen has only a very little money which he inherited from his mother, who was French, and he looks to me to mend his fortunes for him."

Adrian leaned back in his seat and regarded her with perplexity and amusement.

"Yet you still accept his help and his company?"

She shrugged.

"Why not? We needed a man's escort, and there was no one else. He does not know, of course, that I have guessed what he has in mind. Besides, once I have achieved my purpose, I dare say that I will marry him. At least I know the extent of his weaknesses, for we have been brought up almost as brother and sister."

Adrian looked at her, but could find nothing to say. She baffled him, this strange girl with her practical common-sense and her dedicated dreams, her painful awareness of her own afflictions and the humorous resignation with which she accepted them. It seemed incredible that she was the daughter of the foolish, chattering, self-pitying Phoebe Westlake, and he reflected that the father rather than the mother must have had the shaping of Christina's life and character. She misconstrued his silence, and lifted her head defiantly.

"I fear I have shocked you, Captain Clare," she challenged him. "You are thinking, no doubt, that a modest young woman would never speak so, especially to a new acquaintance."

He shook his head, and matched frankness with frankness in his reply.

"I was thinking, Miss Westlake," he said quietly, "that the bond between you and your father must have been very close."

The defiant stare relaxed and her eyes filled with tears, but she forced them back determinedly.

"It was indeed," she replied sadly. "We used to talk together by the hour, and he encouraged me to speak frankly, even though Mamma disapproved most strongly. He used to say that he wished me to be able to think for myself. I have tried to do what he would have wished, but there have been so many difficulties, and I have been so lonely since he died." She broke off, moving her hands in a deprecating gesture, looking up at him with a little wistful smile. "Forgive me, Captain Clare. I presume too much upon a brief acquaintance, but I wish you could have met my father. You would have liked each other, I am sure."

The subdued murmur of voices and laughter from the tap-room swelled suddenly in volume, and there was a clattering of feet in the stone-flagged passage as the soldiers trooped out to resume their fruitless search for Jeremy Brigg. Adrian got up, and took Christina's hand to help her to her feet.

"I am honoured that you should think so," he said gently, "for I can guess, I think, how great a compliment it is. Believe me, I wish with all my heart that I were worthy of it."

6

Old Acquaintance

When he had parted from Christina, Adrian at once sought out Japhet Barnby and informed him that he and his servant would remain at the inn that night, for it was clear that if he were to visit Coombe Royal it would be too late to resume his journey that day. Titus arrived soon after this, and, receiving news of this change of plan with his usual philosophic calm, prepared to wait patiently until he was told, or could discover, his master's reasons for this further delay.

Adrian dined with the ladies and Stephen Ancroft in the oak-panelled parlour, but excused himself as soon as the meal was over. He sent for his horse, and having ascertained the road to Coombe Royal, bade Titus await his return and rode away at a brisk trot.

The directions he had been given brought him a short while later to a pair of tall, wrought-iron gates, their pillars crowned with crouching beasts so worn by time and weather that it was impossible to identify them. The gates stood wide, and beyond them a well-kept drive ran straight as an arrow between an avenue of splendid trees to disappear a furlong or so away over the crest of a slight rise. Adrian spurred forward, between the gates and past the neat lodge, and so came a few minutes later to a point from which the house of Coombe Royal lay full in view.

It was, he judged, some two hundred years old, built of a pale stone which looked almost golden against the greys and browns of the wooded hill behind it. Great mullioned windows flung back the rays of the setting sun, and above the gabled roof, smoke from the graceful chimneys curled lazily into the air. There were lawns about it, and flower-beds empty as yet, and here and there great trees as old or older than the house itself. So this was Christina's heritage, the prize of which the elder brother had been robbed by the younger.

A second pair of gates, smaller and more delicately fashioned than the first, closed the entrance to the gardens, which were separated from the park by a sunken wall, but obviously his approach had been observed, for before he reached them a servant appeared and hurried to open them, and then to take the Captain's horse as he dismounted at the foot of the flight of shallow steps leading to the front door.

Adrian trod confidently up the steps, and was greeted at the top by a butler with the air and presence of a prelate, who bowed him into the house but informed him at the same moment that Mr. Westlake was at present from home. Adrian nodded in response to this information, but said firmly:

"Perhaps Mrs. Westlake will receive me if she is at home. Inform her that Captain Clare craves the pleasure of an interview with her."

The butler bowed gravely and went away, and Adrian was left to take stock of his surroundings. They had passed through the small vestibule immediately within the front door, and he found himself now in what must have been originally the great hall of the mansion. The walls were panelled and hung with antique weapons, logs smouldered in the vast stone fireplaces at either end, and opposite to the door by which he had entered, a broad staircase rose gracefully to serve an encircling gallery. If Helen's goal had been wealth and position, then undoubtedly she had achieved it with her marriage.

The butler returned after a few minutes and conducted Adrian out of the hall and along a wide corridor, pausing at last to throw open a door and announce the Captain's name. Conscious of suddenly quickened heartbeats, Adrian stepped forward into a room all white panelling and pale silk hangings, where the rosy glow of evening contended with golden candlelight. After the dimness of the corridor he was dazzled for a moment, and then his eyes accustomed themselves to the sudden brilliance, and he found himself face to face with Helen at last.

She was standing in the middle of the room, a stately figure in a wide-skirted, rose-coloured gown of some rich silk that shimmered in the candlelight. For a moment she remained thus, staring at him while the servant withdrew and softly closed the door, and then she moved forward with outstretched hand.

"Adrian!" she said softly. "Adrian Clare! Now indeed I can believe in miracles."

"In miracles?" Adrian endeavoured to speak lightly. "Is it miraculous that, being in this neighbourhood, I should give myself the pleasure of waiting upon you?"

He had placed his hand beneath hers to raise it to his lips as formality demanded, but before he could withdraw it her other hand came up to imprison his, and her wallflower-brown eyes, so striking a contrast to the rich tawny gold of her hair, were lifted searchingly to his face, but she did not answer his question. Instead she said in a low voice:

"You have not changed! I would have known you anywhere! Come, sit down, and tell me what brings you to this benighted spot."

Still clasping his hand, she drew him to the couch before the fire, nor did she release it even when they were seated. For a few moments he looked at her in silence, finding her even more beautiful than his memory of her, for, lovely as she had been in her girlhood, her beauty now had ripened to a voluptuous richness that made his senses swim. It swept from his mind all thought of the wounds she had dealt him years before, of the mad follies he had committed in his quest for forgetfulness, even of his meeting that morning with Christina and the strange story he had heard at the inn. Murmuring her name in a broken voice, he freed his hand from hers and caught her in his arms.

She came to the embrace willingly, even eagerly, returning his kisses with an ardour for which he was unprepared. With her cheek pressed to his she said in a whisper:

"I knew that you would come back to me! I knew it! Sooner or later you would have to come!"

There was a note of exultation in her voice, in the certainty of her power over him, that jarred faintly on his senses, though in the intoxication of the moment he barely heeded it. Only later, when he was free of the immediate spell of her beauty, would the memory of it return to trouble him.

"Are you an enchantress, then?" he asked softly. "Did you weave charms to bring me to you?"

She moved so that she lay back against his shoulder, looking up at him through thick, gold-tipped lashes, an enigmatic smile curving her lips.

"Had I witchcraft at my command, my dear, you would not have tarried so long from me. Ah, Adrian, why did you not come sooner? Were not the last words I wrote to you a promise that I would remember you with kindness?"

"No!" Anger stirred swiftly within him at that reminder of the letter which had shattered his hopes and dreams. "You followed the promise with a warning that we must never meet again."

She laughed softly, mockingly, and he realized that she had spoken with intent, that her reference to her dismissal of him had been no unlucky slip of the tongue.

"Yet you are here!" She lifted her hand to his cheek in a light, careless caress. "Dear fool, what would you have had me write? I was but three months wed."

"And now?" he questioned as she paused.

"Now I go my own way!" There was mockery still in her smile, but he felt that it was no longer directed at him. "Marcus does not interfere. What, does that surprise you? Yet such arrangements are by no means uncommon."

"In London, no!" he replied dubiously. "But in the country——"

Her lazy laughter interrupted him; her hand moved caressingly on his sleeve.

"Oh, the country!" she said contemptuously. "My dear, do I have the look of a country housewife?"

The absurdity of the question made him laugh.

"Not in the least, yet I do not think I have seen you in London."

"No, that I have not yet achieved," she replied pensively, "but, by the mercy of Providence, Bath is none so far hence. I contrive to amuse myself tolerably well there during the season, and at other times I fill the house with guests. We are quiet at present, which is uncommon, but now that you have come I am glad of it."

This was going a little too fast for Captain Clare, who felt that until he had decided upon a future course of action it would be wiser not to commit himself in any way. Prudently ignoring the latter part of her remark, he said casually:

"You are fortunate then in having a house which lends itself to entertaining on a lavish scale."

"This monstrous antiquity?" Helen sat up and patted her ruffled curls into place under the little, lace-trimmed cap. "If the choice were mine, the whole place would be torn down and a modern house built in its stead, but Marcus will not hear of it. I am permitted to make my own apartments habitable, and that is all."

"And very charmingly you have done so, if this is an example." Adrian rested his arm along the back of the couch and looked round at the soft, pale colours, the French furniture and fragile porcelain. "It is a setting worthy of your beauty."

He broke off as his idle glance came to rest upon a portrait on the wall facing the window. It was a small, head-and-shoulders study of a young man, and a small table was set immediately below it to bear flowers, two branches of candles and a small velvet case containing a miniature. The whole arrangement had almost the look of a shrine, but it was not that which startled him, and checked the words on his lips. From the pictured face the grey eyes of Christina were gravely regarding him.

" 'Tis striking, is it not?" Helen's voice broke in upon the strange confusion of his thoughts. "It is a portrait of Godfrey Westlake, my husband's elder brother. He killed a man, and was forced to fly the country."

"In a duel, I presume?" Adrian asked casually, feeling that some remark was expected of him. Helen shook her head.

"No, he shot him as he sat over his wine," she replied calmly. "There was bad blood between them, I am told. Godfrey made his escape, and later died abroad."

Adrian got up and walked across to the portrait. A strong resemblance to Christina could be traced, not in the eyes alone, but also in the broad brow and sensitive, rather wide mouth. It was a fine face, strong with a strength spiritual rather than physical, and Adrian had no difficulty in believing that a man with such a countenance would make unhesitatingly the sacrifice which Godfrey Westlake had made for his young brother.

"There were three brothers, but Marcus is the only one yet living." Helen had followed him across the room, and her words seemed to echo the trend of his thoughts. "The youngest, Edmund, was a sickly lad and died when he was barely twenty-three. This is his likeness."

She picked up the velvet case and handed it to Adrian, and he found himself looking down at another face, strikingly similar to the larger portrait but lacking its manly strength. Helen, looking down at the miniature, spoke again, and there was an undertone in her voice which he could not quite define. It sounded almost like secret, mocking laughter.

"They both resembled their mother, who, unless her

portraits lie, was something of a beauty. My husband is wholly different in appearance." The laughter was unmistakable now, and it was not altogether pleasant. "Poor Marcus! He is pure Westlake—a family not generally remarkable for good looks."

Adrian looked from the miniature in his hand to the portrait with the candles burning steadily beneath it, and a faint frown etched itself between his brows. There was something incongruous in the presence of these two pictures in a room so completely Helen's own; they were deliberately arranged to attract attention, and to point, by subtle inference, to the absence of any likeness of her husband. That there was some meaning behind it he felt certain, though he could not guess what it might be. He said lightly:

"If the eldest brother were indeed guilty of such a crime, it is curious to set his portrait in a place of honour. One would suppose that Mr. Westlake would prefer so lamentable an occurrence to be forgotten."

"No doubt he would prefer it!" The laughter still lingered in Helen's voice and eyes. "I found that portrait by chance three years ago, thrust into the darkest corner of a room very rarely used. I chose to rescue it from obscurity."

His brows lifted.

"May I ask why?"

"I find it attractive!" She laid one hand on his arm, and with the other reached across to take the miniature from him and restore it to its place on the table. Her hair brushed his cheek as she turned, and her face was very close to his. "Good looks have always been one of my greatest weaknesses."

He was stirred afresh by the power of her beauty, by the warmth and perfume of her so close beside him, and yet somewhere at the back of his mind the thought formed coldly that this was not the true answer to his question. Then, before either of them could move, or speak again, the door crashed open, rocking back on its hinges, and a sudden draught swept into the room to set the candles flickering wildly.

Adrian spun round to face the man who stood swaying upon the threshold, and knew beyond doubt that this was Marcus Westlake. A big man, ungainly even in repose, with blunt, heavy features topped by a brown tie-wig which was now a trifle askew. He was in riding-dress, his boots and coat-skirts plentifully bespattered with mud, and his face was flushed, with anger or with wine. For a moment he stared evilly at the couple standing beneath his brother's portrait, and then he advanced with unsteady steps, kicking the door shut behind him.

Helen moved away from Adrian, but not hurriedly, or with any sign of confusion at being found in so compromising a situation. She took a few leisurely paces forward and regarded her husband distastefully.

"Is it necessary, when a guest is present, to behave as though my boudoir were a tap-room?" she demanded coldly. "You shame both yourself and me by such conduct. Captain Clare, since I am obliged to present my husband to you, allow me also to make his apologies for him."

With difficulty Adrian suppressed a gasp, flashing a startled glance from one to the other. He fully expected Westlake to answer that challenge with one of graver import, but to his astonishment nothing of the kind occurred. There was fury in the man's eyes, certainly, but it was a baffled fury, as though restraint were imposed upon him against his will. He bowed jerkily in Adrian's direction, and muttered a curt greeting.

Adrian recovered himself sufficiently to return the bow, and tried to follow Helen's lead as she made smooth, social conversation, but he could not shake off a feeling of unreality. Westlake had flung himself into a chair and stretched his booted feet towards the fire, contributing little to the talk save grunts and an occasional monosyllable, and Adrian studied him covertly from time to time.

What he saw in that heavy face puzzled him more than ever. Westlake was vigorous enough in body, but his countenance would have labelled him far older than his fifty-odd years. There were pouches beneath the deep-set hazel eyes, and lines upon the forehead and scored deeply from nose to mouth, while the lips themselves were set in a bitter, down-curving line. It was the face of a man soured and distrustful, whose triumphs had all turned to dust and ashes in his hands, and yet he did not give the impression of one who would be hounded by remorse. "A hard man". Jeremy Brigg's words echoed in Adrian's memory, and he knew that the highwayman had spoken truly. Yet, hard as he undoubtedly was, Marcus Westlake was breaking or had broken upon some obstacle even more unyielding than himself.

As soon as he could do so without an appearance of undue haste, Adrian took his leave. Helen had discovered that he was lodged at the Merry Month of May and was obviously convinced that his stay in Wiltshire would be protracted, for as he bade her farewell, she said with calm certainty:

"We shall see you again before long, shall we not? Remember, if you find Barnby's notions of comfort unworthy of the name, you will be most welcome here."

He thanked her, but made no definite reply, and so left them. As he rode back to the inn through the uncertain moonlight, it was Helen who filled his thoughts, for he had found the old magic as strong as ever, and knew that, come good, come ill, he would not leave England now. Yet ever and anon, through the memory of her beauty and her eager welcome, he found himself challenged by a pair of grey eyes which seemed now to be the eyes he had seen in the portrait at Coombe Royal, and now those of Christina herself. The memory of that clear, direct gaze troubled him in a manner he could not define, and when he reached the inn he went straight to the room prepared for him, for he felt that he could not face it again that night, in fact as well as in fancy.

Titus, coming to pull off his boots and ask if there was anything he desired, found him preoccupied and disinclined to talk, and wondered at it. Adrian paid little heed to him, but sat staring into the fire and trying to solve the problems arising out of his sudden decision to remain in England.

That these would be innumerable, he knew. In the struggle which must soon be joined for possession of Coombe Royal, he was likely to find himself with a foot in either camp, and it did not require his military experience to tell him that this was an unenviable position at any time. More pressing than these possibilities, however, was the question of how he was to live now that he had defied his uncle's express commands, for he had with him only a very little money, no more than would have sufficed for the expenses of the journey to Bristol.

He began to consider his resources, and their sum total was not encouraging. Soldiering was the only trade he knew; he had a devoted servant; a costly and extensive wardrobe; a good horse, and some equally excellent weapons.

It was the accidental proximity of those last two items in his thoughts which suggested a solution to the problem. For some minutes he debated the possibilities to which it had given rise, and slowly amusement crept into his face. He smote his hand lightly on the arm of his chair and turned to speak to his servant, who had come back into the room with wine and a glass on a tray.

"Titus," he said briskly, "I have a task for you! Tomorrow you will ride on to Bristol, have my gear fetched ashore and despatched to me here, and inform the Captain that I shall not, after all, require a passage to Virginia."

Titus poured wine into the glass and bore it delicately across the room to his master. He said placidly:

"As you wish, Captain, but what will my Lord Warham say to that?"

"He may say what he pleases. I shall not be there to hear it." Adrian took the glass, but paused as he detected a faintly disapproving look in his servant's eyes. "Oh, I am grateful to the old gentleman for all that he has done for me, but I can see no reason why I should be driven out of England merely because I abandoned the career he chose for me. A man's life is his own, to live as he chooses."

"That is true, sir," Titus agreed drily. "May I presume to ask how you propose to live yours?"

"Certainly! I am about to embark upon a new career, which will involve me in no expense since I am already equipped for it in all respects. No, that is not entirely true. I lack a mask, but no doubt our good friend Jeremy Brigg can furnish me with one." He raised his glass to his lips, but over its rim he watched comprehension and dismay flood into the servant's face; there were little devils of laughter dancing in his eyes. "Yes, Titus! I mean to try my fortune on the High Toby!"

7

The Prosperous Attorney

From that suddenly formed resolve no persuasion could shift him. Titus used many, for he could see nothing but disaster ahead if his beloved master insisted upon carrying out his purpose. It was not only the dangers surrounding the project which disturbed him, for he had seen Captain Clare risk his life on more than one occasion in the past, but then it had been a soldier's death he faced, carrying with it a measure of glory. This was peril of a very different sort. If the Captain took to the road, and were captured, his fate would be that of any common criminal—the gallows, and his body in chains on some wayside gibbet as a warning to similar offenders.

Finally, however, Titus realized the futility of his efforts, and desisted, leaving Adrian free to concentrate on the details of his plan. His chances of a successful career on the highway were, he thought, uncommonly good. His military training would be of great value, but even more useful would be his acquaintance with Jeremy Brigg and the Barnby family, and the fact that they were already under an obligation to him. He resolved to visit Brigg at the earliest opportunity, take him into his confidence, and seek his advice.

The moral aspects of the matter troubled him very little. It was by no means uncommon for an impoverished gentleman to solve his financial difficulties by such means, and for close upon a century the legend of the highwayman had been growing. He was the aristocrat of the criminal world, the hero of innumerable stories and ballads; very often he combined his activities upon the road with some highly respectable calling, and was in many cases in league with inn-keepers and ostlers, who sent him word of any particularly rich prize leaving their establishments, and warned him when the danger of capture became pressing. It was, in fact, just the sort of life to appeal to a man of Adrian Clare's temperament, with its excitement and danger and the pitting of his wits and resourcefulness against the forces of law and order.

He rose early next morning, and having seen Titus set out for Bristol, mounted his own horse and rode away in the direction of the woods and the cottage they concealed. He had seen nothing of his fellow-guests since the previous day, and though he tried to convince himself that this was mere chance, he knew in his heart that he was deliberately avoiding Christina. Ever since his visit to Coombe Royal he had been conscious of a faint, uncomfortable feeling of disloyalty towards her, and yet what loyalty, in heaven's name, did he owe to a girl whom he had known for barely twenty-four hours? His concern should be for Helen, who would find herself shorn of wealth and influence if Christina's claim to the Westlake fortune were proved. His whole attention should be given to the task of accumulating a considerable sum of money against that day, for that she would remain with her husband once retribution descended upon him, Adrian could not believe.

He left the road for the track leading into the woods, and after several false casts succeeded in finding the beginning of the path which led to the hidden glade. As his horse picked its way down the last, steep slope, the door of the cottage opened and a burly fair-haired man came out. For a moment Adrian thought that it was

Japhet Barnby, but a second and closer look showed him that it was in fact his brother, Reuben, whom he had already met at the inn.

Barnby seemed surprised but not displeased to see him, and answered Adrian's inquiry with the information that Brigg's wound, though still painful, was beginning to heal just as it ought. He then took the Captain's horse and led it away to the makeshift stable, leaving Adrian to step into the cottage alone.

Jeremy Brigg was sitting up in bed, his left arm supported in a sling, considering with a thoughtful and somewhat disparaging eye a collection of objects spread out on the blanket which covered him. As Adrian strolled into the room he caught a glimpse of a watch, a couple of rings, and one or two other trinkets, and then Brigg's sound hand swept them all into a heap as he looked up with a beam of delight at his visitor.

"Well, my friend," Adrian greeted him pleasantly, "your hurts are mending, I hear! I am heartily glad of it."

"All thanks to you, and that man of yours, Captain," Jerry replied promptly. " 'Tis a debt I can never repay, and 'twas a poor return you had for it when you reached the inn. Reuben's just been telling me of it. Never would I have let you take the mare if I'd known the red-coats had got wind of her."

"They never set eyes on her, though, thanks to your kinsfolk's readiness," Adrian replied, pulling forward the only chair in the room and sitting down. "Nor would suspicion have fallen upon me at all save for young Tedburn's eagerness to avenge himself. I am happy to say, however, that his malice recoiled upon his own head."

"The more reason, then, for you to be on your guard, sir, if you mean to stay in these parts," Brigg warned him grimly. "There be a deal I could tell you about young Mr. Gilbert, and none of it pleasant."

"I can well believe that," Adrian replied cheerfully. He nodded towards the little heap of trinkets which Jerry was still absently fingering. "You will be planning, I imagine, to convert those baubles into coin at no very distant time."

"That's right, sir!" The shrewd brown eyes met his frankly, a humorous twinkle stirring behind them. "But I'll ask you to pardon me from saying how or where. There's tricks to every trade, Captain!"

"I am aware of it." Adrian leaned forward and lowered his voice. "Will you teach me the tricks of yours?"

The twinkle vanished, the brown eyes narrowed, and for a long moment Jeremy Brigg neither moved nor spoke. At last he said bitterly:

"Why, sir? For a wager? To amuse yourself, because there's naught better to do?" He shook his head. "No, Captain! It may be no more than a frolic to you, but it's life or death to me, and to those as trusts me. I'm wishful to oblige you, but I'll not do it that way."

Adrian was silent for a moment, and then he said quietly:

"Why do you do it, Jeremy Brigg?"

Jeremy shrugged, and then swore as the movement irked his injured shoulder.

"To live," he said simply. "I were a groom once, at Mereton Hall, till young Mr. Gilbert had me turned off without a character. No chance after that o' finding another place hereabouts, and horses was the only thing I knew. This way I be servant to no man. I know the country for miles around, and I've got some good friends. It's as good a way to make a living as any other."

"Exactly," Adrian agreed, "and there's the answer to your question, my friend. Not for a frolic, not for a wager. I have reasons for wishing to remain in this part of the country, but I lack the means. In short, I have scarcely a penny to my name."

For a little while longer the shrewd gaze searched his face. He met it unflinchingly, and after a moment or two Jerry nodded as though he were satisfied. He said sympathetically:

"Was it the cards, Captain?"

Adrian laughed.

"Among other follies, Jerry," he replied. "There were many of them, and all exceedingly expensive. Well, what do you say? Will you take me as your apprentice?"

"Aye, sir, that I will, and honoured to do it," Jerry replied promptly. "Give me a couple o' days, Captain, and then come here again. Meanwhile, best tell Japhet and Polly what you are about. They'll need to know if you mean to stay there."

"Can I do that without endangering them?"

Jeremy chuckled.

"I've lived there myself, sir, for weeks at a time, and none the wiser. That inn o' theirs be a regular rabbit-warren when you know its secrets, and there's no servants to poke and pry into what don't concern 'em. 'Tis all in the family, ye see! The wenches help Polly in the kitchen, and Japhet and Reuben and the two lads do all else as is needful. All you need to do is find some likely tale to account for staying there. 'Tisn't the sort o' place a gentleman like you would choose in the ordinary way."

"That you may safely leave to me," Adrian assured him, getting to his feet and holding out his hand. "In two days' time, then. I am grateful to you, Jeremy Brigg."

He rode back to the inn well satisfied with the results of his visit to the cottage, and found Christina alone in the parlour. She was seated at the table with a litter of papers before her and a pen in her hand, and she looked up quickly as he entered.

"I am taking your advice, you see," she said when they had greeted each other, "and making copies of all Father's papers. It is a tedious task, but well worthwhile if it will remove the danger of betrayal."

"Worthwhile, indeed!" Adrian leaned his folded arms on the back of a chair drawn up by the table, and looked down at her with a smile. "I take it, then, that you are determined to consult Walter Kelsby?"

"Yes. Diccon is to drive me into Marlborough tomorrow in the gig. That is why I must finish copying these today."

Diccon was Barnby's younger son, a lad of fifteen. Adrian said with a touch of concern:

"You do not propose to go alone?"

"Stephen will go with me, but Mamma does not feel herself equal to the journey. She is far from well today, and is laid down upon the bed."

He had a shrewd suspicion that Mrs. Westlake's indisposition was provoked by the fear that she might be expected to help Christina in her present task, but he expressed civil concern at the news, and a hope that she might soon find herself recovered. Christina made no reply to this, but said, looking down at the pen in her hand:

"Captain Clare, did you see my uncle yesterday?"

"Yes, I did." Adrian paused for a moment, seeing again that scented, candle-lit room and the menacing figure of Marcus Westlake framed in the doorway. It would be difficult to describe the man calmly and disinterestedly, to prevent his own instinctive antagonism towards Helen's husband from distorting everything he might say of him.

Christina was watching him eagerly. He pulled out the chair and sat down, and as impartially as he could recounted his meeting with Westlake and his impression of the man. She listened attentively until he remarked that her uncle seemed to be oppressed by some sort of mental conflict, and then she said indignantly:

" 'Tis conscience, belike! If ever a man had cause to feel remorse, it is he!"

Adrian agreed, and refrained from voicing his own opinion that remorse was an emotion unknown to Marcus Westlake. Instead he said:

"I saw a portrait of your father at Coombe Royal. You are very like him."

She flushed with pleasure, but when she spoke her voice was still indignant.

"Has my uncle no scruples at all? How can he bear to live with so constant a reminder of the brother he wronged and robbed?"

"As to that, I fancy Mrs. Westlake is responsible." Adrian's voice was carefully non-committal. "The portrait hangs in her boudoir, and she has a miniature of Edmund Westlake also."

Christina's eyes glowed.

"Oh, I will bless her for that! She must have a kind heart, for she cannot know the truth, and if she believed my father guilty, she would not have his likeness in her room." She broke off, her face clouding suddenly. "I wish my uncle were not married! For him I have no pity, but she is innocent and I am loth to do her any harm."

Adrian said nothing, but he was conscious of oddly conflicting feelings. He loved Helen, of course; he had loved her for years, in spite of her treatment of him, and yet Christina's warm-hearted outburst seemed in some way to intensify the curious shadow of doubt which had lurked at the back of his mind since the previous evening. He recalled the undertone of mockery in Helen's voice as she spoke of her husband's two dead brothers, and he knew that whatever had prompted her to set their likenesses in a place of honour, it was not kind-heartedness. Helen was not kind; tantalizing, maddening, desirable, but not kind.

"At least they have no children!" Christina's voice broke in upon his thoughts. "I am truly thankful for that! If there had been children, I do not think I could have pressed my claim, even for my father's sake."

He was spared the necessity of replying to this by the entry into the room of Ruth, the younger of the two Barnby girls. She was carrying a letter which she handed to him with the information that it had been brought by a servant from Coombe Royal, who was now in the kitchen awaiting an answer. Adrian ripped it open and found a formally-worded invitation, in Helen's once-familiar hand, to dine next day with her and her husband.

"Bid the man tell Mrs. Westlake I shall be honoured to accept her invitation," he said to Ruth, but then added, as she turned to go: "No, wait! I will write a note for him to carry to her. You will excuse me, ma'am?"

He bowed slightly to Christina and went quickly out of the room. Ruth followed him, and for several moments Miss Westlake remained gazing at the closed door, a very wistful expression in her face. Then she sighed, and picking up her pen, applied herself once more to a task which now seemed even more wearisome then before.

Next morning Diccon drove the gig round to the door of the inn, followed by his elder brother, Clem, leading Mr. Ancroft's horse, and within a few minutes the little party had set off on their way to Marlborough. As they skirted the duck-pond and came to the road, Christina turned to look back over her shoulder, but if she was hoping for a glimpse of Captain Clare's tall, immaculate figure, she looked in vain. Clem was walking back towards the stables, and of the other occupants of the inn there was no sign.

The journey was uneventful, with no incident other than those occasioned by the deplorable state of the roads, but even so, Christina was thankful when at last the town was reached. Leaving Diccon with the gig at one of the humbler inns, she and Stephen walked to the quiet old house where Mr. Beauchamp lived, and where Walter Kelsby still conducted his business.

The young clerk who received them was frankly scornful of so shabby a couple, and the name of Westlake, which Mr. Ancroft announced with a flourish, produced no more than a stare of patent disbelief. Stephen bridled, but before he could speak again Christina laid a restraining hand on his arm and said firmly to the clerk:

"I assure you that Mr. Kelsby would wish to be informed of my presence here. Please be good enough to tell him that Godfrey Westlake's daughter desires an interview with him."

The quiet dignity of this speech was not without its effect, and the youth, waving her somewhat ungraciously to a chair, disappeared through a door on the far side of the room. After a few minutes he returned, bringing with him an elderly man in rusty black, with thin, stooping shoulders and sparse white hair. This worthy trod across the room to where Christina was seated with Stephen standing beside her, and peered at her over the spectacles perched on the end of his nose. Then, ejaculating, "God bless my soul!" he rounded upon his youthful colleague.

"Go to Mr. Kelsby at once," he commanded him, "and tell him that Miss Westlake is here."

The youth gaped, found himself waved imperatively away, and retreated again, this time by way of the door giving on to the hall. As this closed behind him, Christina looked curiously at the old man.

"You, sir, appear to have no doubt of my identity," she remarked.

He shook his head, a smile touching his lips.

"I knew your father, my dear young lady, and your grandmother also. There can be no doubt whose blood runs in your veins. Forty years I have been clerk to Mr. Beauchamp, and I have been with him to Coombe Royal more times than I can recall. To think that you are Mr. Godfrey's daughter! This will be glad news for Mr. Beauchamp, glad news indeed!"

He rambled on in this fashion until his junior returned with the information that Mr. Kelsby would receive Miss Westlake at once, and then he led them out of the room and up the stairs to a lighter and more spacious chamber on the first floor. A large desk, its top covered by a confusion of papers, occupied the most prominent position in the room, and behind the desk was sitting the most repellent-looking man Christina had ever seen.

A broad face of a curiously opaque and unhealthy pallor seemed to rest upon heavy shoulders with no neck to intervene; the wide, almost lipless mouth, like a knife-slit in a piece of dough, was utterly lacking in kindliness or humour, while the prominent eyes of an oddly light and indeterminate colour held no more warmth than two bubbles of pale glass. He got up as she walked towards him, and came round the desk towards her, revealing that despite his breadth of shoulder and enormous girth, he was of less than average height. He was dressed plainly enough, but in materials of the finest quality, and on the fat, pale hand extended to Christina a great ruby glowed.

"So you are Godfrey Westlake's daughter!" he greeted her. "Yes, I can see why my clerk had so little doubt of your identity. The likeness is remarkable. Upon my soul, this is a prodigious surprise to us all!"

His voice was a singularly flat and level monotone, as though it were produced by some mechanical contrivance with no capacity for feeling, and the pudgy fingers which had enveloped her slender ones were cold and faintly damp. It felt like the hand of a dead man, Christina thought, and with difficulty repressed a shudder. She was beginning to regret her decision to consult Mr. Kelsby.

The lawyer was looking inquiringly towards Stephen, and with an effort Christina recovered herself sufficiently to present him, and to explain the circumstances which had led to his presence there. Walter Kelsby's pale, protruding eyes passed expressionlessly from her face to Ancroft's.

"You are fortunate, Miss Westlake, in finding so devoted a friend," he remarked, and neither of them could be sure whether or not he spoke in irony. "Life can be difficult for two women alone in a foreign land."

They were all seated by this time, he behind his desk again, the two young people facing him across it. He leaned back in his chair and clasped his hands across his great paunch as he continued:

"You have some purpose, no doubt, in coming to visit me?"

"Naturally, Mr. Kelsby." Christina spoke calmly, for though fear and repulsion were still strong within her, she had mastered them both. "I have come to England to claim my inheritance, the estate of Coombe Royal. That was my father's dearest wish and his last command to me."

He nodded as though this was the answer he had expected, but said warningly:

"That is a matter which cannot be settled in a day. Such a claim must be thoroughly investigated. It will be necessary to produce proof of your identity, incontestable proof which will withstand the closest scrutiny."

"I am aware of that." Christina produced her packet of papers and pushed it across the desk towards him. "I think you will find there all that you require."

He took up the packet and opened it, but after the most cursory inspection raised his eyes sharply to her face.

"These are but copies."

"Exact copies, Mr. Kelsby, I assure you. The originals are in a place of safety and you may see them if you wish, but they shall not pass out of my hands at this stage. Their value is too great."

He was silent for a moment, and studied her closely as though his first impression of her had now proved false and he was seeking to correct it. There was a hint of respect in his eyes, and she felt a sudden return of confidence as she recognized it. Finally he nodded as though in agreement, and returned to his perusal of the papers.

"Very well, Miss Westlake," he said at last, putting them down again upon his desk. "I will put this matter in hand at once." He thrust back his chair and rose to his feet. "You realize, of course, that I shall be obliged to inform your uncle of it?"

"I had supposed it, sir," Christina replied composedly. "Such information will, I think, come more properly from you than from me, and for that reason we have been at some pains to keep secret our arrival in the neighbourhood. We are lodged at the Merry Month of May."

"Ah, yes! The Barnby family! They always were devoted to your father's interests," he replied, and once again she was baffled by the lack of expression in his voice. "I shall go to Coombe Royal tomorrow, and if it is agreeable to you, avail myself also of the opportunity to wait upon your mother."

It was not particularly agreeable to Christina, who mistrusted her parent's tendency to indiscreet chatter, but beyond replying that she was not certain whether Mrs. Westlake would be well enough to receive a visitor, she did not venture to dissuade him. It would not do, she felt, to antagonize Mr. Kelsby at this stage.

By the act of rising he had seemed to intimate that the interview was at an end. Christina got up also, but after a moment's hesitation said quietly to Ancroft:

"Will you be good enough, Stephen, to wait for me below? There is something I wish to say privately to Mr. Kelsby."

Stephen looked resentful, as though he would have liked to protest, but the firm tone of the request left him no choice but to comply. Christina waited until he had gone reluctantly from the room and then turned back to Kelsby, who had resumed his seat at the desk.

"I will be brief, sir," she said without preamble. "It is my most earnest desire to prove that my father was innocent of the crime which drove him into exile. I believe that you can help me to do it."

"A most natural and laudable desire, my dear young lady," Kelsby agreed after only the very slightest pause. "As to my ability to help you, however——" he left the sentence unfinished, and stared at her with cold, unrevealing eyes. Christina met that chilling regard steadily. She said quietly:

"When I am mistress of Coombe Royal, it will be in my power to reward very handsomely anyone who can provide me with the means to clear my father's name. Remember that, Mr. Kelsby, if you can think of anyone who might so help me."

She curtsied demurely and limped softly from the room without waiting for a reply, and left him sitting, like a fat, pale toad, behind his littered desk.

8

Perilous Enchantment

Captain Clare was surprised, when he arrived at Coombe Royal in response to Helen's invitation, to find that he was not the only guest. Mr. Tedburn was there, with his wife and eldest daughter, and close upon Adrian's heels came another couple, somewhat younger than the Tedburns, who were introduced to him as Sir Edward and Lady Manners. He had not envisaged Helen playing hostess to the local gentry, with whom she obviously had no common interests whatsoever, nor did it seem likely, from what he had seen on his earlier visit, that she was doing it to oblige her husband. He could only suppose that she found even these tedious guests preferable to her own company, and Westlake's.

Although the party had clearly been planned for some time, it soon became apparent that Adrian was the guest of honour, and also that the rest of the company were regarding him with a curiosity which was very faintly hostile. He was aware of speculation in their eyes as they looked at him, and of a significant exchange of glances now and then. He was too well versed in the social arts to betray his consciousness of this, but it roused in him a vague disquiet, which the attitude of his host insensibly increased.

Seated at the head of the table, and somehow contriving to look slightly dishevelled in spite of formal attire and powdered wig, Marcus Westlake was to all outward appearances the genial host, and yet Adrian, encountering his glance across the expanse of snowy damask and glittering glass and silver, discovered in those deep-set, brooding eyes a look of such murderous anger that he felt a sharp sense of shock. This was hatred, naked and undisguised, and yet for some inexplicable reason held rigidly in check.

He had no chance to speak to Helen alone, but all the while he was acutely aware of her, seated beside him at table, and, later, moving among her guests in the big drawing-room. She looked incredibly lovely in a gown of deep blue silk, embroidered with silver stars that gleamed and faded with her every movement, the gold of her hair hidden beneath powder, sapphires glinting in her ears and about her throat. Her beauty and the hunger it awoke in him were a torment almost too great to be endured, and yet in the presence of these others he must let no hint of it appear, must smile and laugh and make idle, meaningless conversation as though his whole being were not racked with the desire to hold her again in his arms, to feel her arms about him and her lips yielding eagerly to his. Only at the very last, when she gave him her hand to kiss farewell, and looked up at him through her lashes in the way he remembered so well, did the suspicion enter his mind that she was deliberately trifling with him.

He returned to the inn in no very amiable frame of

mind, and did his best to listen courteously and with attention to Christina's account of her visit to Walter Kelsby. She was quick to sense his mood, however, and bringing her eagerly begun tale to an abrupt conclusion, bade him a prim goodnight and went to join her mother in her bedchamber. Adrian, irritated by his own lack of sympathy, then drank a bottle of wine which he did not really want, restrained himself with difficulty from picking a quarrel with Stephen Ancroft, and took himself ill-humouredly off to bed.

Next morning saw him again at the cottage, where he found Jeremy Brigg deep in consultation with a stranger, a tall, lean, lantern-jawed individual in sober, well-cut riding-clothes. This gentleman Jerry introduced as Edward Sparrow, another member of the profession Captain Clare was about to enter, explaining that as he was himself incapable at present of initiating the Captain into the mysteries of the High Toby, he had enlisted Mr. Sparrow to do so in his stead.

The two men took stock of each other in silence and with mutual satisfaction. Mr. Sparrow was clearly impressed by the style and elegance of his friend's protégé, while Adrian, whose dealings with his fellow-men had been sufficiently wide to make him a shrewd judge of character, could find no fault with his chosen instructor. He had a merry eye which belied his somewhat melancholy cast of countenance, and a general air of being able to cope with any situation. He had another quality also, one which Adrian recognized.

"Were you ever a soldier?" he asked curiously.

Mr. Sparrow grinned.

"For close on seven years, Captain," he replied frankly, "until the day I had a fancy to be my own master again. But the army had made me lose what little liking I'd ever had for honest work, and that's why I took to the bridle-lay. I've never had cause yet to regret it."

The cheerful impudence of the answer made Adrian laugh, and Mr. Sparrow, regarding him with approval, was moved to remark that the Captain was a right 'un, and no mistake. Jeremy looked pleased at this, but, wasting no further time on an exchange of compliments, came instead to the purpose of the meeting.

"Ned'll set you on the right way to business, sir," he informed Adrian. "There's not a flash ken in these parts where he's not known, and not a track or bridle-path as he can't show you. You work with him for a week or two, and you'll be set up right and tight."

"I'm much obliged to him," Adrian said with a smile, "and to you, too, Jerry." He addressed himself to Mr. Sparrow. "I have a good horse, and my own pistols, but one thing I do lack is a mask. Nor have I the smallest notion where to obtain one."

"That's easy settled," Jerry broke in. "In the chest yonder, Ned. You know where to look." He watched his friend fling open the chest, and then looked again towards Adrian. "As for the horse, sir, it won't do to use your own. You'll need another, and we've took the liberty o' seeing to that, too."

"The devil you have!" Adrian exclaimed. "I am not questioning your actions, but why cannot I use my own mount?"

"Because it'll be known, sir," Ned Sparrow replied, coming back to the bedside with a strip of crêpe in his hand. "You'll be staying at the inn, and riding out on your own horse, but t'other will be stabled here. You'll leave yours in its place when there's work to be done, and fetch it again afore you go back to the inn. That way you'll stand in no danger o' being recognized by your mount."

"Which can happen very easy, Captain, as you've got good cause to know," Jerry added warningly. "Besides, that way there'll be less risk for Polly and Japhet. I don't say as there ain't places at the inn where a horse can be hid, but that's only in time o' danger. 'Twouldn't do for a regular thing."

Adrian admitted the force of these arguments, and went out with Ned to inspect the mount provided for him. This proved to be a magnificent animal, black as night from nose to tail, and built on lines which brought a gleam to Adrian's eyes even while he remarked ruefully that at present he was not in a position to purchase such a horse. Ned chuckled at this, and said with a sly, significant wink that that was a matter which could be settled wholly at the Captain's own convenience.

Adrian remained for some while at the cottage, and by the time he left he had been made free of a good deal of information concerning the trade of highway robbery. Mr. Sparrow, who was clearly of the opinion that no amount of talk could equal the value of actual experience, had charged him to return at dusk, when they would set out together to see what fortune might send them along the Bath road, and Captain Clare had agreed readily to this proposal. Since he was now pledged to his new career, the sooner he embarked upon it, the better.

While he was with his two confederates he had plenty to occupy his thoughts, but as soon as he found himself alone again, the memory of Helen returned to plague him, and on a sudden impulse he turned his horse's head in the direction of Coombe Royal. The need to see her again had overmastered caution, and though he could not entirely forget the uneasiness provoked by his previous visits to the house, it had not the power to keep him away.

This time he was admitted without question and conducted at once to the room where Helen had first received him, but on this occasion he did not find her alone. Her husband was with her, and also, perched grotesquely on one of the frail gilded chairs, an enormously fat man with a pale, repellent face. Adrian had paid sufficient heed to Christina's story the night before to realize that this must be Walter Kelsby, and wished for an instant that he had not come. An already difficult situation was not likely to be improved by this encounter.

Jut how difficult his position was soon became plain to him. Kelsby studied the newcomer with a pale, reptilian stare; Westlake, standing before the fire with both hands clenched upon the mantelpiece and his back to the room, did not even turn his head; but Helen, flushed and stormy-eyed, came up out of her chair like an avenging goddess.

"I wonder, sir, that you dare to show your face here!" was her startling greeting. "Why, in heaven's name, did you not warn us what was afoot? Or are you in league with that designing minx?"

Adrian, who had expected a very different welcome, blinked at her in astonishment. So taken aback was he that for a moment his brain refused to function and he could only wonder which of them had taken leave of their senses.

"Warned you of what?" he stammered. "I do not understand."

With an exclamation of anger and disbelief she turned away, and it was left to Kelsby to play the part of peacemaker. He heaved his vast bulk out of the chair and bowed ponderously to Adrian.

"Permit me, sir, to explain," he said in his flat, monotonous voice. "Mrs. Westlake is in a very natural state of agitation, for she and her husband have received a severe shock. In brief, my dear sir, a claim to this estate has been put forward by a young woman who declares herself to be the daughter of Mr. Westlake's elder brother, who left the country some two-and-twenty years ago. This lady, with her mother and a young gentleman, is at present residing at the Merry Month of May, where, so I am given to understand, you also are lodged."

Light had broken upon Captain Clare before this speech was half completed, but he made no attempt to interrupt it, for he needed a moment or two to collect his wits. He was aware that Westlake had turned at last, and was staring at him with undisguised suspicion, and that Helen's eyes, too, were fixed challengingly upon him, as she stood gripping the back of a chair, one foot, just visible beneath her silken skirts, tapping impatiently on the floor. Adrian looked again at Kelsby.

"I am indebted to you, sir, for the explanation," he said ironically. "I have not, I think, the pleasure of your acquaintance."

The lawyer bowed again.

"My name is Kelsby, Captain Clare. I am Mr. Westlake's man of business."

Adrian bowed slightly in response to this and then turned to Helen. There was something of sternness in his manner.

"So, madam, simply because I am staying at the same inn as this pretender to your husband's fortune, I am accused of complicity in the affair. May I ask why?"

"That her name is Westlake did not, I suppose, appear to you to be worthy of comment?" Helen retorted acidly, and Adrian laughed shortly.

"She would make a great parade of that, of course," he said scornfully, and then for the first time addressed himself to Westlake. "I was aware of the presence of these people at the inn, and have even had some casual conversation with the young man. He told me his name was Ancroft, and I assumed the ladies, who keep largely to their own room, to be his mother and sister."

The explanation seemed to satisfy Westlake almost against his will, for the suspicion faded from his eyes, and he said grudgingly:

"That's likely enough. Barnby and his damned brood would do their best to deceive you, that's certain!"

"Then I owe you an apology," Helen broke in. Her anger had vanished as though it had never been, and she was smiling as she held out her hand towards him. "Forgive me, Adrian! It is true that I am overwrought, and I shall take a turn in the garden to calm myself. You shall escort me to prove that you bear me no ill-will. Mr. Kelsby and my husband will wish to discuss this tiresome affair."

She picked up a wrap of russet-coloured velvet which had been flung down across a chair, and led the way out of the room, and Adrian followed her without question. When the door had closed behind them, Walter Kelsby turned to Westlake with a subtle change of manner. He was no longer the lawyer addressing a client, but a man speaking on equal terms to another.

"That is a new gallant, is it not?" he remarked drily. "Upon my soul, your good lady is insatiable! I marvel at your patience."

"Damn your impudence, have done!" Westlake, his

eyes blazing, turned on him with a kind of suppressed savagery. "My patience is like that of any other man—by no means inexhaustible! Sooner or later it will break, and when that day comes I promise you that you will both have cause to remember it. You, Kelsby, and that wanton jade who makes a mockery of her marriage vows."

He was overpowering in his anger as he towered over the lawyer's squat figure, but Kelsby seemed indifferent to the menace of him. There was no change of expression in his pallid, toad-like face as he raised it towards the taller man.

"Bombast, my friend, sheer bombast!" he said flatly. "Leave these empty threats, and direct your thoughts instead to graver matters. I warn you, Westlake, if this girl is all she claims to be—and it is my belief that she is—your days at Coombe Royal are numbered."

Meanwhile, in the pale March sunshine on the terrace, Helen had paused while Adrian placed the wrap about her shoulders. One of her hands came up to cover his, and she turned her head to look up into his face.

"Forgive me," she said again. "I was angry, and said what I did not mean. I should have known better than to fling such an accusation at you."

He bent his head to press his lips to the slender fingers covering his own, and so avoided the necessity for a reply. A feeling of shame stabbed at him for an instant, but he appeased it with the reflection that just as he had not sought Christina's confidence, so there was nothing to be gained by further explanations here.

"I was jealous, I think," Helen went on as they descended the steps and paced slowly across the smooth lawn towards the shrubbery. "You had come back to me at last, and when they told me of this girl and her absurd pretensions, and it seemed possible that you were somehow bound up with them, it was more than I could bear. I was hurt, and I wanted to hurt you in return."

"I came because I could no longer stay away," he replied frankly, relieved that he could speak the truth at last. "Nor, having seen you again, can I see anything else. I thought I had forgotten you, but I was deceiving myself. One kiss, and you have taken possession of my world."

"Have I? Have I, truly?" Her voice was eager. "Oh, Adrian, I have waited so long to hear you say that! Ever since that miserable day I sent you away from me, all those years ago. But it would never have served, my dear! I was not made to follow the drum, or to wait quietly at home for a soldier husband to come back from the wars."

"No!" Adrian spoke quietly, accepting at last the truth he had refused to acknowledge seven years before. "This was what you wanted, was it not? A great house, servants, all the trappings of wealth and consequence. God knows, I could never have given them to you!"

"You could have given me so much more!" Helen spoke with a bitterness he had never heard in her voice before. "Youth and love and laughter—all the things we shared that summer long ago! All the things I cast away in order to bind myself to a rich man of my father's generation. Wealth is not everything, Adrian, and fetters are none the less fetters because they masquerade as jewels."

They had reached the shrubbery now, and the great yew hedges were rising like solid walls about them to form a haven from prying eyes. He halted and took her in his arms, and with a little sigh of weariness and contentment she rested her head against his shoulder. He was filled with a sudden tenderness which had in it nothing of desire, for this was a Helen he had never seen before, wistful and appealing as a sorrowful child. He laid his cheek against her golden hair.

"My love, my love," he murmured, "have you been so unhappy?"

"So unhappy," she whispered, and caught her breath in a sob. "Adrian, you will not leave me again? You will not deny me some happiness at last?"

"How could I deny you anything?" he said huskily. "Helen, if this claim against Westlake succeeds——"

"It will not," she replied confidently. "Kelsby will think of something. He is clever, much more so than you would suppose, and he has much to lose. But I do not want to think of it, or of him." She took his face between her hands and drew it down to her own. "I do not want to think of anything but you."

Nevertheless, it was Helen herself who broke at last the spell of those stolen, enchanted moments, freeing herself reluctantly from his arms and glancing over her shoulder towards the gap in the massive, green-black hedges which gave a glimpse of the lawn.

"You must go now, my love," she said wistfully. "It will not do to linger here too long." She took his hand in both her own and carried it to her cheek. "I must contrive a little, before you come again, but it will be soon, I promise you." Her eyes lifted sharply to his, a glimmer of anxiety in their brown depths. "You will come, Adrian, when I send you word?"

"I will come," he promised in a low voice. "The devil himself shall not have power to stay me."

He was thinking of that promise some hours later, as he sat his horse in the shadow of a clump of trees some thirty yards from the Bath road, and watched the faint glimmer of a coach's lamps labouring slowly up the gentle slope towards him. Beside him, Ned Sparrow, mounted on a big, rangy grey, sat statue-still, staring in the same direction, and a finger of moonlight, finding its way between the branches overhead, gleamed on the barrel of the long horse-pistol in his hand.

Adrian's own weapon was drawn and ready, his other hand held in check the splendid animal he bestrode, and the crêpe mask felt close and unfamiliar across the upper half of his face. Watching the maddeningly slow approach of this, his first victim, he was conscious of an inward crawl of excitement, an almost unbearable tension such as he had sometimes felt upon the eve of battle.

The lights were closer now, they were almost level with the clump of trees, and the faint moonlight showed the coach as a black shadow crawling along the white ribbon of the road. Then Ned Sparrow said in a sharp whisper, "Now!" and at the same moment set spur to

his horse. Adrian followed suit, and together they swept
down upon the unsuspecting travellers.

In accordance with a pre-arranged plan, Adrian fired
a shot over the heads of the men on the box, and thun-
dered on to bring his mount plunging to a halt across
the road in front of the coach, while Sparrow rode up
to the vehicle itself. The coachman was fully occupied
with a team of horses terrified by the noise and flash of
a shot so close at hand, while the footman, staring in
dismay at the menacing, masked figure barring the way,
sat as though petrified and made no attempt to reach his
own weapons. Adrian covered them both with his second
pistol and marvelled at the ease with which the thing
had been accomplished.

Mr. Sparrow went about his business with an efficiency
born of long practice. The two gentlemen the coach contained were obliged to alight and speedily relieved of
purses, rings and watches, which disappeared into the
capacious pockets of Ned's riding-coat, and the two highwaymen then drew off, having met with no resistance
whatsoever.

Matters were not, Mr. Sparrow warned Adrian a few
minutes later, always as simple as this, and travellers
sometimes put up a very spirited defence of their property.
In proof of this he cited the present plight of Jeremy
Brigg, and confessed that he had himself sustained injuries
on several occasions. Adrian accepted this caution calmly,
and earned his mentor's approval by remarking that a
trifle of danger merely added spice to the game.

Only one other traveller came their way that night, but
even so they returned to the cottage richer by some thirty
pounds, and trinkets to the value of half as much again.
Ned was inclined to look disparagingly upon the night's
haul, but Captain Clare felt that his first venture as a
highwayman had not been entirely unsuccessful.

Next day they were out again, in daylight this time,
when, since more people were abroad, both the gains and
the risks were greater. During the afternoon, while they
were busy with a post-chaise occupied by a well-dressed,
middle-aged gentleman and his two young sons, Ned

caught sight of a party of mounted men approaching, who, as soon as they saw the chaise and its assailants, spurred forward to render assistance.

"Draw off, Captain!" he shouted hoarsely. "Riders coming up!" and without more ado wrenched his horse round and made off at a gallop.

Adrian followed suit, and since Ned knew every inch of the countryside, and their pursuers did not, they made their escape without difficulty. That warning shout, however, lingered in the memory of one of the two boys, and since he was an observant lad he was able to report, when his father laid information with the authorities, that one of the robbers had been dressed like a gentleman, with a gold-edged hat, and lace at throat and wrist, and that he had been addressed by his companion as "Captain".

Adrian, unaware of this and untroubled by any of the forebodings which afflicted his servant, informed Titus on his return from Bristol that he found his new life very much to his liking. Titus, resigned by now but by no means easy in his mind, received this information in silence, and, since it was clear that time would now hang heavily on his hands, went to Japhet Barnby and offered to make himself useful about the inn when not occupied with the Captain's affairs. Japhet accepted the offer readily, and Titus was soon accepted into the family circle.

Three days had now elapsed since Adrian's last visit to Coombe Royal, and he was possessed by an impatience which not even his adventures on the High Toby could dispel. No word had come from Helen, and he had almost resolved to go there again without waiting for a summons, when the message so eagerly awaited arrived at last. He came back to the inn late on the afternoon of the third day to find a man whom he judged to be a groom sitting on the bench outside the door. Adrian dismounted, handed his horse over to Diccon to be led away, and was about to go into the house when the man on the bench got to his feet, pulled off his hat and said respectfully:

"Captain Clare?"

The Captain admitted it, and found a folded scrap of

paper put into his hand. It bore no direction, but when he opened it he found, in Helen's handwriting, the single word, "tonight".

His heart leapt wildly and he crushed the paper in his hand. The messenger, looking not at Adrian but at a point an inch or two above his left shoulder, said softly:

"Not by the main avenue, Captain. There's a field gate a quarter of a mile beyond, and a lane leading to the stables. At ten o'clock, sir."

Adrian nodded, and dropped a coin into the man's hand before going into the inn. On the stairs he encountered Christina, and replied to her greeting in so absent and preoccupied a manner that she halted and watched him out of sight with surprise and dismay.

Since the entire Barnby family were aware of his association with Jeremy and Ned, no surprise was felt at his request to have his horse saddled at a late hour. Following the directions he had been given, Adrian came by a devious route to the vicinity of Coombe Royal, and was met a furlong or so from the stables by the man who had brought him the message. This individual took charge of the Captain's horse, and indicated a path which he said would bring him to a side door where someone was waiting to admit him.

The mansion loomed silent and ghostly in the moonlight, with only a faint glimmer of light showing here and there, but as Adrian reached the door to which the path had led him, it was opened from within, and the gleam of a candle showed him the figure of a woman whom he took to be Helen's maid.

Without a word she led him along an unlighted corridor and up a narrow spiral staircase tucked away in an angle of the building. Another corridor, with the shadowy figure of his mysterious guide moving silently before him, until at last she halted and scratched softly upon a door. A moment's pause, and then she opened it and stood aside to let him enter, and closed it noiselessly behind him.

The room in which he found himself was warm and perfumed, and glowed with pale colours like the inside of a sea-shell. Only a single branch of candles burned on a table beside the silk-hung bed, but the light of a blazing fire filled the room with a shifting, shimmering radiance, through which Helen, her shining hair falling about her white shoulders, came to him with outstretched, welcoming arms.

9

Captain Gallant

The information laid against Adrian by the gentleman in the chaise was the first intimation the authorities received of Captain Clare's activities, but it was by no means the last. Repeatedly, in the days that followed, similar complaints were made, and though highwaymen were no novelty upon that or any other road, it soon became clear that this particular one was something out of the common. His victims were as eloquent in describing the elegance of his attire and his courtly manners as they were in condemning his audacity and the frequency of his attacks, for unlike most highwaymen, who would make a haul, and then refrain from further depredations until it was spent, the Captain let scarcely a day pass without taking toll of some unlucky traveller. Ned Sparrow, passing rapidly from the rôle of leader to that of follower, shook his head with grim foreboding and warned against the folly of tempting fortune too far, but he spoke in vain. Adrian was not concerned merely to make a living; he wished to accumulate sufficient funds to withdraw from the game should the need arise.

Recklessness was not the only complaint Mr. Sparrow had to make of a pupil who was in many ways a credit to his teaching, for Captain Clare possessed, in his opinion, far too many extraordinary scruples. There was, for instance, the occasion during the first week of their association when they stopped an opulent-looking coach which proved to contain only three very youthful and frightened ladies in the charge of an apprehensive governess. Adrian no sooner discovered this than he apologized profoundly and bade the coachman drive on, commanding Ned to let them pass in a tone of voice which that worthy had not heard addressed to him since his army days. When, later, he protested at the loss of this rich prize, he was informed curtly that it was not Captain Clare's intention to rob women or children, and that if he wished their partnership to continue he must resign himself to that fact.

To that principle Adrian was to hold throughout his career upon the road. Any woman travelling alone was permitted to go on her way without surrendering so much as a single trinket, and even those in the company of male relatives were treated with as much courtesy as the situation allowed. The gentlemen might prove aggressive, even violent, and be dealt with accordingly, but their fair companions were never involved. As time passed and the fame of the mysterious and daring highwayman grew, it was this persistent chivalry as much as anything else that earned him the name by which he presently became widely known, the name of "Captain Gallant".

Vigorous efforts to capture him were made, but it was like trying to lay hands on a will-o'-the-wisp, for no one could guess when or where he would strike next. By day or night, sometimes alone, sometimes with one or even two companions (for when Jeremy Brigg's injury healed he occasionally joined forces with Adrian), he would appear out of nowhere, make a lightning attack, and vanish again amid the rolling chalk downs or the fastnesses of some wooded valley. Tales of his daring, his gallantry, his generosity to anyone in need who chanced to cross his path, passed from mouth to mouth and grew more fantastic with each telling, until those who had not seen him began to regard him as an almost legendary figure, an idealized epitome of every highwayman who ever stopped a coach.

Yet there were many who had seen him, had heard the pistol-shots and the ringing command to halt, had glimpsed the black horse and the striking figure of its rider, the shining top-boots and the froth of lace, the powdered hair beneath braided hat, and knew that Captain Gallant was no figment of popular imagination. They surrendered their money and their jewels and drove on to make furious complaints in Bath or Marlborough or to the country Justices.

These complaints carried weight, for Gallant's victims were all people of wealth and influence; the humbler travellers he never despoiled, confining his attentions exclusively to the rich people of fashion travelling to and from England's most famous spa. The indignation he provoked, however, was felt far more acutely by the authorities than by the man they sought. The secret of Captain Gallant's identity was well guarded.

For this Adrian was largely indebted to the Barnby family and the resources of the inn they kept. At the very first, Japhet had suggested to him that he should move from the bed-chamber he now occupied to another in the older part of the house, and when Adrian protested that he was very comfortable where he was, said in an oddly significant tone:

"You'll be a deal more comfortable in the other, Captain. Come with me now, and I'll show you what I mean."

Intrigued, Adrian had followed him to a room over the parlour, and Japhet, having closed and locked the door, led him across to the fireplace and showed him the trick of a sliding panel in the wall, and a narrow spiral stair which curled down into the darkness against the side of the great chimney.

"It leads down into the cellars, sir," he explained. "There's only a bit o' the old house standing above ground, but the cellars be all there and you could hide a score o' men in 'em. There be another way out, too, among the trees back o' the barn. Let me but light a candle and I'll show you the way."

"Jerry told me this place was a regular rabbit-warren," Adrian remarked as he prepared to follow his guide down the stair, and heard Japhet's deep chuckle come echoing back to him.

"This be a road he's used more than once when the red-coats was after him," he replied in a whisper. "Quiet now, Captain! There be another panel here as leads into the parlour."

The gleam of the candle showed Adrian a mechanism similar to the one Japhet had demonstrated to him in the room above, and then they were past it and descending into the chilly depths of the hidden cellars. At the extent of these he could only guess as he followed the inn-keeper along a narrow passage which terminated at length in a short flight of steps, and a flagstone which turned on some kind of pivot to close an opening hidden in the midst of a thick clump of trees and bushes, with the high walls of the barn rising a score of feet away and forming a barrier between the opening and the house itself.

Adrian had not so far been obliged to use the secret way, although the knowledge of it stayed reassuringly in his memory. He adhered always to the plan outlined by Brigg at their early discussions, leaving one horse at the cottage while he rode out as Captain Gallant, and fetching it again before he returned to the inn. He had given his fellow-guests to understand that a matter of business was keeping him in the neighbourhood, and if they wondered what manner of business it might be, they were too well-bred to inquire.

Miss Westlake and her companions had, in fact, other matters to occupy their thoughts during those weeks while they awaited the result of Walter Kelsby's investigation of Christina's claim. News of her presence at the inn had somehow leaked out, and a good deal of curiosity was felt in the district concerning her. Titus, whose years of soldiering had given him the knack of ferreting out information, reported to his master that among the humbler folk Miss Westlake's arrival had been greeted with relief. Marcus Westlake was a hard taskmaster and heartily disliked, and it was hoped that the young lady's claim would succeed. The older folk remembered her father with affection, and old and young alike felt that any change would be for the better.

There were other things, too, that Titus learned, but

these concerned the present lady of Coombe Royal and he had the wisdom to keep them to himself. It had not taken him long to discover how matters stood between Captain Clare and Helen Westlake, but if half the things which were said of her were true, it would not be long before the Captain found them out for himself. To inform him of them at this stage would do no good, and merely invite a storm of anger to break about his own head.

Had Titus but known it, however, the process of disillusionment had already begun. For years Helen had been enshrined in Adrian's memory as his one true love, and had they never met again would no doubt have remained so, a lost and perfect dream against which all other women must be measured and found wanting, but now, against his will, he was beginning to see her as she really was, selfish, demanding, and wantonly, needlessly cruel.

It was that last failing in her which repelled him, for he was himself incapable of deliberate cruelty and it was a thing he could not forgive. Ironically enough, his discovery of it in Helen was made through Marcus Westlake, whose attitude all along had been so inexplicable. It was an attitude that Adrian found vaguely disquieting. He felt certain that Westlake was aware of his relationship with Helen, since from the very first she had made no secret of her feelings, and though his nocturnal visits to Coombe Royal were made with all the outward trappings of secrecy it was unlikely that they could have remained undiscovered.

He was fully prepared to receive Westlake's challenge and to give him satisfaction, but the challenge had not come, even though whenever they chanced to meet, the same murderous hatred glared at him from the other man's eyes. Adrian was baffled. From all that he had seen and heard of Marcus Westlake, he had not supposed him to be the type of man to endure with complaisance his wife's infidelity.

At length he spoke of it to Helen. She looked at him for a moment with an expression he could not read, and then laughed softly on the same note of mockery he had heard her use before in speaking of her husband.

"I told you, my dear, I go my own way," she said lazily. "Marcus does not interfere."

"I was right, then?" Adrian questioned after a moment. "He does know?"

"Of course! He is not a fool!" Helen's voice was cool, still with that undertone of mockery. "But he will do nothing. He cannot. I have made sure of that." She laughed again, and lifted her hand to smooth away the frown of perplexity between his brows. "My poor Adrian, do not look so puzzled! I have learned that to bend another person completely to one's will, one has only to discover their most jealously guarded secret. It is an infallible weapon."

He continued to frown at her, but he was no longer perplexed. Marcus Westlake's most jealously guarded secret must be the means he had used to cheat his brother of Coombe Royal, and if Helen knew and had threatened to betray that, it was small wonder that he was powerless in her hands. He remembered suddenly the portrait of Godfrey Westlake in its shrine-like setting of flowers and candles, and the thought of that needless refinement of cruelty filled him with revulsion.

Yet in spite of his lost illusions he found himself powerless to break away. On the occasion of his first visit to Coombe Royal he had accused Helen of witchcraft, and now he recalled with bitterness those idle, jesting words, for it was indeed as though some enchantment bound him to her. Again and again he vowed that he would go to her no more, and each time the resolve was lost in his need of her. He came near to hating her for the power she had over him, which he could not find the strength to resist, and hated and despised himself for his own weakness.

In these tormented moods he turned with relief to the gentler influence of Christina. At the beginning of his association with Ned Sparrow and Jeremy Brigg he had seen little of her, for when he was not riding with Ned in the guise of Captain Gallant, he was exploring the countryside and acquainting himself thoroughly with every mile of it, since in the trade he had adopted such knowledge might mean the difference between life and death. As time passed, however, he was more often at the inn, and so became aware of a circumstance which puzzled him a little, until he perceived the purpose behind it.

This was the frequent presence at the inn of Gilbert Tedburn, whose family had chosen to range themselves on the side of the new claimant to Coombe Royal. They had come in force to visit Mrs. Westlake, much to that lady's delight, and Gilbert had very humbly begged Christina's pardon for his conduct at their first meeting. Civility obliged her to give it, and after that his visits became an almost daily occurrence. Very often his eldest sister accompanied him, to sit silently by while Mrs. Westlake chattered incessantly, and it was not long before Gilbert and Stephen struck up a friendship, but Christina, finding no pleasure at all in the acquaintance, formed the habit of slipping out of the house whenever the weather was fine, and retreating to a haven she had discovered during one of her solitary walks.

From the crossroads where the inn stood, one way led south-westwards along the hillside towards Coombe Royal, and about a quarter of a mile along it a lesser road sloped steeply down between high, wooded banks to ford a stream. This lane was seldom used, and Christina had taken a liking to the little, grassy, flower-strewn hollow where the stream crossed the road. Here she was safe alike from her mother's querulous demands and Gilbert's clumsy gallantries, and could read, or sew, or merely dream, according to her mood.

She was lingering there one day when Captain Clare came riding down the opposite slope. He had almost reached the stream before he saw her, and then he swept off his hat and bowed in greeting, and so came splashing through the shallow water to draw rein beside the boulder where she sat. Looking down at her with a smile, he said lightly:

"You are very solitary here, Miss Westlake. One might almost suppose that you have forsworn society altogether."

"I have forsworn the present society at the inn," she replied frankly. "Gilbert Tedburn is there with his sister, but fortunately Betsy warned me of their arrival and I was able to slip out without being seen."

"In that event I applaud your prudence, and will ask leave to bear you company awhile." She made a slight, shy gesture of assent, and he swung out of the saddle, leaving his horse to crop the rich grass beside the stream. "I fear that young man does not improve upon acquaintance, and while I have nothing against Miss Tedburn, I do not find her an enlivening companion."

Christina laughed.

"No more do I," she confessed, "and they will try to thrust her upon me. I would seek to discourage any intimacy with her family, but Mamma is so pleased to find us already accepted by them that I have not the heart to spoil her pleasure."

He raised his brows.

"A pleasure which you do not share?"

She shrugged, and spoke with a hint of bitterness.

"Only in that their eagerness for our friendship implies a belief in the success of my claim. Gilbert Tedburn, I have no doubt, comes to vie with Stephen as a suitor for Coombe Royal."

He thought it very likely, but found it was a matter on which his mind did not care to dwell, for of late the question of what would happen if and when Christina's claim were proved had become oppressive to him. He contrived to change the subject, and presently had the satisfaction of knowing that he had persuaded her out of her somewhat melancholy mood.

That was the first of many such meetings, for though no rendezvous was ever made, he knew that almost every afternoon when the weather was fine, he would find her there by the stream. During those pleasant, springtime days he came to know her well, and to find in her qualities far deeper and more rewarding than the beauty for which she sighed in vain, honesty and courage and loyalty, and a quaint humour which was entirely her own. Godfrey Westlake had been unable to give his daughter wealth, but in the things of heart and mind he had made her rich indeed. From Christina, Adrian learned enough of her father to marvel that Marcus Westlake could have had such a brother, and to feel a deep and lasting regret that he himself had never known him.

Almost without realizing it, he came to value Christina's friendship beyond anything in his present life. From the hazards of his adventures as Captain Gallant, and the torment of his passion for Helen, he turned to her in search of the peace he could find nowhere else. He wondered sometimes what her reaction would be if she knew he was the highwayman of whom the whole neighbourhood was talking, but he resisted the temptation to take her into his confidence. Such knowledge would mean danger, and that was the last thing he wished to bring upon Christina. Where she was concerned, his instincts were wholly protective.

Yet in the end she had to learn the truth, and that in a manner he would have given much to avoid. On a certain bright afternoon towards the end of May he stopped a private chaise on the Bath road. The smartness of the carriage, the liveries of the postilions, and the quality of the glossy beasts they bestrode, seemed to herald plunder of no common kind, and as Adrian, his command to halt having been obeyed, rode up to the chaise, the window was let down with a crash and the face of the sole occupant appeared in the aperture.

It was a face to linger in the memory, no matter how fleeting a glimpse was caught of it; an arrogant, aristocratic face with a high-bridged nose and thin lips, and slanting black brows in sharp contrast to its pallor and the powdered curls which framed it. Eyes of a cold, greenish-grey regarded his assailant, and a voice as cold said softly:

"The celebrated Captain Gallant, I believe? It is time someone rid this highway of you, my friend!"

The raising and firing of the unsuspected pistol which accompanied these words had the swiftness of a snake striking, but some instinct for danger had made Adrian rein back. He reeled in the saddle as the bullet struck his arm, and then the horses, wild with fright at this second explosion so close beside them, plunged forward out of control, and the chaise went rocking and lurching away down the road.

Adrian wrenched his horse round and made for the shelter of some trees a short distance away, where he paused to take stock of his injury. It was slight enough in itself, a flesh wound high in the right arm near the shoulder, but it was bleeding profusely, and an attempt to knot his handkerchief about it with his sound hand and his teeth proved unsuccessful. The only thing to do was to make for the inn and seek help there. The cottage in the woods was nearer, but he knew that Jerry would not be there, and it needed another pair of hands to check the bleeding.

He made what speed he could, but there was some way to go and the necessity of avoiding farms and villages made the distance longer. The blood was soaking into his sleeve and running in trickles over the back of his hand, and he found it increasingly difficult to concentrate. He set his teeth and urged the horse to a gallop across a wide stretch of meadowland, but the landscape was beginning to shift and swirl before his eyes as he fought desperately against a weakness which grew greater with every passing minute. It was an instinct deeper and more primitive than conscious thought which brought him at last to the narrow lane sloping down through the woods to a shallow stream, and the hollow beyond where Christina was waiting beneath a cascade of hawthorn blossom.

She looked up eagerly at the sound of his approach, and then sprang to her feet with a stifled cry. While he forded the stream and halted on the further bank she stood as though transfixed, one hand pressed to her lips and her grey eyes wide and frightened above it, but when he slid out of the saddle and took a stumbling pace towards her she recoiled in alarm. It did not seem possible that Christina should look at him with terror in her eyes, and only when he brushed his left hand across his brow in an attempt to clear his vision did he realize that he was still masked. He tried to pull off the concealing crêpe, but the effort was too much for his failing strength and before he could accomplish his purpose he pitched forward and fell in an inert heap at her feet.

He came slowly back to consciousness to find his head pillowed in Christina's lap while she held a wet handkerchief to his forehead. The mask was off, and so was the powdered wig he wore over his own fair hair as part of his disguise, and the perilous secret was hers whether he would or no. He looked up at her and found that she was gravely regarding him.

"Do not try to move," she said quietly, "I have bandaged your arm and the bleeding has stopped. You will feel better directly."

For a few minutes he made no attempt to disobey, for he felt curiously content, and the gentle touch of Christina's fingers on his brow brought a sense of ineffable peace. Then slowly, as a measure of strength returned to him, it brought with it a realization of danger, not only to himself but to her. With a sigh he dragged himself into a sitting position and forced himself to take stock of his present plight.

That it was fraught with danger was plain, for the black horse alone was enough to betray him as Captain Gallant, even without his disordered appearance. Christina had wisely not attempted to remove his coat but had fastened her bandage above it, using his neckcloth for the purpose. The blue cloth sleeve was dark and sodden with blood, and there were further stains on the skirts of his coat and on his buckskin breeches. He must be a gruesome spectacle, he reflected ruefully, and when he looked again at Christina was not surprised to see her even more pale than usual, and with some lingering horror in her eyes.

"I frightened you, my dear," he said gently. "Forgive me!"

She shook her head.

"A little at first," she admitted in a low voice, "but only until I realized who you were."

She was shaking out the damp handkerchief as she spoke and did not look up. He would never know how far that was from the truth, how insignificant had been her alarm at sight of a masked and bloodstained stranger compared to the agony of terror she had felt when in swift suspicion she had pulled off the mask and discovered who it was who lay so deathly still at her feet. He must never know how much he meant to her, how completely he had filled her world since the moment of their first meeting.

"Tell me what to do now," she said after a moment. "Shall I fetch help?"

"No." Adrian pressed his sound hand to his head and endeavoured to think clearly. "I must try to get back to the inn, so that this wound may be dressed and I can get fresh clothes."

"You cannot go back!" There was dismay in her voice. "Mr. Tedburn is there, and Gilbert."

"There is a hidden way into the house," he explained, "and if you will help me I should be able to reach my room unobserved. Will you do that?"

"I will do anything." She got to her feet, concerned now only to get him to a place of safety. "Do you think you can mount your horse?"

He shook his head.

"The horse must stay here. It is too well-known. Lead it among the trees and tether it there."

She did as he bade her, and then came back to help him to his feet. The effort made his head swim, but Christina was clinging with both hands to his sound arm and after a moment or two he conquered the weakness. Slowly they made their way up the hill, and, taking advantage of the cover of the trees which grew thickly there, came at last to the clump of bushes behind the barn. With her help he contrived to raise the flagstone, and when Christina had lighted the lantern which was always left in readiness just within, they descended into the darkness of the subterranean cellars.

The distance between the entrance and the foot of the spiral stair seemed unaccountably long to Adrian, and weakness was clawing at him again by the time the stair was reached. Only by a tremendous effort of will did he succeed in dragging himself up it, and at the top he fumbled ineffectually with the catch until Christina squeezed past him and released it. The panel slid back with a faint creaking sound, revealing a room filled with late sunlight, and Titus in the act of hanging one of his master's coats in the big oaken press.

The slight sound brought him swinging round. He stared in astonishment for a moment or two, and then dropped the coat and sprang forward as Christina stepped carefully into the room, disclosing behind her Adrian's bloodstained figure. By the time she had extinguished the lantern and set it down in the hearth, Titus had half-led, half carried his master to a chair and was bending over him with the utmost concern.

Adrian was finding it increasingly difficult to focus his gaze on the anxious face above him, but his mind was still sufficiently clear to realize what must be done. He said with an effort:

" 'Tis less serious than it looks, my friend. Tell Japhet my horse is hidden in the wood by the ford. He will know what to do. And fetch me some brandy."

Titus knew better than to waste time in protests or idle questions, and with a swift glance at Miss Westlake went quietly out of the room. Christina came across to the chair and stood looking down at Adrian.

"You are in good hands now, and so I will leave you," she said quietly. "I do not think I need to tell you that your secret is safe in my keeping."

He took her hand and gripped it for a moment, leaning his head with closed eyes against the high back of the chair.

"It is a secret which could bring you into danger," he said wearily, "and God knows I never wished that. I did not mean you to know."

There was a moment's silence, and then she said with an odd little catch in her voice:

"I would never betray you, never! I would sooner die!"

She freed her hand from his, but he had the impression that she bent over him for an instant. He tried to look up at her, but before he could find the strength to do so she had gone, her light, uneven footsteps receding quickly and ending in the sound of a softly closing door.

10

Suspicion

It was the following afternoon before he saw her again, and then, ignoring the advice of his servant and Mrs. Barnby, he rose and dressed and went down to the parlour. Their care and a night's rest had done much to restore him, and though he was a trifle pale, and had to use his right arm with caution, he hoped that no one but Christina would observe it. In any event, he felt that it would be likely to arouse suspicion if a sudden indisposition kept him in bed at a time when a notorious highwayman was known to have been wounded, for whoever the unknown man in the chaise might be, he was not likely to have kept his adventure secret.

How right he was in his supposition was proved before an hour had passed. He found only the two ladies in the parlour, and, answering Christina's anxious glance with a reassuring smile, sat down by Mrs. Westlake and inquired after that lady's health. This was a subject which she was delighted to expound to anyone, and particularly to Captain Clare. She was very well disposed towards the Captain, and had been so from the first. He was so charming, so considerate, so very much the gentleman. She would have liked to think that his continued presence at the inn was prompted by regard for her daughter, but had regretfully decided that this could not be the case. Christina was too plain and unaccomplished, nor had she made the least attempt to capture his interest, practising towards him a reserve which cast her mother into despair. She had no suspicion of those meetings in the hollow by the ford, or of the fact that away from her own depressing influence, Christina was a very different person from the quiet, dutiful girl she knew.

Presently, from Mrs. Westlake's aimless chatter, Adrian discovered that Stephen Ancroft had ridden into Marlborough at Christina's request to see Walter Kelsby and learn, if possible, how his inquiries were progressing. Nearly three months had passed since matters had been left in his hands, and no news had as yet been forthcoming. Adrian guessed that Christina was finding it increasingly difficult to eke out their slender resources, and though he felt sure that Japhet and Polly would not press for a settlement of their score, the suspicion troubled him. He found it intolerable to think of any extra burden being cast upon those slight, courageous shoulders.

Soon after this Stephen returned, bringing with him Gilbert Tedburn and his sister, whom he had met on their way to the inn. As soon as greetings had been exchanged, he produced a letter which he handed to Mrs. Westlake with the information that it had been entrusted to him by Mr. Kelsby. The widow thanked him, but put it aside and entered into a one-sided conversation with Miss Tedburn, ignoring her daughter's anxious, meaning glance. Christina said nothing, and her manner as she responded coolly to young Tedburn's clumsy overtures was admirably composed, but Adrian could guess and sympathise with the impatience which must be consuming her. It was not long, however, before his attention was claimed elsewhere as Stephen remarked casually:

"There is a clamour of gossip in Marlborough today. Rumour has it that the highwayman calling himself Captain Gallant was shot yesterday by one of his intended victims."

From the corner of his eye Adrian saw Christina start, and look up sharply from the sewing with which she was engaged. He said lightly:

"There will be many eager to claim the credit for that, to say nothing of the reward. A hundred pounds, is it not?"

Stephen shrugged.

"So I believe," he said ungraciously, "but it is likely to lie unclaimed yet longer. The rogue was but wounded, if the tale I heard is true."

"It's true enough," Gilbert broke in. "My father had word of it this morning. Gallant stopped Sir Deryk Mandeville's chaise not five miles from here and in broad daylight. Mandeville had a pair of pistols ready loaded, and winged the fellow with his first shot, but his horses took fright and bolted before he could make a second. By the time the postilions had control of them again, Gallant had made off and has not been seen since. A search is being made, of course."

"Of course," Adrian agreed blandly. "A wounded man should not be hard to find."

"That depends, surely, upon the seriousness of his injury?" Christina cast him a reproving glance, and spoke quickly to forestall Gilbert's next remark. "Was he badly wounded, Mr. Tedburn?"

"It seems unlikely, ma'am, since he has so completely disappeared. We heard that Sir Deryk is believed to have shot him in the right arm or shoulder."

Courtesy had obliged Gilbert to address his reply to Christina, but after the barest glance in her direction his inimical and faintly suspicious glance returned to Captain Clare. The Captain's snuff-box was in his hand. He took a pinch, and with an airy gesture flicked a speck or two of snuff from his ruffles, using his right hand for the purpose. Gilbert watched him morosely.

"This Mandeville," Adrian said casually. "Does he live in these parts?"

"No, but he is well known here." There was a faintly sneering note now in Gilbert's voice. "He is often at Bath, or at houses in the country around. At Coombe Royal, for instance, he has been a frequent guest."

Adrian raised his brows with only a faint show of interest, and the subject was allowed to drop. For a little while longer he remained in idle conversation with Christina and the two young men, and then found an excuse to withdraw, for Ancroft and Tedburn always bored and irritated him, and today he was conscious of these emo-

tions to an unusually marked degree. He attributed this
lack of patience to his injury, which ached in a dull,
persistent way which was extremely trying, and which
was not improved by the necessity of using the injured
arm as though nothing were amiss.

Gilbert watched him leave the room, and even after
he had gone remained staring at the closed door in a
manner so abstracted that Stephen was moved to chaff
him about it. Gilbert brought his gaze back to the speaker,
and regarded him with an air of grave portent.

"I was just thinking," he said in answer to the banter,
"that I would give much to know whether our fine friend
yonder is hiding a recent wound under that dandified
coat."

Stephen gaped at him, but Christina's heart gave a
sickening lurch of dismay, for this was the thing she had
been dreading most of all. Gilbert had never forgiven
Adrian for the humiliation at their first meeting, and if
his suspicions were seriously aroused he would not rest
until they were proved. Somehow she contrived to make
her voice light and faintly amused as she said:

"Surely, sir, you are not suggesting that Captain Clare
and this highwayman are one and the same?"

"I am suggesting, Miss Westlake, that there is something infernally mysterious about Captain Clare," Gilbert
replied in an affronted tone. "There was the question of
the chestnut mare on the day he arrived here. You know
as well as I do that he was riding such a mare that day,
even though it pleased you to pretend otherwise."

She looked at him coldly, masking the sick apprehension
she felt with a show of disdain.

"My purpose in that was to spare Captain Clare any
needless inconvenience," she retorted icily. "You may
recollect that upon that day I stood somewhat in his debt."

A dark, angry flush rose in his cheeks, and for a moment
she wondered uneasily if she had been foolish to refer
to an incident in which he had cut so poor a figure. She
believed that policy would persuade him to endure such
caprice on her part, but his was a nature which would
cherish a grudge for a long time in the hope of settling it.

"Be that as it may," he said ungraciously, "the mare was never seen again, and the gelding the soldiers saw was Ancroft's horse, not Clare's. I, for one, would like to know what lay behind that affair."

Christina shrugged.

"It is mystifying, certainly, but since Captain Clare's usual mount is grey, and Captain Gallant, so I have heard, invariably rides a black horse, I do not see what bearing it has upon your previous remark."

"Oh, Tedburn's suspicions are prompted by malice, not by reason," Stephen put in with a laugh. "He will be trying to convince us next that 'tis highway robbery which keeps Clare lingering here, even though the real reason is known to every gossip in the neighbourhood. It's my belief he is jealous!"

Gilbert gave a snort of contemptuous laughter.

"What, of Clare's conquest at Coombe Royal?" he said derisively. "I thank you, no! Those favours are too widely bestowed for me to covet them. As for Clare, if the one thing is true of him, as undoubtedly it is, why not the other? Helen Westlake is not so dainty that she would let a trifle like highway robbery stand in the way of her desires."

Christina sat as still as death, her sewing lying forgotten in her lap and hot colour rising in her cheeks. Gilbert, perceiving this and mistaking the reason for it, began to stammer an apology into which Stephen broke with a touch of impatience.

"Oh, Miss Westlake will forgive your outspokenness, never doubt it! 'Tis time she was made aware of the truth, so that she need waste no more needless pity on her uncle's wife." He turned to Christina, keeping his voice low so that the words did not reach Mrs. Westlake on the far side of the room. "Everyone knows that Clare is her lover, nor is he the only man so favoured. The woman's lightness is a by-word! You need not fear that she will lack protectors when Coombe Royal passes into your keeping."

Christina realized that her hands were trembling; she

gripped them tightly together and lifted her grave, searching regard to Ancroft's face.

"Is this the truth, Stephen?" she asked in a low voice.

"The truth, upon my honour!" he replied earnestly.
"Do you think I would so slander any woman unless I
were certain the charge was just?"

She shook her head.

"No," she said, half to herself. "No, I do not think
you would." As though scarcely aware of what she was
doing, she laid her sewing aside and got to her feet. "But
I did not realize . . . this has been a great shock to me.
Forgive me!"

She barely waited for them to reply, but brushed past
them and went quickly out of the room. Stephen smiled
to himself. He had for some time suspected Miss Westlake of a certain tenderness towards Captain Clare, and
would have disillusioned her earlier had he not felt certain
that to do so would do his own cause more harm than
good. He was grateful to Gilbert Tedburn for doing his
work for him. He knew that he need have no fear of
Gilbert as a rival, but Adrian Clare was a very different
matter, and had been causing him some uneasiness. He
had no wish to see the rich prize of Coombe Royal slip
through his hands and into the Captain's.

Outside the parlour door Christina paused for a
moment. She had no idea what had become of Adrian,
nor did she feel equal to facing him at that moment, but
it was imperative that he should be told of Gilbert's
suspicions. After a little consideration she found Titus
and bade him warn his master to be on his guard against
young Mr. Tedburn. Then, feeling that she had done
her duty in that respect, she retired to her bedchamber
and remained there in confused and unhappy meditation
until her mother came in search of her, bringing with
her Walter Kelsby's letter.

The tone of this was decidedly encouraging, for it informed them that Mr. Kelsby's inquiries were nearing
completion, and that he saw no reason to doubt that a
few weeks more would see Miss Westlake established as
the heiress of Coombe Royal. Her mother was jubilant

at this news, and Christina endeavoured to show a like enthusiasm, although for her the long-awaited tidings were overshadowed by the discovery she had made earlier.

For the rest of that day she was even more quiet and withdrawn than usual, and went early to bed, but by morning she was in command of herself once more. This composure was the hard-won fruit of many sleepless hours, during which she had forced herself to face the situation disclosed to her by Stephen and Gilbert, and to recognize the fact that it changed her own position not at all. She had known all along that she could never hope for anything more than friendship from Adrian, and if she had cherished a dream of something deeper, it had been with full knowledge of her own folly, and of the pain she was courting in thus giving her love where it was neither sought nor desired.

So it was that when they met that afternoon at the hollow by the stream, and he thanked her for the warning she had sent him, she was able to answer him with outward calm, and to describe to him the reasons which Gilbert had given for his suspicions. Adrian listened thoughtfully, and nodded.

"More spite than solid fact," he remarked when she had done, "but even spite can be dangerous when it is used to whip up suspicion. I wish young Tedburn would cease dwelling upon the business of the mare. You are too closely concerned in that for my peace of mind."

She brushed this impatiently aside, and answered him as she had answered Gilbert himself the previous day.

"What has the mare to do with Captain Gallant?"

Adrian laughed.

"Nothing—and everything! One might almost say that but for that animal there would have been no Captain Gallant." He smiled ruefully into her puzzled face. "Perhaps one day it will be possible for me to tell you the whole story, but there are others involved whose confidence I have no right to betray." He paused, but she made no reply, and after a little he added in a more serious tone: "Now that you know my secret, there is so much more that I would tell you if I could. It might perhaps help you to understand Captain Gallant, even if you could not forgive him."

She knew a moment's fear that he meant to speak to her of Helen, and that, she knew, would be more than she could bear. Looking down at a spray of hawthorn blossom which she had plucked from the tree beneath which they stood, she said quietly:

"It is not for me to judge him, Captain Clare! I want only to be his friend, as I hope I am yours, and true friendship, surely, should not ask for reasons or justification?"

Adrian stood looking down at the dark, bowed head and wishing that he could see her face. He felt himself shaken by emotions he could not define, but foremost among which was a sudden, disquieting sense of his own unworthiness. After a pause he said, with a diffidence strange to him:

"You will at least let me thank you for all you did for me two days ago? Without your aid I could not have reached safety."

Still she did not look up."

"Nor does friendship ask for thanks," she replied in a low voice. "If it is ever in my power to help you, I will do so gladly."

He was silent again for a space, and then he took her hand, blossom spray and all, and lifted it to his lips.

"Captain Gallant's life lies here," he said quietly, looking down at the slender fingers, "and Adrian Clare is very content that it should be so."

11

The Road to the Ford

That night, for the first time, he failed to keep an assignation with Helen. It was not an easy decision to make, but one which caution forced upon him whether he would or no, for if news of Captain Gallant's injury had reached Mereton Hall, it would be known at Coombe Royal also, and it would not do for Helen to discover that he was nursing just such a wound. Remembering how she had bent Marcus Westlake to her will by discovery of his secrets, Adrian resolved that she should not acquire a like power over him. That Christina knew the identity of Captain Gallant was a source of comfort rather than anxiety; for Helen to know it would rob him for ever of any security or peace of mind.

Of that reflection others, even more disturbing, were born. He had believed that he loved Helen, but surely there could be no love where there was no trust. He had allowed himself to be swept headlong into an intrigue with her, but that alone he had never desired. It had been his hope that when Westlake could no longer furnish her with all the trappings of wealth she would be willing to leave him, that together she and Adrian might leave England for some country where he could turn his military training to good account, and where, since no one knew them, she could pass henceforward as his wife. It was with that thought in mind that he had embarked on the trade of highwayman, so that he might acquire the means for such a journey, but now the cherished dream had faded, and its passing brought no regrets.

Wherein did the fault lie? He asked himself the question that night as he lay staring at the shifting pattern of moonlight on the wall of his room. In himself, or in Helen, or merely in the passing of time which had changed them both? Perhaps she had always been selfish and cruel, and he had not known it, seven years ago. Or, knowing it, he had refused to believe it, as he had no choice but to believe it now. Yet, in spite of all, he could still desire her, feel himself caught in the evil enchantment of her beauty, and know a haunting doubt that he would ever be free of its spell again.

He moved restlessly in the darkness, contemptuous of his own weakness, and the thought of Christina came suddenly into his mind. Was it there, perhaps, that salvation lay? Could there be love without desire, and peace and gentleness and shared laughter to drive out the tormenting memory of a shattered dream?

Next morning he startled his servant by announcing that he intended to leave the inn for a time. Until his arm was completely healed he would make Jeremy Brigg's cottage his headquarters, and anyone who inquired should be told that he had gone on a visit to friends in the next county.

It was not long before he took to the road again, and any exasperated soldier or harassed Justice who had supposed that Sir Deryk Mandeville had dealt once and for all with Captain Gallant knew that they had rejoiced too soon. The incident appeared merely to have made him more audacious than before.

Jeremy was delighted to have the Captain under his roof again, and to aid and abet him in his raids upon passing travellers. Unlike Ned Sparrow, Jerry had no fault to find with Adrian's methods. It was his own ambition to retire from the High Toby as soon as he had saved enough money, and he was willing to take a few extra risks if by doing so he could hasten that happy day.

One evening, as they sat over a meal in the oak-beamed kitchen, their talk turned to the Westlake family and the future of Coombe Royal. Jerry shared the general enthusiasm for Christina's claim, but was less hopeful than most that its success would mean any improvement in the lot of tenants and servants.

"For what do a young maid know of the proper ordering of an estate," he demanded, "and her reared in foreign parts, as Miss Westlake was? They may prove she's the heiress—I'm not saying as they won't—but d'ye suppose her uncle will loose his hold on Coombe Royal because o' that?" He shook his head, and wagged his knife, with a sizable piece of meat impaled upon it, in Adrian's direction. "You mark my words, Captain! Him and that fat toad, Kelsby, have had their claws too deep in it these twenty years to be got rid of so easy."

"Kelsby?" Adrian's eyes narrowed as he regarded the speaker's knowing face. "What has he to do with it?"

"That's what I'd give a deal to know," Jerry retorted, "but I'll tell you this, Captain! Twenty years ago Kelsby was that poor he'd scarce a decent coat to his back, and none o' the gentry hereabouts ever thought o' consulting him until Marcus Westlake quarrelled wi' Mr. Beauchamp and gave Kelsby the handling of his affairs. Now he has a finger in every pie, and rides in his own coach as fine as a lord, wi' jewels on his fat fingers and his ugly carcase decked out in silk and velvet. And who's stood behind him all these years and helped him to climb up from the gutter?" He nodded sagely, and answered his own question. "Squire Westlake, that's who."

Adrian continued to stare at him with narrowed eyes. So the bond which Christina had suspected between Kelsby and her uncle did exist. He said slowly:

"Why should Marcus Westlake befriend a poor attorney?"

Jerry shrugged.

"Gratitude, belike, or maybe fear. Kelsby was there when Mr. Edmund died." His shrewd glance met Adrian's across the table. "Reckon we're both thinking the same thing, Captain, but thinking's one thing, and proving it's another. There's one thing certain, though! The little lady back at the inn'll be no match for 'em, not on her own, she won't. 'Tis a mortal shame she ain't wed."

Adrian made no reply. Jerry's words had pointed to an

obvious truth, and he wondered why it had never occurred to him before. Christina was only nineteen; until she came of age, or married, her affairs must be the responsibility of some legal guardian, and who was the obvious choice for that rôle if not her uncle? The old lawyer, Beauchamp, was the only person who might have helped her, and he was still gravely ill. Westlake and Kelsby would have a clear field.

"They'll plot some devilry between 'em, depend on it!" Jerry's voice put the thought into words almost as it formed in Adrian's mind. "I'm a peaceable man, Captain, as well you know, but by God! if I had the good luck to stop Kelsby's coach, I'd be sore tempted to put a bullet through his black heart. There's not another man within twenty miles as is hated and feared as he is." He helped himself to another generous portion of meat, and chuckled grimly. "I've got no kindness for Squire Westlake, but I reckon it's little enough peace he has, what wi' Kelsby on the one hand, and that wife of his on the other. She's made him the laughing-stock o' the whole parish, flaunting her fine lovers for all the world to see. 'Tis a wonder he's not taken a whip to her, the shameless hussy, but there! it's true there's no fool like an old fool!"

He picked up his tankard and drank deeply, apparently unaware of his companion's sudden stillness, or the clenching of his hand on the table's edge. Then he set the vessel down, wiped his mouth on the back of his hand, and began to talk of other matters as though the conversational possibilities of the previous subject had now been thoroughly explored.

Adrian answered him somewhat at random, and as soon as the meal was over got up and went out of the cottage, to pace to and fro beneath the trees in a mood of bitter self-contempt. He had no doubt that Jerry's seemingly innocent reference to Helen's conduct had been deliberately made, and he was consumed by shame and fury as he realized in what light he must appear to everyone in the neighbourhood of Coombe Royal.

He did not doubt the truth of the allegation, and could only despise himself for not having recognized it long before. He was no inexperienced schoolboy, and the guarded messages, the discreet servants, that convenient private staircase to her apartments, would all have shrieked it to him had he chosen to listen. It was vanity alone which had deafened and blinded him, and if he had been deceived, it was as much by his own fault as by Helen's.

He writhed under the goad of that reflection for another four-and-twenty hours, until the thought of self was banished by a message from Titus, brought to the cottage by Diccon the following afternoon. Titus, it seemed, was extremely uneasy, and would be grateful if the Captain would return to the inn without delay. Just what was amiss Diccon did not know, but he thought that in some way it concerned Miss Westlake.

Adrian stayed for no further questions. He had implicit trust in his servant, and he knew that only something very disquieting could have prompted such a summons. He sent Diccon to saddle his horse, and after a brief word of explanation to Jerry made what haste he could back to the inn.

His servant's news did nothing to quell his uneasiness. The day before, Christina had come into the inn in some distress, and, chancing to encounter Titus before anyone else, had told him that while sitting in the hollow by the stream she had been startled by a noise amid the undergrowth on the bank above her. Looking up, she had discerned the figure of a man who, as soon as he realized he was observed, had made off with every appearance of haste and secrecy, while Christina, made uneasy by this, and by the solitude of her surroundings, had hurried back to the inn.

Titus, advising her to say nothing to anyone else, had gone immediately to the spot, where he found unmistakable traces of the man's presence, traces, moreover, which suggested that this was not the first occasion upon which he had lurked among the trees and bushes. Returning to the inn, he had suggested to Miss Westlake that she should not in future venture out alone, a warning which he had repeated that morning. By this time, however, she had recovered from her fright and was disposed to make light of the matter, perceiving which, he had resolved to inform his master of the incident.

"For there's no denying, sir, that it's common knowledge now that Miss Westlake's claim is likely to succeed," he concluded, "and it would suit her uncle very well if some accident befell her. I wouldn't take the liberty of saying as much to the young lady myself, for fear of frightening her, but it's my opinion there's some villainy afoot."

"You are very probably right," Adrian agreed. "I will find Miss Westlake, and see if she will accept a word of advice from me."

To find Christina, however, was less easy than he expected, but at last Ruth Barnby volunteered the information that she had gone out for a walk. There was little doubt of her destination, and Adrian, remarking casually that he would go in search of her, strolled out of the inn and along the road towards Coombe Royal.

Once out of sight of the house he quickened his pace, but even so Titus overtook him before the fork in the road was reached. Adrian nodded his approval, and said softly:

"We will go through the wood, I think, and not by the road. If fortune favours us, we may take our bashful friend by surprise."

They entered the wood and moved cautiously among the trees, but before they had gone a dozen yards a sudden sound brought them to a halt. Somewhere not far away a horse had snorted and tossed its head, the jingle of its harness coming clearly to their ears. For a few seconds they stood motionless and scarcely breathing, and then Adrian stole forward in the direction of the sound and gently parted an intervening screen of leaves.

He found himself looking into a little open space where, for some reason or other, a few trees had been felled, a space separated from the road by only a thin screen of foliage and almost filled at present by a light travelling-coach to which four powerful horses were harnessed. A big man, muffled to the eyes in a high-collared greatcoat and with his hat pulled low upon his brow, was crouching behind a bush near the road and peering down the hill towards the ford.

Adrian was aware of Titus looking over his shoulder, and motioned to him to withdraw again. When they had retreated a safe distance they halted and looked at each other in grim foreboding.

"By God, sir, we are only just in time!" Titus said in a whisper. "What does he intend? An abduction?"

"It looks very much like it," Adrian agreed in the same tone. "There is probably an accomplice hiding near the ford. Go back and keep watch on the coach, and I will endeavour to intercept Miss Westlake before she reaches the bottom of the hill. She cannot be far ahead of us. You are armed?"

Titus nodded grimly and patted the pocket of his coat, and then turned to retrace his steps. Adrian went on down the hill, keeping to the shelter of the trees until certain that he was out of sight of the watcher by the coach, and then he slid and scrambled down the bank to the lane.

It was on the steepest part of the hill that he caught up with Christina, where the road ran straight down to the stream between banks which at that point were between fifteen and twenty feet high. She swung round in alarm at the sound of his footsteps, but when she saw who it was the dismay faded from her face, to be replaced by a swift, unguarded radiance.

"Captain Clare!" she exclaimed. "Oh, how you startled me! I did not know that you had returned."

"I arrived a bare half-hour ago," he replied, wondering how to warn her of her danger without causing her too much alarm, "but what I heard from Titus brought me in search of you. It is no longer prudent for you to walk alone in this fashion."

Even as he spoke he was aware of sounds from the top of the hill which told him that the coach had emerged from its hiding-place into the lane. He slid his hand into his pocket and closed it about the butt of his pistol, looking swiftly about him in search of the accomplice he felt convinced was lurking somewhere close at hand. Then he realized that the coach was descending the hill at no ordinary pace, and knew, in an instant of horrified revelation, that he had been too confident of Marcus Westlake's intentions. A faint, hoarse shout of warning from Titus was drowned in the rattle of wheels and the thunder of galloping hoofs, as Adrian spun round to see death hurtling towards them down the narrow, sunken road.

12

The Suitor

In such a spot there was only one slight chance of escape, and he took it instinctively, without conscious thought. Catching Christina about the waist he tossed her up to his shoulder and sprang desperately up the steep bank beside them. The ground crumbled beneath them as he fought frantically for a foothold, and for one hideous instant it seemed that they must slip back into the path of the maddened horses, and then his free hand encountered the stout root of a tree and clenched hard upon it. Their downward slide was checked, and though his muscles seemed to crack beneath the strain he succeeded in maintaining his hold while the coach rocked past them with only inches to spare, to splash through the ford and disappear up the farther slope at a gradually slackening pace.

Long before it was out of sight, Adrian's fingers had slipped from their precarious hold, and he and Christina slid down to the road again amid a mass of loosened earth. She had clung tightly to him during the interminable moments of danger, but now as he dropped to one knee and lowered her gently to the ground, her arms loosened their hold and she looked up at him with dazed, horrified eyes. She was trembling violently, her face, drained of all colour and smeared with dirt, was close to his, and on a sudden impulse he bent and kissed her lips. Just for an instant he was aware of her swift response, and then with a sob she thrust him away and buried her face in her hands.

Titus came running down the hill through the settling clouds of dust, white-faced, the pistol he had not dared to use still in his hands. He found Miss Westlake crouched, weeping, at the foot of the bank, and Captain Clare, still on one knee beside her, both dusty and shaken but miraculously unhurt. Adrian looked up as he approached, and the servant saw that he was very pale, with a set look about his mouth.

"We were mistaken, Titus," he said quietly, getting to his feet. "It was not abduction that was planned, but murder."

"It was, sir," Titus agreed in a shaken voice. "I watched him shift the coach out on to the road, but until he whipped the horses to that wicked speed, I never guessed his purpose. By God, Captain, I had my heart in my mouth as I came down the hill, not knowing what I should find!"

"You find us safe, my friend," Adrian replied grimly, "but it was a devilish close thing, closer than I should care to risk again." He bent over Christina and lifted her to her feet. "Come, my dear, let us take you back to the inn."

She obeyed without protest, as though the shock of their narrow escape had for the time being deprived her of all spirit, and went silently up the hill between them, leaning heavily on their supporting arms. Only when they reached the spot where the coach had been hidden, where trampled grass and broken branches betrayed its passing, did she speak, and then, not looking at Adrian, she said in a low voice:

"Was it . . . my uncle?"

He glanced compassionately down at her averted face. His heart ached with the desire to comfort her, to protect her, to take upon his own shoulders all the difficulties and dangers with which she was surrounded, but a barrier had sprung up between them and he knew it was of his own making. Cursing his folly in yielding to an impulse as yet scarcely understood, he replied quietly:

"I fear it was. The man was of his height and build, and he would not risk entrusting such a task to another."

A strong shudder shook Christina's slight body, and she stumbled as though she could not see very clearly. Instinctively he tightened his grip to steady her, and was curiously hurt by her immediate, involuntary withdrawal.

They came into the inn by way of the yard and the kitchen, where Polly hurried to greet them in quick concern at sight of their dishevelled appearance and Christina's white, tear-stained face.

"An accident!" Adrian said briefly in explanation. "Miss Westlake will tell you of it. Look after her, Mrs. Barnby! She has had a bad fright."

He waited until Christina had been shepherded out of the room in Polly's care, and then turned to Titus. His mouth was still set in a hard line, and there was a look in his eyes which the servant recognized as boding ill for someone.

"Go saddle my horse while I rid myself of this dust," he said briefly. "I am for Coombe Royal, and a word or two with Westlake. I've no doubt he recognized me, and the time has come for some plain speaking." He paused drumming his fingers on the table and staring straight before him with frowning eyes. After a moment or two he added softly: "And, Titus, I desire you to keep a close watch over Miss Westlake henceforth. There is Walter Kelsby to be reckoned with as well as her uncle, and I trust the one as little as the other."

Mrs. Barnby took Christina up the back stairs to her bedchamber, and made her sit down there while she questioned her gently concerning the nature of the accident. The story she heard, though broken and disjointed, was clear enough to horrify her, but instead of dwelling upon it she applied herself to the task of soothing and comforting Christina. After a while, when Miss Westlake was more composed, she told her that Mr. Kelsby had arrived at the inn during her absence, and was now with her mother in the parlour.

This news had the effect of diverting Christina's thoughts. She directed a startled glance at Mrs. Barnby, and said anxiously:

"I must go down! It must be something important if Mr. Kelsby has come himself to see us. Help me to tidy myself, Polly."

Some fifteen minutes later, clad in her best gown, her hair becomingly arranged by Polly's skilful fingers, she went slowly down to the parlour. An anxious scrutiny of her face in the mirror had shown her that she was still rather pale and heavy-eyed, but she hoped that this would pass unnoticed by Mr. Kelsby. Her mother, she felt sure, would as usual be too absorbed with herself to remark it.

She found them engaged in earnest conversation, but this was broken off as she entered, and the lawyer heaved himself up out of his chair and came forward to greet her. Once again she endured the clammy touch of his hand upon hers, and met the cold, unrevealing stare of the pale eyes, while the repulsion and distrust which she had not entirely succeeded in conquering roused again within her.

"I bring you good news, Miss Westlake," he informed her in his flat, monotonous voice. "Your claim has been proved beyond all doubt. Coombe Royal and all that goes with it is yours."

A surge of exultation brought the colour to her cheeks and a sudden mistiness to her eyes, as her thoughts flashed to her father and the gladness that news would have given him. For a few seconds triumph wholly possessed her, and then an ugly memory came to turn her mind in a new direction.

"Does my uncle know, Mr. Kelsby?" she asked in a low voice.

The lawyer nodded.

"I have written to inform him of it. I shall visit Coombe Royal before I return to Marlborough, but there are many matters to be discussed, and I wished him to have time to accustom himself to the situation before we met."

Christina nodded, sinking down into the chair he drew forward for her, but her thoughts had gone back to the

narrow, woodland road, to the coach and its four maddened horses plunging down the steep hillside. Marcus
Westlake must have been planning that trap for days,
and when Kelsby's letter reached him he knew that he
must delay no longer. If Adrian had not followed her,
this news of her success would have come too late.

"In Heaven's name, Christina, is that all you have to
say?" Her mother's querulous tones broke in upon her
troubled thoughts. "Have you no word of gratitude for
Mr. Kelsby, no thanks for all the trouble he has taken
on your behalf?"

"Of course!" Christina looked up, flustered, to meet
the lawyer's unreadable gaze. "Forgive me, Mr. Kelsby!
I——I am a little overcome. I have dreamed of this day
for so long."

"Naturally, Miss Westlake. I do not seek for thanks."
Kelsby's voice told her as little as his eyes. "There are
certain matters, however, which need to be made clear,
so if I may have your attention for a few minutes——"
he paused inquiringly, and Christina collected her wan-
dering thoughts with an effort and fixed her eyes resolutely
upon his repellent face.

"You have it, Mr. Kelsby," she assured him quietly.
"Pray continue."

He inclined his head in assent.

"Briefly, then, my dear young lady, the situation is
this. Coombe Royal belongs to you, but you are no more
than nineteen years old, and until you come of age, or
marry, someone will have to act as your guardian, and
administer the estate. The most obvious person to do
that is your uncle." Christina opened her lips to speak,
but he lifted an admonitory finger to check her. "Bear
with me a moment longer, I beg. Mr. Westlake has handled
the affairs of Coombe Royal most ably for more than
twenty years, and these are matters of which neither you
nor your mother has any experience at all."

"In any event, my health would not be equal to it,"
Mrs. Westlake put in languidly. "I shall take your advice,
Mr. Kelsby, and go to take the waters at Bath as soon as
this affair is satisfactorily settled."

"Mamma, you cannot be thinking of leaving me?" Christina exclaimed in dismay. "How can I live at Coombe Royal alone? For I will not have my uncle as my guardian, I swear! He cheated Father of his rights, and——" she broke off, remembering in time her resolve to say nothing in her mother's hearing of her recent narrow escape, "and he wishes me no good, I am sure," she concluded lamely.

There was a pause, Christina clasped her hands tightly together and sat staring down at them, fighting against the panic which Kelsby's suggestion had aroused. Marcus Westlake her guardian? Marcus, who not an hour since had tried to kill her? Was she then to be placed completely in his power by Kelsby, who was almost certainly his accomplice? Was her mother to be persuaded to take up residence in Bath, and she left at Coombe Royal in the nominal care of Helen, Adrian Clare's beautiful, wanton mistress?

"No!" she said aloud, startling them with the vehemence in her voice. "No, I will not! I do not trust them."

"Since you feel so strongly upon the subject, Miss Westlake," Kelsby said smoothly in answer to that outburst, "it is fortunate that an alternative course offers itself. You will recall that I said 'until you come of age, or marry'. In that latter event, of course, the estate will pass to your husband, and Mr. Westlake can no longer be in any way concerned."

"You see, Christina, these tantrums are quite unnecessary," Mrs. Westlake added fretfully. "I wish you will learn to restrain yourself, and remember that the least excitement oversets my nerves. A little patience on your part, and we should have been spared this exhibition of hysteria. However, I do not mean to rebuke you on so auspicious an occasion. I am sure that it will answer very well."

"What will answer?" Christina looked from one to the other in bewilderment. "I do not understand."

"Bless my soul, child, where are your wits?" her mother demanded despairingly. "Mr. Kelsby has been so obliging as to make you an offer of marriage. Very properly, he came to seek my consent before addressing himself to you."

Christina came slowly to her feet, bewilderment giving way to disbelief, which was in its turn succeeded by sheer horror. For a moment her gaze rested with undisguised loathing upon the fat, toad-like figure of her suitor, and then turned incredulously towards her mother.

"And you have given it?" she said in a stricken whisper. "No, you do not mean it! Even you could not expect such a thing of me."

"Christina, mind what you are saying!" Extreme agitation lent the widow an unwonted energy, and starting up from her chair she seized her daughter by the wrist and dragged her across to the far side of the room, flinging an almost incoherent word of excuse and apology over her shoulder to Kelsby as she did so. By the window she halted and jerked Christina round to face her. A spot of colour was burning in either cheek, and she spoke in a hissing whisper.

"Do you want to ruin all, you foolish, ungrateful girl? Make an enemy of him, and he will throw in his lot with your uncle, and who knows then what the end will be? Why, pray, should you not marry him? He is a man of sense and fortune, who will think more of increasing your wealth than squandering it on extravagant follies as a younger man might do, so what matter if he is not entirely to your taste as a husband? I dare say you have a fancy to wed some handsome young spark like Captain Clare, but let me tell you, my girl, that men of his stamp look for more in a bride than you have to offer. You will do as I bid you, so let us have no more of this defiance!"

Christina wrenched herself free and swung round to stare blindly from the window, struggling to calm the tumult of anger and dismay seething within her. She heard Kelsby's soft tread approaching—in spite of his girth, he was surprisingly light of foot—and then his level, expressionless voice addressing her mother.

"This matter, madam, has not perhaps been handled as delicately as one would wish, but I believe the harm is not past mending. If you will give me leave to speak to your daughter alone—yes, I am aware it is not usual——" for Mrs. Westlake had made a faint, protesting sound "——but in this case I believe that all our interests will best be served by setting convention aside for a few minutes."

There was a pause while Mrs. Westlake obviously struggled with her sense of what was proper, and then with a resigned word of assent she turned and went slowly out of the room. Kelsby closed the door behind her and returned to stand by the table in the middle of the floor.

"I make you my apologies, Miss Westlake," he said flatly. "I would not have worded my proposal in the terms your mother chose to use, but then, I have not taken her completely into my confidence. Will you do me the favour of listening to what I have to say?"

Reluctantly, drawn by the hint that there was more to this matter than had yet been disclosed, Christina turned to face him. He waved her back to the chair she had left, and because she was too proud to let him guess that she feared him, she limped back to it and sat down. Mr. Kelsby nodded as though in approval.

"First, let us clearly understand each other," he began, seating himself in a chair facing her, "for I suspect that your instant rejection of my offer springs largely from misapprehension of its nature. A marriage between us would be purely a matter of convenience. I wish you to become my wife in law, nothing more. Do I make myself clear?"

Christina nodded without speaking, feeling with dismay the hot colour flooding into her face. Mr. Kelsby regarded her confusion with an irony which served only to increase it, and to make her feel that she had been behaving like a hysterical schoolgirl.

"Coombe Royal is the only thing I desire," he resumed after a pause, and now for the first time she could detect the faintest trace of feeling in his voice. "It is more than five-and-twenty years since I first set eyes on it, and in all that time I have never ceased to covet it. The dream of my life has been to make myself master of it, but it was a dream without hope of fulfilment until the day you made yourself known to me."

Another pause, while Christina sought for something to say, and could find nothing. She did not doubt that Mr. Kelsby was speaking the truth in so far as his desire for Coombe Royal was concerned, but the conviction did not wholly banish her distrust. As though he realized this, the lawyer continued in a dispassionate, reasoning tone:

"It is not such a bad bargain I am offering you, after all. You may depend upon me to guard your interests well, you will have no more to fear from your uncle, and since I am some thirty years your senior it is highly probable that you will find yourself free again while you are still comparatively young. My most potent argument, however, which I have kept until the last, is this." He thrust his hand into the breast of his coat and brought out a folded paper. "On the day you marry me, that shall be yours, to do with what you will."

Doubtfully Christina took the paper and unfolded it, disclosing a page of writing in a hand she recognized as Kelsby's. At the bottom, however, above the lawyer's signature and that of Marcus Westlake, she beheld, in feeble, wavering letters, the name of Edmund Westlake. In sudden excitement she returned to the top of the page, and a glance at the opening lines was sufficient to tell her that here was a confession to the murder of Giles Carew.

"Your uncle Edmund dictated that to me when he lay dying," Kelsby's unemotional voice informed her, "and only I, and his brother Marcus, knew of it. It has been in my possession ever since."

Christina lifted wondering eyes to his face.

"And you will allow me to publish it, if I marry you?"

He shrugged his fat shoulders.

"Its value as a threat against Marcus Westlake ceases when Coombe Royal passes out of his hands. You told me, did you not, that you would reward most handsomely anyone who could clear your father's name?"

"But if I refuse your offer?"

He leaned forward and twitched the paper out of her hand again before she realized his intention.

"Then I shall destroy it," he said calmly. "As I pointed out, its value will be gone."

"No, wait!" She spoke urgently, fearful that he might put his threat into execution there and then. "Wait! Let me think."

He paused, the paper held up between finger and thumb, regarding her inquiringly while she twisted her hands together in an agony of indecision. In spite of his bland assurances, the prospect of becoming his wife filled her with dismay, yet it was the price she must pay for possession of that priceless document and the establishing of her father's innocence. What, after all, was she asked to sacrifice, save freedom? With a sinking heart, but her head held proudly high, she made the bitter choice and gave him her answer.

"Very well, Mr. Kelsby," she said in a resolute voice. "If those are the terms you demand to make known the truth, I have no alternative but to accept them. I will marry you."

13

The Scapegoat

As Adrian rode to Coombe Royal, his anger against Marcus Westlake mounted steadily. Ever before his mind's eye hovered the hideous picture of what would have happened that day if Titus had not been watchful, or if he himself had delayed his return to the inn, for had she been trapped alone in the sunken road, Christina, lame as she was, would have had not the smallest hope of escape. The brutality of the plot sickened him; he could not conceive how any man, no matter how greedy for wealth, could deliberately condemn a defenceless girl to a frightful death beneath trampling hoofs and wheels.

He rode fast, consumed by a burning impatience to confront the man, to inform him that his infamy was known and Miss Westlake by no means lacking in protectors. The fact that where Marcus Westlake was concerned his own position was decidedly equivocal never even occurred to him, for, temporarily at least, Helen was forgotten as completely as though they had never met, and it was the intended crime against Christina which filled his thoughts to the exclusion of all else.

He was admitted to the house without question, and though the butler was undoubtedly taken aback by his demand for Mr. Westlake, he was too well trained to show it. Blandly requesting Captain Clare to be seated, he went to inform his master of the visitor's arrival.

Adrian half expected Westlake to deny himself, and was fully prepared to force his way into the man's presence should the need arise, but when the butler returned it was with the information that Mr. Westlake would receive the Captain immediately. He then led the way to the library, ushered Adrian within, and closed the door regretfully upon what promised to be an uncommonly interesting conversation.

Westlake was standing before the empty fireplace, his hands clasped behind his back and his head thrust aggressively forward. He stared evilly at Adrian from under lowering brows, and a sneer twisted his lips.

"It is not often that Captain Clare chooses to recall my existence," was his ominous greeting. "To what do I owe the honour on this occasion?"

"To a reason which I fancy is as well known to you as to myself," Adrian replied curtly. "Surely our encounter earlier today is worthy of further comment?"

A guarded look flashed into the hazel eyes, but that was the only betrayal. Westlake said sourly:

"If you intend to talk in riddles, I beg that you will hold me excused. I have neither the time nor the patience to unravel conundrums."

"Nor I the patience to pose them," Adrian retorted coldly, "so we will have the matter in plain words. I refer to the attempt you made a short while since to murder your niece."

"Plain words indeed!" Westlake's voice was harsh. "You should set a more careful guard on your tongue, Captain."

Adrian shook his head.

"It is not I who need to practise caution," he said contemptuously. "Miss Westlake herself caught a glimpse of you yesterday when you spied upon her in the woods, and this afternoon I and my servant saw you skulking there beside your hidden coach. Had I guessed your vile purpose, we could have overpowered you then." Recollection of what that purpose had been, and the narrow margin by which it had been thwarted, was vivid in his mind, and he took a pace forward, his voice shaking with the fury that possessed him. "My God, Westlake, have you no pity at all? She is lame, and little more than a child!"

"She is old enough to dispossess me," Marcus retorted callously. "I have been master here for more than twenty years, and now I am expected to step aside so that a slip of a girl may take my place. Hell and the devil! am I expected to make her welcome?"

"You are expected, I believe, to give up that which was never rightly yours," Adrian replied sternly. "Whatever crime your brother was suspected of committing, Coombe Royal was his and passed from him to his daughter. You have been no more than a steward here, Westlake, and now the rightful owner has come home."

The insult of these words was deliberate, for in his present mood he would have liked nothing better than to provoke Westlake into challenging him. The overwhelming anger and disgust he felt towards the man could be appeased, he thought, by nothing less. For a moment or two he thought he had succeeded, for Westlake took a pace forward, his attitude decidedly menacing.

"You damned, impertinent young jackanapes!" he exclaimed furiously. "Do you have the infernal impudence to tell me what I should or should not do? By what right, I wonder? Your intrigue with my wife does not give you the right to thrust yourself into my family concerns!"

"I came here to warn you!" Adrian's voice was cold now, in contrast to the other's hectoring tones. "Understand this clearly, Westlake! Your niece does not lack friends. You are neither liked nor trusted at the Merry Month of May, and after what happened today there is not a soul there who will not be constantly on the watch for any further threat to her safety." He paused, and then added softly: "As to our private differences, if you have any further comment to make upon that score, I shall be happy to accommodate you."

Westlake stared at him, his face working, a hell of baffled fury in his eyes, and then he swung round and strode across to the window, where he stood with his back to the room and his hand gripping and twisting the heavy curtain beside him as though he wished it were the Captain's throat. Ignoring Adrian's last words, he said over his shoulder:

"You have no proof!"

"I can soon obtain it," Adrian retorted, "make no mistake about that. You drove that coach today, and I have no doubt the horses were from your own stable. A few questions among your grooms will soon establish that, and I am sure that Mr. Tedburn would be happy to ask them if the facts were laid before him. He has shown some interest in Miss Westlake's welfare."

Marcus gave a harsh, mirthless laugh.

"So I have heard. He hopes to secure Coombe Royal for his loutish son."

"Very likely, but that matters not at all. What is important is that he is a magistrate, and has the authority to see that inquiries are made. And made they will be, I give you my word, if you make the least move again to harm your niece." Adrian paused, studying with some perplexity that broad, unrevealing back. "You failed in your attempt today, and you should give thanks for it, for had you succeeded you would certainly have lost more than Coombe Royal. Good God, man! did you think you could murder her, and no questions be asked? You are the first person upon whom suspicion would fall. If your friend Kelsby was party to the plot, then he is less shrewd that I would have supposed, and gave you false counsel."

"Kelsby!" Marcus spun round to face him, spitting out the name as though it were an oath. "That fat fool has given me no help in my present plight. Any lawyer worthy of the name would have found some means of disproving the girl's claim, and making me secure in possession of the estate. God knows he has had favours enough from me in the past!"

He spoke as though he had forgotten the identity of his hearer, as though his burning resentment against Kelsby must find an outlet in words if it were to be endured. Adrian said quietly:

"And with what did he purchase your patronage? His silence?"

"Silence?" Westlake started, becoming aware of him again. Suspicion and a hint of alarm kindled in his eyes. "What the devil do you mean?"

"I mean that belief in your elder brother's guilt is by no means universal. It is remembered that only you and Kelsby were present when your younger brother died, and that your close friendship with Kelsby dates from that time. That only you, and Godfrey, and Edmund knew the truth concerning the murder of Giles Carew." He paused, looking sardonically at the elder man. "These things are not forgotten, my friend, and neither is the esteem in which Miss Westlake's father was held by all who knew him. You would do well to remember that, and also to bear in mind that if silence can be purchased, so, too, can speech."

He saw the suspicion deepen in Westlake's eyes, and smiled grimly to himself. It would do no harm to foster dissension between the two confederates. That relations between them were already strained was made clear by Westlake's outburst, and the reason for this was not hard to guess. Walter Kelsby cared for nothing save his own interests, and was shrewd enough to realize that these could best be served by giving his support to the lawful owner of Coombe Royal. Marcus Westlake stripped of wealth and influence was of no further use to him.

"It is always so when fortune fails," he said quietly.

"Remember the adage of the rat and the sinking ship."

Westlake did not reply. He had turned his head as though something outside had caught his attention, and was staring again from the window. Adrian could see his face in profile against the light, the blunt nose and heavy, aggressive jaw, the bitter, down-trending line of the mouth. An unscrupulous man, he thought, but not a clever one; the events of the day bore witness to that. A man goaded to desperation by the thought of all he was about to lose, and by the defection of the confederate whose keener wits might have saved the situation for him.

Westlake was still staring into the garden and seemed to have forgotten the Captain's presence. His hand was clenched again upon the curtain, clenched so hard that the muscles stood out upon its back like cords, and shaking with the violence of some suppressed passion. Impelled by curiosity, Adrian moved forward a little so that he, too, could see into the garden.

Beyond the window was the wide, stone-flagged terrace, and beyond and below that a stretch of smooth green turf bounded by a thick yew hedge. Midway along this was a statue of Cupid, poised to let fly an arrow, and beside its pedestal Helen was standing, her gown of ivory and palest pink shimmering against the dark foliage behind her. Her golden curls were bare, for the wide straw hat which should have covered them hung behind her shoulders, held there by the ribbons about her throat, and she was looking down at the cluster of roses in her hand as she listened to the words of the man beside her. He stood leaning forward, one hand on Cupid's pedestal, his head with its powdered curls bent towards Helen, the rich crimson silk of his coat glowing in the sunshine. Posed there in that setting of clipped hedge and shaven lawn, beneath the statue of the blind, winged god, it seemed to Adrian that for a moment they had the unreality, the fragile, ephemeral quality of figures fashioned in porcelain, or painted upon a silken fan.

The man paused, and Helen lifted her head at last, looking up at him with languorous, remembered grace. He swept her into his arms and she went willingly, the roses falling to the ground as her own arms came up to cling and to caress. Beside him, Adrian heard Westlake draw in his breath with a sharp, hissing sound of pain and fury, but no knife of jealousy twisted in his own heart. He felt only a cold disgust, directed as much against himself as against Helen, and mingled with it a profound relief that the spell she had cast over him so long ago was broken at last.

He turned away, moving back to the centre of the room, and as though the movement had recalled his presence to Westlake's mind, the other man turned, too, to follow him with his eyes.

"You see, Captain, indifference does not serve where Helen is concerned," he sneered. "There is always a rival eager to take one's place. You have neglected her of late. Do you wonder that you find yourself supplanted?"

His tone was an indescribable mixture of rage and pain and malicious triumph, as though he found some salve to his own outraged feelings in Adrian's supposed discomfiture. He came away from the window and stood leaning upon the back of a chair, eyeing the younger man malevolently.

"Your day is over, Clare," he informed him harshly. "Helen is prudent, and looks to the future, and whatever your resources may be, it is not likely that they can compare with your successor's. My money bought her, and when I have it no longer she will leave me for a man who has as much, and more, to lavish upon her." He paused, staring straight before him now, his lips twisting in bitterness and fury. "My God! must I lose her along with everything else?"

Adrian looked incredulously at him. It was unbelievable that after her treatment of him, her shameless infidelities and her deliberate cruelty, any tender feelings for his wife could survive in Marcus Westlake's heart, and yet now he had the look of a man upon the rack. An hour ago Adrian would have scorned the notion that he could ever feel pity for Christina's would-be murderer, but now as he looked at him he was aware of a reluctant stirring of compassion, and shame at his own part in the man's betrayal. There was nothing that he could say, and after a moment he turned and went quietly out of the room, leaving Westlake alone with the torment of his thoughts.

The abruptness of his departure took the servants unawares, and he was obliged to wait for some minutes while his horse was saddled again and brought to the door. He was already mounted, and about to ride away from the house, when from a tree-lined walk nearby Helen appeared on the arm of her new gallant.

That this encounter with Captain Clare came as a shock to her was evident, for she halted at sight of him, her eyes widening with surprise, displeasure and even a hint of dismay, but at first Adrian scarcely glanced at her. He was staring instead at the face of the man in the crimson coat, seen clearly now for the first time, a pale, arrogant face with cold, green-grey eyes beneath slanting, jet-black brows, and realizing with a stab of startled recognition that this was the man whose ready pistol had so nearly ended the career of Captain Gallant.

Helen recovered herself immediately and moved forward again, towards the spot where Adrian sat his horse in the sunshine. He bowed from the saddle as she approached, but there was a look of such icy comprehension in his eyes that it pierced even her armour of self-confidence, and brought a touch of angry colour to her cheeks.

"I was not aware, sir, that you had chosen to honour us again with your presence," she said, and there was a decided edge to her voice. She turned to her companion. "Sir Deryk, permit me to make known to you Captain Adrian Clare. Sir Deryk Mandeville."

The gentlemen exchanged bows, but when Adrian spoke it was Helen to whom the words were addressed.

"I have been out of this neighbourhood for a time, Mrs. Westlake, which must be held sufficient excuse for my absence, but I cannot flatter myself that it has been greatly felt. A trifle of business with your husband brought me here today, but as that is now completed I will intrude upon you no further. I bid you a very good day, madam!" He glanced at Mandeville. "Sir Deryk, I am charmed to have made your acquaintance."

He bowed again and touched his horse with the spur, moving away towards the gates leading to the avenue. They both stood looking after him, Helen resentfully, Mandeville with sardonic amusement.

"So this is where Captain Clare has been hiding," he remarked softly. "The mystery is solved."

"Hiding?" Helen turned quickly to face him. "From what?"

"From his relatives, presumably. The young fool avoided a debtors' prison by a hair's breadth, and old Lord Warham, his uncle, settled his affairs on condition that he left England for good. He was to take ship from Bristol, but at some point on the journey from London he disappeared, and nothing has been heard of him since. The affair was the talk of the town three months ago."

Helen's expression was puzzled.

"I thought he came into an inheritance five or six years ago?"

Sir Deryk shrugged.

"Very possibly he did. Fortunes have been squandered in far less time than that." He paused, looking with a faint frown after Adrian's receding figure. "Strange! I have never met Captain Clare before, and yet there is something oddly familiar about him which I cannot quite define. However, memory is an elusive thing, and more likely to bear fruit if left to itself." He turned, proffering his arm. "Shall we go within?"

Half an hour after Adrian's departure—they had, in fact, passed each other upon the road—Walter Kelsby drove up to the door of Coombe Royal. He was admitted at once to Marcus Westlake's presence, but they had barely had time to greet each other when the door opened again and Helen came into the room. Her husband regarded her sourly.

"We have business to discuss, madam, and desire to be private."

Her brows lifted.

"I have some interest in the matter, I suppose? If we are to be driven out of our home by this niece of yours, I desire know what arrangements are being made."

Westlake scowled.

"So that you may make others on your own account?"

"Perhaps," she replied mockingly, and turned to the lawyer. "Well, Mr. Kelsby, what news do you bring? Do we go, or stay?"

He spread out his hands in an apologetic gesture.

"My dear lady, what can I say? This young woman is, beyond all doubt, the lawful daughter of Godfrey Westlake and Phoebe, his wife. Her claim to Coombe Royal is undeniable, and to contest it further would be worse than useless."

Her deceptively soft brown eyes regarded him speculatively.

"You appear to be singularly unconcerned, Mr. Kelsby. Can it be that you have persuaded Miss Westlake to let all the business of the estate remain in your hands?"

He bowed his head in assent, but before he could speak Marcus said eagerly:

"The girl is under age, is she not? For the next two years, at least, she will need a guardian."

"And in two years, who knows what may happen?" Helen added softly. "Surely so shrewd a man as Mr. Kelsby has not overlooked that obvious solution?"

"No, Mrs. Westlake, I have not, but the question does not arise." The level voice was as unemotional as ever; the pale eyes revealed nothing of resentment or of triumph. "The young lady is to be married."

"Married?" Helen's voice sharpened suddenly. "To whom?"

Kelsby leaned back in his chair, clasping his hands across his stomach, the corners of his thin-lipped mouth lifting in the travesty of a smile.

"To me, Mrs. Westlake," he replied ironically. "Whom did you suppose?"

Her lips parted in astonishment, but for several seconds she seemed bereft of speech. Westlake's jaw dropped and he stared unbelievingly at his erstwhile accomplice, who returned the look blandly, enjoying their stupefaction. Then, very softly, Helen began to laugh.

"I congratulate you, Mr. Kelsby," she said in a voice

shaking with mirth. "I do indeed! That was a master-stroke, no less!"

"It was a damned treacherous piece of double-dealing," her husband broke in furiously. "By God, Kelsby, if you think I will step aside and watch you thrust yourself into my place, you are mistaken!"

"You are mistaken, not I," Kelsby replied calmly. "Miss Westlake has done me the honour of accepting my hand in marriage, and her mother fully approves the match. There is nothing that you can do to prevent it."

"Tell me, Mr. Kelsby," Helen said curiously, "what persuasion did you use? I have no wish to' offend you," her voice was mocking, "but surely you had rivals who might have been thought more likely to succeed?"

"True, madam, but I have one overwhelming advantage. Miss Westlake is devoted, almost fanatically so, you understand, to her father's memory, and it is her dearest wish to see his innocence established in the eyes of the world. Happily for the success of my suit, I am in a position to gratify that wish."

"Edmund's confession!" Helen said softly. "I see!"

"You're mad, Kelsby!" Westlake's voice was rough with anger and with fear. "To publish that confession is to admit how it came into your hands. It would destroy us both!"

"Use your wits, my dear Marcus!" Helen said in a bored voice. "The confession is to be made public after the marriage has taken place, not before. Am I not right, Mr. Kelsby?"

"Naturally, madam." The lawyer's pale, protuberant eyes met hers in a look of mutual understanding and approval. "I am not fool enough to give it to her until we are safely wed."

"Or even—at all?" Helen laughed again as she rose to her feet, shaking out her silken skirts that were the colour of a wild rose. "Your wits do not stand in need of sharpening, my dear sir. Well, you have told me all that I desired to know, so I will leave you now to your matters of business."

Marcus Westlake said nothing. He seemed stunned by

the completeness of the disaster which had overtaken him, and listened apathetically while Kelsby talked and planned, showed him papers and demanded signatures. Even when their business was done and the lawyer had left him, he remained seated at the table, his arms resting on the polished wood, his chin sunk in the folds of his neck-cloth while his brooding eyes stared dully before him. For a long time he sat thus, but at last the heavy head was lifted, the expression of despair changed to one of firm resolve, the inert hands clenched into fists. So for a few seconds he remained, and then with an air of purpose he rose to fetch pen and paper. Sweeping aside the other papers which still littered the table, he seated himself again and began to write.

Meanwhile, Walter Kelsby was being driven back towards Marlborough through the lengthening shadows of evening. He sat at his ease, hands clasped across his middle, one foot braced against the opposite seat to steady him against the jolting of the coach, and meditated with satisfaction upon the events of the day. So absorbed was he in contented thought that he paid no heed to the passing of time or distance, and when the quiet of the summer evening was shattered by a thunder of hoofbeats and the crack of a pistol-shot, his awakening was as rude as though he had in fact been soundly asleep.

The coach lurched to a standstill, and in alarm and dismay Mr. Kelsby heaved himself forward to peer from the window. He had just had time to identify his surroundings as a lonely hillside not far from the Bath road when a big, black horse was reined in alongside the coach, and the afterglow of sunset revealed to him the unmistakable figure on its back. Mr. Kelsby had never before seen Captain Gallant, but he had heard him described too often and too accurately to be in any doubt of his identity now.

"No tricks, my friend!" said a quiet, deadly voice. "I do not ride alone tonight."

The crash and tinkle of breaking glass behind him brought Kelsby's head round with a jerk, and framed in the shattered window on the other side of the coach he beheld the head and shoulders of a second masked man, whose levelled pistol was steady as a rock. Captain Gallant leaned down from the saddle and wrenched open the door.

"Step down, Mr. Kelsby," he ordered sternly in a voice as cold as death. "Our business will not delay you for long."

The lawyer hesitated, looking up at him. Behind the slits of the black mask, the highwayman's eyes glittered strangely, icy and menacing; the well-shaped mouth was set in a hard, uncompromising line; the gloved hand holding the long horse-pistol made a slight, meaningful movement. Mr. Kelsby had not a great deal of physical courage. He scrambled down from the coach.

14

No Divided Heart

The garden at the Merry Month of May was large, and devoted for the most part to fruit, herbs and vegetables, but one corner of it, that nearest to the old part of the house, was a survival of earlier days. Here was a stretch of smooth turf, bounded on one side by the house itself, on two others by a high brick wall, and on the fourth separated from the rest of the garden by a tremendous yew hedge. Flowers grew there in many-coloured profusion, and in the farthest corner, where a silver birch tree trailed its delicate branches, was a little arbour smothered in climbing roses.

In this shadowy, scented retreat Christina sat on the morning following her betrothal to Walter Kelsby. She had brought a piece of sewing with her, but this lay neglected in her lap and was no more than a pretext for her presence there, something with which she could pretend to be occupied if anyone stumbled upon her hiding-place.

She had felt an overwhelming need for solitude, for a respite from her mother's incessant chatter. The news that Christina's claim to Coombe Royal had succeeded, followed by the added satisfaction of her betrothal, had roused Mrs. Westlake at last from her abyss of depression and self-pity. She was full of plans, for their removal to Coombe Royal as soon as Marcus Westlake and his wife could be dislodged therefrom; for Christina's wedding; for her own removal to Bath as soon as the marriage had taken place. To Christina, worn out by conflicting emotions, this sudden excess of energy was harder to bear than the previous obsession with ailments and illnesses.

Almost as bad as her mother's ceaseless talk was Stephen's glowering silence. There had been an ugly scene with Stephen last night, when she broke to him the news of her betrothal. His first reaction had been genuine horror at the thought of such a marriage, for he was not altogether unfeeling, and he and Christina had been closely acquainted since childhood.

Although fully aware of the hopes he had cherished of securing her fortune for himself, she was sufficiently touched by this evidence of concern to explain to him the true nature of her bargain with Kelsby, but instead of reconciling him to the match, the disclosure seemed merely to increase his bitterness against it. He berated her unmercifully for what he called her "morbid occupation" with her father's wrongs, and the readiness with which she had agreed to hand over the wealth of which he had been deprived to one of the men who had cheated him of it.

His rage inspired an answering anger in Christina. Her head came up, and she faced him with blazing eyes and the colour rising in her cheeks.

"At least Mr. Kelsby is frank and honest in his proposals," she retorted hotly. "It is Coombe Royal alone that he desires, and he does not pretend otherwise. Do you think I have no pride? I would a thousand times rather agree to such a marriage as he offers me than listen to protestations from you which we both know to be lies! I am neither a child nor a fool, Stephen! I know that I lack those attributes which make a woman desirable in the eyes of men—God knows I have never been encouraged to deceive myself on that score—but I know, too, that an heiress need never lack a husband! If I can use my inheritance to purchase justice for my father's memory, I shall account it well spent."

He stared at her, resentment and chagrin smouldering in his eyes. He had been very sure of success, so sure, in fact, that he had of late been living considerably beyond his means, entering recklessly into the pursuits and pleasures of Gilbert Tedburn and his friends. The thought of his commitments, which without help he would certainly not be able to meet, made him feel rather sick, and of his desperation was born the spiteful desire to hurt Christina, who had destroyed all his hopes.

"I suppose," he sneered at length, "that I would have fared better had I come to you with the sort of cold-blooded bargain you have agreed to make with Kelsby?"

"It would have been more honest," she replied fiercely. "Do you think I enjoy compliments and gallantries which I know to be sheer hypocrisy? Gilbert Tedburn might be forgiven for making that mistake, but you should know me too well to imagine you could prevail with me by such means."

"Yes, I know you," he said scornfully, "better, perhaps, than you suppose. You are not as cold and fastidious as you pretend, are you, Christina? You may be indifferent to my wooing, and to Tedburn's, and prefer your empty bargain with Kelsby to an honest marriage with either of us, but it would be a very different matter if Clare glanced in your direction. He could have you upon any terms he chose!"

With that he left her, striding out of the room with a fine show of disdain, slamming the door upon whatever answer she might make. In fact she made none. Her anger vanished like a pricked bubble and she sank down into the nearest chair, overwhelmed not so much by the truth of his words as by the thought that he had discovered her secret. Were her feelings then so transparently plain? Had anyone else guessed that she had been foolish enough to lose her heart to Captain Clare? How many of the inhabitants of the inn knew it, and regarded her with pity or with contempt?

The mortification induced by questions such as these stayed with her throughout the night, and plagued her still as she sat in the dim green hollow of the arbour, but there was one thought she could not bring herself to face. It had lurked at the back of her mind since the previous day, unbearably humiliating, mocking her with the certainty that whoever else had or had not realized the truth, Adrian himself must have guessed it after their narrow escape from death in the woods above the ford. Whatever emotion had prompted him to kiss her then, relief or pity or merely the desire to reassure and to comfort, she did not know, but the memory of her own eager, instinctive response had remained with her ever since, shaming her almost beyond endurance.

Desperately, in defence against such thoughts as these, she turned her mind towards the future, but even there scant comfort was to be found. Yesterday she had convinced herself that the only sane and sensible course was to accept Kelsby's bargain, to hand over to him the cares and responsibilities as well as the riches of Coombe Royal, but since then doubts had begun to creep in. Try as she would, she could not overcome her instinctive distrust of the man, and though she reminded herself sharply that he could not be blamed for his repulsive appearance, that it should fill her with pity rather than abhorrence, she shrank from his mere presence as she would from the toad he so closely resembled. The prospect of being thrust constantly into his company, deprived even of the meagre support of her mother's presence, grew more forbidding every hour, while from the nagging, unacknowledged dread that his word was not to be depended upon she shuddered away in horror.

She closed her eyes, overcome by a sense of loneliness so devastating and so complete that it was like a cold, black tide rising to engulf her, and when she opened them again a shadow had darkened the entrance to the arbour, and Adrian was standing there under the heavy clusters of roses. It was their first meeting since he had brought her back to the inn the previous day, and she sat as though turned to stone, hearing only the hammering of her own heart.

"I have been looking for you," he said. "There is something I wish to give you."

He stepped forward and dropped a folded paper into her lap. For a moment or two she sat staring at it, and then as though in a dream took it up and unfolded it. From the foot of the page, Edmund Westlake's wavering signature seemed to leap out in letters of fire. As her eyes lifted in bewildered wonder to Adrian's face, he said lightly:

"Mr. Kelsby had the misfortune to be held up on his way home by Captain Gallant."

It needed a few seconds longer for the full magnitude of the service he had done her to dawn upon Christina, but when at length realization came, when she knew that the precious document was there in her hands, without any need for sacrifice or bargain, the relief was so overwhelming that her rigid self-control snapped at last. Her head went down, and a great sob burst from her lips.

Adrian's bantering manner fell from him like a cloak. In an instant he was on one knee beside her chair, his hands covering hers in a strong, comforting clasp as he said gently:

"Christina, my dear, there is no need to weep. How could I let Kelsby hold that threat over you to force you to accept his vile bargain?" His fingers tightened painfully upon hers; his voice was unsteady. "He will never know how close he came to death last night!"

She looked up at him in piteous bewilderment, her eyes wet with tears.

"But you did not know," she said wonderingly. "You could not have known."

"I did know," he assured her quietly. "Before I left here yesterday to visit your uncle I commanded Titus to keep watch over you, and warned him that Kelsby was as little to be trusted as Westlake. Then he learned that Kelsby was in the parlour with your mother." He smiled faintly. "Titus is very conscientious. Throughout your entire conversation with Kelsby he was behind the panel, on the secret stair, and he heard every word. When I returned he greeted me with the news. I had passed Kelsby on the road to Coombe Royal. All we had to do was to wait for him to make the journey home, and stop his coach at the most convenient spot." He paused to take the paper, to fold it, and to close her fingers over it again. "Keep it safe, my dear, until the time comes when you can make use of it."

She nodded, dashing the tears from her eyes with her free hand.

"I owe you so much," she said unsteadily. "First you saved my life, and now—this! How can I ever thank you?"

He shook his head, and, rising to his feet, looked down at her with a smile.

"True friendship does not look for thanks," he reminded her. "Did you not tell me so yourself, upon a similar occasion?"

A faint, tremulous smile was her only answer, but his words, recalling as they did a time when he, and not she, had stood in mortal danger, turned her thoughts in a new direction. Bestowing the paper carefully in the bosom of her gown, she rose to her feet and lifted an anxious gaze to his face.

"What if Mr. Kelsby becomes suspicious of you? If he learns that I have the paper, he is bound to guess the identity of Captain Gallant." Horror at the thought of what such a suspicion might mean seized upon her; she laid a trembling hand on his sleeve. "Oh, you should not have taken such a risk! I would never forgive myself if any harm came to you through me."

Adrian laid his hand over hers.

"You must not trouble yourself on that score. Kelsby might suspect, but he would never dare to accuse me. To admit to any knowledge of that paper would be to admit also that he is as guilty as your uncle in suppressing the truth of Giles Carew's death, and robbing your father of his rights."

"But he promised to make it public, if I married him!"

He shook his head.

"To keep such a promise would have destroyed him, Christina. For more than twenty years all the revenues of Coombe Royal, which by right belonged to your father, have been flowing into his pocket, and Westlake's. The sum involved must be enormous."

"Then he never meant to keep faith with me!" Christina spoke in a shaken whisper and shuddered violently, covering her face with her hands. "Dear God! from what have you saved me? My uncle with his murderous schemes was the more merciful of the two!"

She turned away from him and stood in the mouth of the arbour, under the crowding blossoms, looking out across the sunlit garden. There was silence, broken only by the humming of bees busy among the roses, and the sound of Betsy or Ruth singing to herself in the distance as she went about her work.

"I am afraid!" Christina said simply at last. "Afraid of them both! It seemed so easy in the beginning. Right was upon my side, and I had courage and confidence enough. Now both are gone. I know what it is to be hated, and I cannot fight it alone any longer."

She spoke as though to herself, her voice quiet and unemotional and indescribably desolate. She leaned her hand against one of the posts supporting the arbour and rested her forehead upon it, and one of the roses above her, so full-blown that a breath would have shattered it, let fall its red petals upon her. They drifted all about her, some settling on her dark hair, others clinging to her white dress like great drops of blood.

Adrian took a swift pace forward so that he stood close beside her. He knew the truth of his own heart at last, had recognized it yesterday in the white-heat of his fury against the men who would have harmed her, in the utter indifference with which he had looked upon Helen in Deryk Mandeville's arms, but now a strange uncertainty made him hesitate. She was young and inexperienced, and overwrought by the events of the past twenty-four hours, and it would be fatally easy to frighten her yet further. He must be patient and gentle, and use the utmost delicacy in all he said and did, if he were to convince her of that truth without destroying the bond which already existed between them. He set his hands lightly on her shoulders, turning her to face him again.

"Not alone, Christina," he said in a low voice. "Let me fight it for you. Give me that right. I will guard you well, I promise you, and keep you safe from harm. You need never be afraid again."

Christina's heart seemed to stop beating for a moment. This could not be happening; it was a dream, a delirium, or else she had read into his words a meaning he did not intend. Not daring to look up at him, she said in a breathless whisper:

"I do not understand."

"I am asking you, very humbly, to be my wife," he said gently. "It is a thing I have very little right to ask. I have no fortune of my own, I make my living on the high road and you are the heiress of Coombe Royal. All I can offer you is protection from your enemies, and my devotion always." He paused, looking down at her with some anxiety. She was trembling and her face was paper-white. "You have become very dear to me, Christina. Your safety and happiness will always be my foremost concern."

It was not a dream. This incredible, unbelievable thing was really happening. She felt incapable of coherent thought. He was still holding her lightly by the shoulders, and she was conscious of his touch through every fibre of her being, just as she was conscious of the warmth of the sunshine and the piercingly sweet scent of the roses.

He was waiting for her answer. Slowly, almost timidly, still half afraid to believe, she looked up at last, into the handsome, reckless face and the blue eyes which, laughing no longer, were watching her with such unwonted gravity.

"I will marry you," she whispered.

She saw the sudden light leap in his eyes, and as his hands on her shoulders drew her towards him she closed her own eyes and lifted her face for the expected kiss. For a second that seemed an eternity she waited, and then felt his lips, very gentle, against her forehead.

"You have made me very happy, my dear," he said quietly. "Very happy, and very proud."

She stood as still as death, not understanding, scarcely even feeling, numb with bewilderment and shock. Yesterday he had kissed her lips, his own warm and compelling upon them, yet now, to seal their troth, he bestowed on her an embrace he might have given to a child. He was speaking again, and she forced at least a part of her mind to concentrate on what he was saying.

"It will be best, I think, if we say nothing to your mother at present. Or to Ancroft, for that matter. They might consider it their duty to inform Kelsby, and it will do no harm for him to believe you still safe in his trap, at least until you are firmly established at Coombe Royal." He lifted his hand to brush away one of the rose petals which still clung to her hair. "It may be necessary to see him again," he warned her. "Can you bring yourself to do that, Christina? To deceive him a little, until the moment comes when I can tell him that you are promised to me?"

She nodded, but moved away from him and stooped to pick up her sewing from the ground. She took it out and then folded it with unnecessary care, smoothing it between her hands. Looking down at it, she said reluctantly, as though the words were torn from her against her will:

"What of Helen Westlake?"

There was a long moment of silence, of mounting, unbearable tension. The challenge seemed like a tangible thing, like a sword, menacing and double-edged, thrust suddenly between them, wounding them both. At last Adrian said very quietly:

"You know, then?"

She was still intent upon the sewing.

"Stephen told me. He said everyone knew of it. Then

I remembered the day we first met, when you told me
that you had known her long ago, before her marriage.
There was something in your voice when you spoke of
her——" she broke off, gripping the sewing tightly between her hands, no longer even pretending to be aware
of it. When she spoke again the words were stifled, almost
inaudible. "You had come in search of her, after all
that time. You must have loved her very much."

He did not reply at once. How could he make her
understand the irony of his love for Helen, the early
betrayal, the years of folly culminating in a crazy quest,
the bitter disillusion which had followed the fulfilment
of his desire? These were things beyond her comprehension, and to try to tell her of them could only add
to the burden of doubt and uncertainty she already had
to bear.

"It is over, Christina," he said gravely at last. "It was
a fever, a madness that lasted for seven years, but now
I am healed of it at last, that I swear to you. It is no
divided heart I offer you, my love."

She turned quickly to face him, her lips parted, her
eyes imploring reassurance, but whatever she would have
said of question or entreaty was never uttered. While
Adrian spoke, a shadow had fallen across the sunlit grass
outside the arbour, and a light footfall, soundless on the
close-cropped turf. Even as Christina turned, there was
a low laugh, and a sweet, mocking voice said softly:

"Yes, it is over, rest assured of that! You have not
delayed long before seeking consolation, have you, my
dear Adrian?"

The two within the arbour spun round as though jerked
by a single, invisible cord. Framed in the rose-hung arch-
way, her flame-coloured riding-dress a splash of vibrant
colour against the green, calm and assured in the insolence of her great beauty, Helen herself was enigmati-
cally regarding them.

15

The Serpent in the Roses

Christina had not a moment's doubt of the newcomer's identity. She had tried often to visualize what Helen must be like, but the woman confronting her now was lovelier by far than anything she had imagined, and for a moment or two she was conscious of no feeling other than astonished admiration. The plainness of Helen's present attire enhanced rather than detracted from her beauty, the well-cut coat moulding her magnificent figure, the perfection of her features emphasized by the severity of drawn-back hair beneath a black tricorne. She looked insolently at the couple before her, and a smile of languorous mockery touched her lips.

" 'No divided heart'," she quoted lightly. "A charming sentiment, my dear, and charmingly expressed. You always did command a pretty turn of phrase."

Adrian stepped forward out of the shade of the arbour, and confronted her in the strong, bright sunlight. He was very angry, but beneath the anger was a small stirring of fear, less for himself than for Christina. Helen was utterly heartless. He knew that now beyond all doubt, and he was certain, too, that her present lazy mockery was a cloak for a mood of venomous spite against which the younger girl would have no defence at all.

"Why have you come here?" he demanded sternly, and Helen's brows lifted at the tone he used.

"Because it pleased me to come," she retorted coldly. "Do I need any other reason?"

She did not wait for his reply, but lifting the slender riding-whip she carried she put him contemptuously aside and looked past him into the arbour, where Christina stood silent and unmoving.

"I desire to make the acquaintance of my husband's niece," she announced. "Come, child, do not hide there in the shadows! There is no need to feel confusion because you were tempted to listen to Captain Clare's pretty speeches. You are not the first woman to do so, as I dare say you know."

Christina laid her sewing down carefully on the chair, and limped slowly forward to Adrian's side. Helen watched her, her gaze travelling deliberately from the pale face with its heavy crown of dark hair, down over the slight, immature figure, and lingering with studied cruelty on the lame foot just visible beneath the muslin skirt. A faint, scornful smile curved her lips.

"Now I understand," she said softly. "My wits must be growing dull, or I should have guessed the truth before." She gave them no time to ponder the meaning of these cryptic words, but went on without a pause, speaking now directly to Christina. "So you are Godfrey Westlake's daughter, the new mistress of Coombe Royal! I must congratulate you, I suppose, though that was not my purpose in seeking you out. I came to warn you."

"To warn me?" Christina was pale as death, but her voice, at least, was calm and composed. "Against what, madam?"

"Against Adrian, of course!" Helen replied, and laughed. "It is really very amusing, is it not? Yesterday, quite by chance, I discovered that he has scarcely a penny to his name, and having some experience of his powers of persuasion, I considered it my duty to inform you of the fact. An heiress, my dear, must be constantly on her guard against fortune-hunters."

"If you are hoping to make mischief by these means, Helen, you will be disappointed," Adrian said shortly. He was white with an anger held rigidly under control. "I have made no secret to Christina of my lack of means."

"And she does not care, having now more than enough for both," Helen concluded mockingly. "A generous, if somewhat unworldly point of view. But you mistake me, my dear Adrian! I did for a short while suppose that the estate of Coombe Royal might be a prize you could not resist, yet I could not rid myself of the feeling that such opportunism was not in keeping with your nature as I knew it. Now I see that I was right in that. You have not changed at all, have you?"

He was aware of Christina's puzzled, questioning glance turning towards him, but he, too, was baffled by Helen's words. His uneasiness grew, for he knew her to be capable of any cruelty. She was still smiling with her lips, but her eyes were cold and venomous.

"I am reminded of a day seven years ago," she resumed pensively after a moment. "Do you remember, Adrian? We had ridden out from Tunbridge with a party of friends, and chanced upon some village louts tormenting a half-grown puppy, which you must needs rescue. Then you insisted on carrying it home with you, and when in spite of all your care it died, you were quite ridiculously grieved. It was an unlovely little creature, as I recall, but all that mattered to you was that it was maimed and friendless." She laughed gently, and glanced sidelong under thick lashes at Christina. "No, you have not changed! Your pity is still fatally easy to arouse."

A deathly silence succeeded this flow of honeyed spite. Adrian was almost afraid to look at Christina, for the purpose of the anecdote, and the cruel comparison drawn by barbed words and mocking tone, were unmistakable, and when with a feeling of sick misgiving he turned towards her, she was staring at him with stricken, tragic eyes. Her lips moved soundlessly, and when in quick concern he put out his hand to her, she dashed it aside and, turning, went at a stumbling run towards the house.

He took a couple of paces after her, and then halted and swung round again to face Helen, who recoiled involuntarily from the look in his face. She recovered herself in an instant, and spoke boldly to cover that betrayal of alarm.

"Yes, you would like to murder me, would you not? But that would not mend matters, my dear. I doubt that anything can do that."

He recognized the truth of what she said, and anger perished in bitterness and disgust. He said wearily:

"Why, in God's name? I do not flatter myself that jealousy was the cause. Do you just love cruelty for its own sake?"

She disregarded the question, answering it with another.

"Why did you leave me, without a word? When I sent to discover what had become of you, the people here said that you had gone away."

He shrugged.

"That was quite true. I returned only yesterday."

Helen's lips tightened.

"It did not occur to you to inform me of your intention? I am not accustomed to such cavalier treatment, Adrian, and I do not like it. What brought you to Coombe Royal yesterday?"

"I told you. Business with your husband."

"With Marcus!" she repeated scornfully. "Are you sure it was not to spy upon me?"

He raised his brows.

"You flatter yourself unduly, Helen, but even if I had come seeking you, what I saw would have been sufficient to overcome any such desire. Mandeville may be content to be one of a retinue of admirers. I am not."

The colour rose angrily in her cheeks under the sting of his contemptuous tone, and her eyes narrowed spitefully. She said with dangerous calm:

"Indeed? It must be consoling, then, to know that in your present pursuit you need look for no rivals. It will need all the wealth of Coombe Royal to gild that pill, will it not?"

He shook his head, curbing his anger still, making of it a cold and deadly weapon to parry the malevolence of the woman confronting him.

"Your earlier shot came nearer to the mark, Helen. I am not dazzled by the glitter of Christina's inheritance."

"You amaze me!" she said with a sneer. "I should imagine you would find it amusing to squander it as you squandered your own."

"It is not quite the same," he replied swiftly. "I admit that I squandered my own patrimony. I flung it away in every kind of senseless extravagance, because I believed then that I had lost the most precious thing in life and that in a ceaseless round of pleasure I might find a measure of forgetfulness. I know now how mistaken I was. The thing I had lost was utterly worthless."

Now at last he had avenged in part the attack upon Christina, for those words had wounded Helen in the most vulnerable facet of her nature—her vanity. She went white with rage, and the hand holding the whip lifted in a slashing blow which would have laid open his face had it landed. He caught her by the wrist, thwarting the intention and twisting the whip from her grasp with his free hand. Holding her thus prisoner, he looked down into her furious eyes.

"I spoke the truth to Christina just now, when I told her that I was healed of my madness at last," he said quietly. "I should be grateful to you, Helen! For seven years I cherished a dream, a delusion of lost happiness, and might have dreamed it to my life's end had I not come seeking it again, and found reality instead. It is not Christina's fortune I covet. It is not pity I feel for her. I love her, and I will spend my whole life, if need be, striving to win her love in return."

For several seconds after Adrian paused there was silence, and then Helen wrenched herself free and spoke in a vicious, contemptuous tone.

"So you love her, do you? Yes, I believe it! It is just the sort of weak, romantic folly I would expect of you. You love her, and will continue to do so until the end of your days! Do you expect me to envy her on that account? No, life is short, and God preserve me from the tedium of constancy!" She paused, and slowly the fury in her eyes faded, cooling and changing to an expression of mocking, malicious satisfaction. She laughed, and it was not a pleasant sound. "Yes, Adrian," she said again, "I believe that you truly love her, but do you suppose you will ever be able to make her believe it—now?"

She stood looking at him, watching comprehension and dismay come into his eyes, and then she stooped and picked up the whip from where he had let it fall. Straight-

ening up again, she drew the lash of it gently across his
cheek in the scornful travesty of a caress.

"Good-bye, Adrian," she said lightly, "and good fortune
in your wooing," and, turning, she went with leisured
grace towards the inn, her flame-coloured skirts whispering
across the grass, and the echo of her laughter drifting
back to taunt him with a sense of failure and defeat.

Helen went swiftly through the house, ignoring Mrs.
Barnby's suspicious, disapproving glance, and emerged
again into the sunshine beneath the swinging, faded sign.
Her groom, that discreet and self-effacing personage, was
waiting with the horses under the sleepy gaze of Reuben
Barnby, who was leaning against the wall with his hands
thrust deep into his pockets and his eyes half-closed
against the glare of the sunlight. Helen swept past him
and mounted her horse, and with the servant at her heels
skirted the pond and turned along the road towards
Coombe Royal.

Reuben continued to watch them until they passed out
of sight, and then with a grunt of satisfaction he straightened his back and returned to the stables, there to resume
the work which their arrival had interrupted. Captain
Clare had not spoken idly when he warned Marcus Westlake that a constant watch would be kept at the Merry
Month of May.

Helen rode fast, her restless mood communicating itself
to her horse, but was presently checked by an encounter
with Mr. Tedburn. He was obviously big with news, and
poured into the lady's indifferent ear an account of Walter
Kelsby's misadventure the previous evening, the most
singular feature of which appeared to be the fact that
this was the first robbery committed by Captain Gallant
so far from the main Bath road. In view of this, Mr.
Tedburn added, it would perhaps be prudent if Mrs.
Westlake did not ride abroad without adequate protection;
his wife and daughters would certainly not be permitted
to do so.

Helen raised her brows.

"But is it not true that Captain Gallant has never yet
attacked an unescorted woman? I shall not skulk at home

on his account, I assure you, nor shrink from the possibility of an encounter with him." She looked at Mr. Tedburn under her lashes. "In fact, it might be amusing to
discover whether he is worthy of the name he has been
given."

She laughed into the magistrate's shocked and disapproving face, and touched her horse lightly with the
whip. It bounded forward, the servant following, and
Mr. Tedburn was left gasping in a cloud of dust raised
by the plunging hoofs.

For another two or three furlongs Helen maintained
a reckless pace while her thoughts darted here and there
like angry wasps among the events of the morning. The
news concerning Walter Kelsby afforded her a moment's
malicious amusement, for she disliked the man even
though she respected his cunning, and she reflected with
a chuckle that Captain Gallant's appearance must have
come as a rude awakening after his triumph over Marcus
and his betrothal to Christina.

His betrothal! Her thoughts jerked to an abrupt halt
as she recalled the scene she had witnessed in the arbour.
True, she had heard no talk of marriage, but from what
Adrian had told her later it was unlikely that he would
approach Christina with anything else in mind. Yet Christina was promised to Kelsby, and held fast by his promise
to publish Edmund Westlake's confession and so clear
her father's name. Or was she so held? Since the previous
day, had some blow been struck to free her, and by
whom?

Sudden excitement woke in Helen's mind, and she
checked her horse to a walking pace the better to consider
the facts known to her. Christina would never have accepted Kelsby's bargain without a glimpse of the precious
paper, so he must have been carrying it with him yesterday; and on his way home he had been stopped, and
robbed. A document such as that would have had no
value to an ordinary highwayman, but no one had ever
suggested that there was anything ordinary about Captain
Gallant.

She tried to remember how long it was since Gallant's

first appearance. Only a few months, she felt sure. Adrian Clare had come to Wiltshire three months ago, having by his own confession squandered his entire fortune, yet not once during that time had he appeared to be short of money. It would be very like Adrian to take to highway robbery to mend his fortunes, and every description she had heard of the debonair highwayman could be applied with equal accuracy to Captain Clare.

A little smile of vindictive satisfaction curved her lips. Chance, and her own shrewdness, had placed a powerful weapon in her hands, and Adrian should come to regret most bitterly the treatment he had accorded her. Vanity, most potent of all her feelings, had been grievously wounded and must be avenged.

Sir Deryk Mandeville was waiting for her when she reached Coombe Royal. He came to help her down from her horse, forestalling the groom in performance of that duty, and proffered his arm to lead her into the house. They mounted the steps together, and beneath the cloak of formal ceremony he said very softly, bending his head so that his lips were close to her ear:

"They tell me your husband is from home, and will be gone several days. Will you not come away with me now, before he returns? Have I not been patient long enough?"

She smiled, and her fingers tightened on his arm, but she shook her head.

"Wait just a little longer, my dear! I promise you it will not be more than a day or two at most. Marcus can do nothing to hinder me, and there is something I wish to see accomplished before I leave Coombe Royal for ever."

They were in the great hall now. She released his arm and turned to face him, and he saw that her eyes were very bright.

"I am told that Captain Gallant robbed my husband's lawyer last night, not far from here," she said lightly. "You have seen this highwayman, Deryk. What is he like?"

He looked at her with surprise and a trace of impatience.

"I had but a fleeting glimpse of him," he reminded her. "Young. I should say, and sat his horse well. A gentleman, by his dress."

"Would you know him again, do you think?"

He shrugged.

"Who can say? I might, if I saw him on horseback."

"If you saw him on horseback," she repeated. "I see!" She drew a deep breath of satisfaction, and laughed very softly. "Bear with me a few minutes longer, my dear. There is a trifle of business which I must attend to without delay."

She touched his cheek lightly with her fingertips in a fleeting caress, and hurried away. Coming to her boudoir, she paused only to strip off her gloves before sitting down at her writing desk and taking out pen and paper. The letter she wrote was a long one, covering several pages, and when it was finished she summoned her maid and sent her to fetch the groom who had ridden with her to the inn.

While she waited, she read quickly through the letter, made an alteration here and there, and added a brief postscript. When the groom came into the room she was occupied in fixing the seal, and said without looking up:

"I desire you to carry this to Mr. Kelsby without delay. After his misadventure last night, you will probably find him at his house, but if he is not there, then seek him in Marlborough or wherever else he may be. Do not return until you have placed it in his hands." She raised her head, holding the letter out towards him. "Tell him that I am certain of the information it contains, and desire him to act upon it without delay."

16

"On Any Terms—"

Christina, fleeing blindly from the silken malice of Helen's words, sought refuge in the house, where she was thankful to find the parlour unoccupied. Dropping into a chair, she covered her face with her hands, the tears trickling between her fingers as the brutal taunt hammered relentlessly in her ears. "Maimed and friendless. Your pity is still fatally easy to arouse."

Pity! All her life she had hated it, had shrunk from seeing it in the eyes turned upon her, from finding it in the words and bearing of those who, by pointedly ignoring her affliction, seemed somehow to focus attention upon it. She had taught herself to make no sign, to betray none of the burning resentment consuming her, but it was none the less fierce for being repressed. Now resentment became despair, for if pity was all that Adrian felt for her, how could she ever marry him?

Then, as she grew calmer, Stephen's angry gibe came into her mind. "On any terms," he had said, and now with sudden self-knowledge she knew that it was true. Adrian might pity her, but at least it was not the contemptuous pity she had come to dread; he had offered her the protection of his strength and worldly experience, and promised to make her happiness his foremost concern. What right had she to look for more? These things were already more than she had ever dared to hope for.

Carefully she dried her eyes, trying to compose herself, reminding herself sharply that she had much for which to be thankful. Yesterday she had forced herself to accept Kelsby's loathsome bargain, and to face a future indescribably bleak, charged with nameless dread. Now, freed of that hated contract, the proof of her father's innocence secure in her possession, herself the promised wife of the man she loved, she should be on her knees thanking God for her deliverance, rather than bewailing the fact that she did not fill Adrian's heart and mind and world as completely as he filled hers.

Not even for a moment did she consider Helen's other accusation, that it was her inheritance which had prompted Adrian's proposal. She knew instinctively that there was not the slightest truth in it, and she would be more than thankful to place the whole of her fortune in those loved and trusted hands. She had obeyed her father's wishes and fought untiringly to recover her birthright, but she had been secretly appalled at the weight of responsibility which possession of Coombe Royal would thrust upon her. Now that burden would be lifted from her shoulders, but more important by far than her own peace of mind was the fact that it would no longer be necessary for Captain Gallant to ride the Wiltshire roads. That alone, she thought, should outweigh all other considerations. To know him safe from discovery and arrest, to be free of the fear which had haunted her day and night ever since she learned his secret, should be consolation enough.

So, presently, when Adrian came in anxious search of her, he found her composed, if a trifle withdrawn. She greeted him with a smile, and a grave apology for her abrupt departure.

"I behaved absurdly," she concluded, in a calm voice belied only by her nervously-twisting hands. "Heaven knows I should be accustomed by now to clumsy references to my lameness."

"It was not clumsiness, Christina, but deliberate cruelty," he said quietly. "What she said was unforgivable."

"It is no wonder that she hates me. I have heard that wealth and great position mean much to her, and these she had as mistress of Coombe Royal. I have taken them from her." She hesitated, not looking at him. "Then, too, she was displeased by what she overheard."

"Christina!" Adrian came to stand beside her chair, resting one hand on its back. "It was her vanity alone that was touched. She considers it her right to make an end, as and when she chooses, and she will never forgive me for breaking the hold she had upon me."

"Are you sure?" Christina's head was still bowed so that he could not see her face. "Pain and jealousy could cause cruelty that is not meant."

"Will you be her advocate, in spite of all?" Adrian's voice was very gentle, and his hand moved from the chair-back to touch her dark hair. "She neither needs nor deserves your sympathy on any count. Sir Deryk Mandeville is at Coombe Royal, and he, I am told, is exceedingly rich. I have no doubt that he is Helen's chosen protector for the immediate future."

"I see!" Christina spoke in a whisper, the words scarcely reaching his ears. So that was the truth at last! Adrian had visited Coombe Royal yesterday, and no doubt his arrival had taken Helen by surprise. He had discovered her true worth, and in a revulsion of feeling turned to one who was her opposite in every way, who would make no demands upon him, but accept gratefully the pity and the protection which was all he had to offer her. He had offered them honestly, with no pretence at a deeper emotion, and she should be glad that he had not tried to deceive her.

"Christina!" He spoke compellingly now, and his hand came beneath her chin, turning her face up towards him. "I told you the truth just now in the garden. It is over. Helen no longer has any place in my heart or in my life. Do you believe me?"

"I believe you," she said faintly, and closed her eyes against that blue, compelling gaze. She felt unutterably weary, worn out by the storm of emotion which had been tossing her to and fro for hours, and was perilously close again to tears.

Something of this Adrian read in her white face and trembling lips, and the further avowal he had been about to make remained unuttered. What might have been said before Helen's arrival was better left, perhaps, till another day. He let go her chin, and took her hand, lifting it to his lips.

"Thank you, my dear," he said gently. "Now I will plague you no more. We can talk of these things another time."

They were to have no further opportunity to talk of them then, for almost as Adrian spoke, Stephen came into the room. He looked with swift suspicion from Adrian to Christina, obviously taken aback at finding them in such close and intimate conversation, though he said nothing at the time. Later, however, chancing to have a moment alone with her, he remarked with a sneer that since she was now betrothed to Walter Kelsby, it would be more seemly if she were to spend less time with Captain Clare.

"That is my concern, Stephen, and Mr. Kelsby's," she retorted crisply. She had had time to compose herself, and had never at any time stood in awe of Mr. Ancroft. "Perhaps your criticisms should be addressed to him. I've no doubt they would amuse him."

Stephen answered her petulantly, and took himself off in a very ill-humour indeed. He was exceedingly worried, harassed by his financial obligations and unable, rack his brains as he might, to see any way out of his difficulties. All the fine hopes and plans with which he had come to England had proved to be mere delusions, and he could see no alternative to secret, ignominious flight, and a return to the hand-to-mouth existence of which he was heartily tired.

These anxieties continued to plague him for the rest of the day and far into the night, when, too harassed even to think of sleep, he sat half-dressed on the broad window-seat in his bedchamber and stared morosely out over the countryside, placid and peaceful in the light of a full moon. It was a still, warm night with scarcely a breath of wind stirring, and the shadows lay black and dense beneath the trees. The duck-pond was a sheet of burnished silver, and beyond it the cross-roads showed like four white ribbons stretching away into the darkness.

What time it was Stephen neither knew nor cared. The house seemed to have been sunk in slumber for hours, and only he was wakeful, keeping vigil over the ruin of his vanished hopes. In all the silent, silver night, no one else was stirring.

Yet, was he the only one? Suddenly a faint, elusive sound, gone too swiftly to be defined, pierced his preoccupation, and he looked up sharply, straining his ears yet hardly knowing for what it was he listened.

At last it came again, the faint creak and jingle of a horse's harness, not far away and yet unaccompanied by any sound of hoofbeats. He stared about him in perplexity, and then the explanation dawned upon him as a rider emerged from the thick shadows of the road leading to Mereton Hall, his horse stepping silently upon the grass bordering the lane.

Stephen drew back sharply into the shelter of the curtain. There were two men on the horse, and the one in the rear slumped oddly against his companion, who held him there by one arm drawn forward about his own waist, but it was upon the foremost rider and upon his mount that Stephen's startled, incredulous gaze was fixed. A black horse, a proud and splendid beast, and in the saddle a tall figure debonair in fashionable riding-clothes, with lace at throat and wrist and a sword at his side. Powdered hair beneath a black tricorne, and the upper part of the face concealed behind a broad black mask. The notorious Captain Gallant, without a doubt.

The apparition circled the pond and passed out of Stephen's view as it halted before the door, but he heard the creak of leather and the faint jingle of spurs as the highwayman dismounted, then, soft but very clear, the whistled fragment of a tune. Three times, at intervals, the signal was repeated, and then a window opened somewhere above. No word was spoken, but Stephen could imagine the occupant of that upper room peering out, gesturing perhaps for caution, and then vanishing again.

He rose and stole softly across to the door, and opened it a little way. For two or three minutes he waited, and then there were hushed footsteps, and at the turn of the passage, where the stairs twisted steeply down to the square, stone-flagged hall, the gleam of a passing candle.

Overcome by curiosity, and with a faint, nebulous hope

of turning the chance discovery to good account, Stephen crept in pursuit. He had already discarded his shoes, and his stockinged feet made scarcely a sound on the solid oaken floor. Peering cautiously around the last turn of the stairs, he saw that Japhet Barnby, bare-footed, his breeches pulled hastily on over his night-shirt, was silently loosing bolts and chain from the door. Then a stair creaked somewhere above, and Stephen realized with horror that someone else was descending from the upper part of the house.

He had only one slight chance of escaping discovery. At the foot of the stairs, and below them, was a recess which might be large enough to conceal a man. Japhet was still busy at the door, his back towards him, and the person above yet out of sight on the twisting stair, though the growing gleam of a candle betrayed their coming. Holding his breath, Stephen whipped down the few remaining stairs and a moment later was crouched uncomfortably in the recess, pressed as far back into its concealing shadows as he could go.

The door swung open and Captain Gallant supported his companion into the hall. The other man, too, was dressed for riding, but he was hatless, his clothes torn and dusty, his head drooping and his right arm hanging useless at his side. Japhet closed the door and turned quickly to Gallant's aid, while the person descending the stairs reached the hall and hurried forward, revealing himself as the manservant, Titus.

"It is Ned Sparrow," Gallant explained briefly, and the quiet, familiar tones crystallized Stephen's vague suspicions into triumphant certainty. "I found him on the road. His horse was shot under him during the evening and he was trying to make his way to the cottage on foot. I fear his arm is broken."

They had lowered the injured man to a seat on a big oak chest against the wall, and Titus was bending over him, seeking the extent of his hurts. The highwayman stripped off his mask and stood looking on, and the hidden watcher could see his proud, reckless profile clear against the dark panelling behind him. Captain Adrian Clare. Captain Gallant.

There was another footfall on the stairs, a light, uneven step that could belong to only one person, but the men on the other side of the hall did not seem to have heard it. Japhet said dubiously:

"The cottage might have been a safer hiding-place, Captain. Lord knows I don't grudge poor Ned shelter, but 'twill have to be the cellars, I'm thinking, and they be no place for a sick man."

Adrian nodded.

"I know it, Japhet, and tried to take him there, but there are soldiers between here and the woods. The whole countryside is swarming with them tonight."

"What, sir, all on account o' Ned?" Japhet's tone expressed mild surprise, and Adrian laughed softly.

"I fancy my venture last night has something to do with it. Kelsby is an influential man. Well, Titus?"

"A broken arm, sir, as you said," his servant replied imperturbably, "and sundry scratches and bruises. He seems to be totally exhausted."

"Small wonder at that!" Gallant's voice was grim. "It is no pleasant thing to be hunted like an animal, with the hue and cry at one's heels. I will leave him in your care, then, and Japhet's. With so many red-coats abroad, the sooner I am away from here, the better."

"Adrian!" It was Christina's voice, urgent and anxious, speaking softly from the foot of the stairs. He swung round and then came quickly across to her, and Stephen pressed himself even farther back into the recess. Christina moved forward, and they met within a yard or two of his hiding-place. Japhet and Titus exchanged glances, and bent once more over Mr. Sparrow.

"You should not be here, Christina," Adrian reproved her gently. "It would be safer for you to know nothing of this matter."

"I could not sleep," she replied, "and then I heard the others come down, and I was afraid that something might be wrong. Who is that man?"

"A comrade who is hurt and hunted," he said quietly.

"I have brought him here for shelter. Japhet knows him well. Go back to bed, my dear! There is nothing to fear."

"Is there not?" She stood looking up at him, a slight, childish figure with her dark hair in a heavy braid over one shoulder, her left hand clutching the shabby grey cloak about her over her night attire. The right she put out towards Adrian. "You said that there are soldiers abroad tonight."

"So you heard that, did you?" He took her hand in both his own, looking down at her with a smile. "Well, it is true, but my horse is swifter, and my familiarity with the country greater than theirs, and I promise you they will not capture Captain Gallant tonight. But that same horse is tethered now before the door, and if it were seen there it would bring trouble down upon all of us. I must not linger."

"I know," she said in a whisper, and stifled a sigh. "Go, then, but oh, Adrian! be careful, I beg of you. I shall pray for your safety."

"That will be my surest safeguard." Adrian glanced over his shoulder, but Japhet and Titus were still discreetly intent upon the injured man. He bent and kissed her cheek. "Sleep well, my love!"

He turned and went back across the hall, taking the mask from his pocket as he went, pausing for a word with the other men while he fixed it across his face again. From the door he looked back at Christina, lifting his hand in farewell, and then he was gone, and Japhet moving to fasten bolts and chain once more.

Christina went slowly up the stairs again, and presently Titus and Japhet bore Ned Sparrow away in the direction of the kitchen. As soon as the hall was dark and silent once more, Stephen emerged from the recess, stretched his cramped limbs, and returned stealthily to his own room. Once there, he flung himself down, still in shirt and breeches, on the bed, and, clasping his hands behind his head, lay there considering all that he had learned during the past half-hour. Properly handled, his discoveries ought to provide him with a solution to all his problems, and show a handsome profit into the bargain.

17

The Conspirators

By morning, his plans were laid, and he told Christina that he wished to speak to her alone. She looked at him coldly, for she was in no mood to humour him. Adrian had not returned, and though Titus assured her that there was no cause for alarm, and that the Captain knew plenty of safe hiding-places should the need arise, she could not conquer her anxiety, or an illogical feeling of impending disaster.

"I do not think, Stephen, that we have anything to say to each other," she told him shortly. "Your opinion of me has already been made abundantly plain."

"Nevertheless, it is imperative that we should talk," he insisted. "Come into the garden, Christina, where we can be private. Believe me, you will regret it if you do not."

She sighed, and did as he asked, but when he would have led the way to the arbour, she halted abruptly. That spot held too many memories.

"Not there," she said quickly, and turned aside to lean against the trunk of the silver birch, watching him impatiently. "Well, what is it? Make haste and tell me, for I have a great deal to do."

"Yes, to be sure!" Stephen's voice was mocking. "You must make your preparations to move to Coombe Royal, and after that, I suppose, you will be thinking of weddings. When may we hope to see the dashing bridegroom again?"

Christina's lips tightened.

"If you have brought me here merely to jeer at Mr. Kelsby, Stephen, it was labour lost. I will not listen."

"Would I describe Kelsby as dashing? I referred, of course, to the Captain."

Christina's heart gave a lurch of alarm, and to her dismay she felt hot colour rushing to her cheeks. Trying to turn this to good account, she said angrily:

"Such jests are unseemly and unbecoming! Captain Clare——"

"Or Captain Gallant," he interrupted softly. "They are one and the same."

She gasped, and the colour faded from her face as quickly as it had come, leaving her deathly pale. Stephen regarded her with grim satisfaction.

"You were not the only one, Christina, who could not sleep last night. I saw and heard everything. This is a pretty little nest of outlaws, is it not?"

She did not answer, but only stared at him with wide, horrified eyes. Stephen went on pensively:

"I had always laughed at Gilbert Tedburn's suspicions, but his wits are sharper than I thought. How many highwaymen frequent this place, Christina? Gallant I know, and poor Ned Sparrow who must lie in the cellar despite his broken arm, but are there others? It does not matter greatly, of course! That Gallant is known and sheltered here will be sufficient."

"Sufficient?" The words were forced in a whisper between bloodless lips. "Sufficient for what?"

"For the authorities," he replied brutally. "There is a price on Gallant's head, and I am a poor man."

"No!" It was a cry of desperation, of an anguish that told him more clearly than any words how completely her heart had been given. She started forward, clutching the front of his coat with frantic hands. "Stephen, for God's sake, have pity! You would not sell his life for a hundred pounds?"

"Why not?" he retorted callously. "His life means nothing to me."

"But it is not Adrian alone. 'Tis Polly and Japhet and all their family. You have met with great kindness here. Would you repay it by destroying them?"

"That is for you to say." His hands came up to grasp her wrists, gripping them so hard that she gasped with pain. "You were prepared to give your whole inheritance to purchase from Kelsby the proof that your father was no murderer. How much more is Clare's life worth to you than your father's innocence?"

She was still now, looking up into his face, striving desperately for calmness, for the wit to avert the hideous danger threatening her love. She said faintly:

"If Kelsby demands my whole inheritance, what is there left to give?"

He released her abruptly, thrusting her away from him so that she staggered back against the trees again, and leaned there gasping for breath. Stephen looked down at her with a sneer.

"Do not trifle with me, Christina! Kelsby was robbed by Gallant, and no longer has anything to sell. That paper you prize so highly is in your possession now, or Clare's."

"What do you want?" she said imploringly. "Tell me, in pity's name!"

"Oh, be easy! I do not demand that you should marry me instead. It crossed my mind, I confess, but I am not fool enough to suppose that I should live long enough to lead you to the altar. Clare would force a quarrel on me, or I should be murdered by one of his cut-throat comrades." He paused, eyeing her sardonically. "No, you will not be called upon to sacrifice yourself for him. The Law has valued his life at one hundred pounds. I set it higher. At ten thousand."

"Ten thousand pounds?" she repeated incredulously. "How could I pay you such a sum?"

"You will contrive, once Coombe Royal is in your hands. I am prepared to wait until then, but do not mistake me, Christina. All that I learned last night is set down in writing, and it goes to Mereton Hall, with the command that should any unforeseen accident befall me, it shall be opened and read. When you pay me ten thousand pounds, that letter shall be returned to you, unopened."

There was a pause. Christina twisted her hands together, looking about her in a hunted way. A little breeze shook the delicate foliage above her, and the bees hummed busily among the roses.

"You give me no choice," she said hopelessly at last. "I will do as you ask."

Stephen drew a long breath of triumph, and a self-satisfied smile curved his lips.

"I thought you would," he said smugly. "It shows your good sense, but I warn you, Christina, do not try to play me false. Tedburn is very eager to capture Captain Gallant."

He left that warning to ring ominously in her ears and returned to the house. Christina followed him with dragging steps, and, seeking out Titus, told him how his master's secret had been discovered. The news filled Titus with grave forebodings, but he dissembled these and did his best to reassure her, promising that he would carry a warning to the Captain without delay.

When he reached the cottage in the woods, however, it was Jeremy Brigg who came to greet him, and shook his head at the servant's demand for Captain Clare.

"He had an hour or two's rest, and a bite to eat," he explained, "and then he was away to carry word to Ned's wife o' what's happened, and to see if she and the little ones lack aught."

He paused, looking shrewdly at Titus, and then turned and led the way indoors. Filling two pewter tankards with ale from the barrel in the corner, he said laconically: "What's amiss?"

Titus told him, for Brigg was as closely concerned in the affair as anyone. He listened in grim silence, and when the tale was done, stood for some time staring down into his tankard, his brown eyes preoccupied and his brow creased in thought.

"When do you suppose the Captain will be back, Jerry?" Titus asked at last, rousing himself from his own thoughts. "He ought to be warned what's afoot."

Jerry looked up under his brows.

"Maybe he should," he said slowly, "and then again, maybe he shouldn't. Maybe you and me can settle this business without troubling the Captain."

Titus looked narrowly at him.

"There's some plan in your head, is there?" he hazarded, and Brigg nodded.

"There is that!" he agreed briefly, and came to seat himself at the table. "We'll need a third in it, and I reckon Reuben's the one to help us, him having no family to consider, like Japhet has. Polly's my sister, and I'm main fond of her, but there's no denying she's got a plaguey sharp tongue at times."

It was some while before Titus left the cottage, but when he did, the plot had been hatched in all its details, and all that remained was to set it in motion. His first action on reaching the inn was to find Miss Westlake and caution her to say nothing to Captain Clare of Ancroft's demands, explaining that to do so would inevitably provoke an open quarrel between the two men which might lead to the Captain's betrayal. Having received her assurance on this point, he then took Reuben Barnby aside and remained for some time in close and confidential talk with him.

As a result of that conversation, Stephen found himself approached by Reuben during the afternoon. The weather had turned sultry, with a hint of thunder in the air, and Mr. Ancroft, feeling the effect of the heat as well as of his disturbed night, was dozing on his bed when he was roused by a tap on the door. Somewhat irritably he gave permission to enter, and Reuben came in to inform him that somebody wished to speak to him. Stephen stared.

"To speak to me? Who is it?"

Reuben shook his head.

"That I can't say, but I give you my word 'tis important. You'd best come, sir. He be waiting in the barn."

"In the barn?" Stephen's surprise deepened to suspicion as he stared up at the speaker's stolid, pugnacious face. "What tomfoolery is this?"

" 'Tis no tomfoolery, sir!" Reuben came closer, lowering his voice. "It be to do with Captain Gallant."

Stephen sat up abruptly, suspicion now fairly blazing in his eyes.

"Why the devil should I be interested in a damned highwayman?" he demanded sharply.

Reuben shrugged.

"Seems like you was interested enough this morning, when you talked to Miss. She thought so, at any rate, enough to send him warning." He paused, watching consternation flood into Ancroft's face. "Be easy, sir, the message never reached him. That's why you're wanted now. Will you come?"

"Yes, I'll come, confound you!" Stephen swung his feet to the floor, groping for his shoes. "But if this is some trick——"

"'Tis no trick!" Reuben picked up his coat and held it for him. "I can tell you, sir, Gallant's not as well liked as he believes."

Stephen looked at him rather hard, and followed him with no further protest. In the barn, Jeremy Brigg was sitting on an upturned bucket, drawing patterns on the ground with a stick, but he rose as they entered and took off his hat respectfully to Stephen. In the shadows behind him, the chestnut mare turned her head and pricked an inquiring ear. Reuben nodded to Jeremy and went out, pulling the heavy door shut behind him.

"Well?" Stephen spoke sharply. "Who are you? What do you want with me?"

"Jeremy Brigg's the name, sir," the other man replied frankly. "I be Polly Barnby's brother."

"Indeed?" Stephen's glance rested thoughtfully on the mare. "And in the same trade as Captain Gallant, I imagine?"

Jeremy chuckled.

"I'm not denying it, sir. We be partners, in a manner o' speaking." He looked sharply at Stephen. "Did Reuben tell you o' the young lady's message to Gallant this morning?"

"He did!" Ancroft replied abruptly. "How come you to know of it?"

"It reached me instead o' Gallant. He's away towards Bath, and won't be back yet awhile." He paused, regarding Stephen knowingly. "You turned your luck to good account, Mr. Ancroft, and ten thousand pounds is a fair prize, but I might help you to a greater one." He leaned forward, lowering his voice to a conspiratorial whisper. "To Coombe Royal itself."

Avarice gleamed for an instant in Stephen's eyes, but he said scornfully:

"Coombe Royal belongs to Miss Westlake, and will go to the man she marries. To Adrian Clare, in fact."

"But if he was taken——"

"I would have nothing left with which to bargain, and she would die sooner than marry the man who betrayed him. I know her too well to suppose otherwise. Besides, she is promised to Kelsby, and he has her mother's support in his claim."

Jeremy chuckled derisively.

"Maybe, but he's lost the paper as made Miss accept his dirty bargain. Gallant saw to that."

"So I suppose, but Kelsby is still the only living man, other than Marcus Westlake, who knows the truth concerning Giles Carew's death. He might make Miss Westlake believe he could still prove her father's innocence."

Jeremy set a foot on the bucket and leaned an elbow on his bent knee. His shrewd, bright eyes glanced up sidelong at Stephen's face.

"Suppose Gallant killed Kelsby afore they captured him?"

Stephen's jaw dropped and he could obviously find nothing to say. Jeremy proceeded to elaborate his question.

"Suppose Kelsby had word from Gallant that he was willing to bargain for the return o' that bit of paper? He don't know who Gallant is, and we took his money and jewels and all his other papers that night, so as he'd not guess our real purpose. He'd have no call to be suspicious. D'ye think he'd accept the invitation?"

Stephen shrugged.

"In his place, I'd not be able to resist it. What then?"

"Gallant names a time and place, and Kelsby drives up in his coach. He's expecting to strike a bargain, so he makes no move to defend himself. Gallant could shoot him and be away afore the servants knew what was happening, but next day, acting on information received, the red-coats surprise and capture him. That'd be the end o' Captain Gallant."

Stephen had been listening with rapt attention, enthusiasm kindling in his eyes, but when Jerry paused and looked inquiringly at him, he said, with a short, contemptuous laugh:

"A pleasant fantasy, Mr. Brigg, but that is all. I cannot believe that Gallant would be so obliging, particularly as he has no reason to murder Walter Kelsby."

Jeremy's grin broadened.

"No one's ever seen Gallant's face," he said significantly. "You're not far short o' his size, and I could put you in the way o' borrowing his horse and clothes."

"You could——" Mr. Ancroft seemed to be having some difficulty in enunciating the words. "Are you suggesting that I should murder Kelsby?"

"That Gallant should murder him," Jeremy corrected him reproachfully. "What matter who be behind the mask?"

Stephen shook his head.

"It's impossible," he said, but his tone lacked conviction. Jeremy leaned forward persuasively.

"It'd be possible enough. Wi' Kelsby dead and Gallant taken, what's to prevent you marrying the young lady and making yourself master o' Coombe Royal?"

"The young lady herself," Stephen said shortly. "You do not know her. She is the type of woman who would remain true to Clare's memory to her dying day."

Jerry drew a long breath of exasperation.

"Lord save us, sir, there be ways o' persuading an unwilling female. Make off with her, and keep her prisoner for a few days. I could put you in the way of a quiet little inn where no questions'd be asked." He winked knowingly and dug Stephen in the ribs. "Don't tell me as she'd dare to come home without a ring on her finger."

Mr. Ancroft accepted both the suggestion and the familiarity without protest. Excitement was growing in him, and he took a turn about the barn as he tried to subdue it. Halting again in front of Brigg, he said abruptly:

"Why are you so eager to help me to a fortune?"

Jeremy grinned at him.

"Your fortune's no concern o' mine. 'Tis Gallant I'm wishing to be rid of. There was a tidy living to be picked up in these parts afore he took to the High Toby, but now all the rich prizes fall to him, and there's naught left for the rest of us but stage-coach travellers wi' thin purses. Yet if 'tweren't for me, he'd never have took to the road."

He described his first meeting with Captain Clare, but that was as much truth as his story contained. According to Jeremy, Adrian had used his discovery of Brigg's trade to force him into an unwilling partnership, treating him like a lackey and taking the lion's share of the plunder. He was a born actor, and poured out his grievances with a vehemence that was wholly convincing.

"Thinks he be still in the army, and me one o' the poor devils serving under him," he concluded bitterly. "Lording it here at the inn, too, and Polly and Japhet afeared to cross him because he knows too much about 'em. I tell you, sir, 'twill be a glad day for all of us when Gallant takes his last ride."

"You certainly have no cause to love him," Stephen admitted, "but why choose me for your accomplice? Why not take Gallant's place yourself?"

"Because for one thing me and Reuben lack the learning to write the offer to Kelsby. For another," he took his foot from the bucket and stood upright. He was half a head shorter than Stephen. "I lack the inches. Gallant's even taller than you."

"And Reuben Barnby is a deal too stout," Stephen added thoughtfully. "Yes, I can appreciate your difficulty." He turned away, and began absently to fondle the mare. Over his shoulder he added: "What profit do you look for, besides freedom from Gallant?"

Jeremy shrugged.

"Freedom's enough for me, sir. O' course, if you care to make me a little present after you're wed, I'll not refuse it. And there's always the reward."

"Which you, of course, will claim." Stephen nodded, running his hand down the mare's glossy neck. He was silent for a space, while Brigg waited patiently, and then with an air of decision swung round again to face him. "So be it, then! What must I write to Kelsby?"

Jerry beamed delightedly at him.

"Just tell him you're willing to come to terms for the return o' that confession, and bid him be at Oliver's Mill tomorrow night at eight. D'ye know the spot I mean?"

Stephen nodded.

"I have seen it. A derelict ruin of a place about four miles from here. An excellent spot for an ambush."

"Ye're right, Mr. Ancroft! That's why I chose it. The mill stands in a hollow, and there's a spinney on t'other side o' the road where we can wait for him."

"Yes, I remember it. Do we meet there?"

"What, and have to stay for your own horse and gear once the deed is done?" Jeremy looked shocked. "No, we'll meet well before that, somewhere not far from here. D'ye know the road to Mereton Hall?"

"Naturally!"

"Then maybe you recall a track leading off to the right, into the woods, a quarter of a mile from here?" Stephen nodded, and Jeremy went on: "There's a thick clump o' holly trees just beyond the second bend. I'll be there at six wi' the disguise, and Gallant's horse. You'd best come on foot."

"As you wish," Stephen agreed indifferently. His thoughts seemed to be elsewhere, and after a moment's hesitation he put them into words. "Suppose Clare chooses to ride out tomorrow evening. What then?"

Jeremy chuckled.

"He won't, Mr. Ancroft. Trust me for that. Our fine Captain'll spend the evening where no one won't see him, and he'll never be able to prove as he weren't at Oliver's Mill."

Stephen nodded, apparently satisfied on that score, but there was still another point which troubled him.

"I understand why you wish to be rid of Gallant, but what of Kelsby? What grudge do you bear him?"

Jeremy's face hardened.

"The same as everyone else in these parts, sir. He's a

cunning, grasping, upstart rogue wi' not an ounce o' pity in him, and it'd be an ill day for all of us if he ever became master o' Coombe Royal. Squire Westlake's a hard man, but he's a babe in arms compared wi' Kelsby." He spat in token of his infinite disgust, and nodded solemnly at Stephen. "You go write that letter, Mr. Ancroft, and Reuben'll bring it to me here. I'll see it reaches Kelsby afore dark." He paused, eyeing Stephen shrewdly. "There was talk, so Miss said, of another letter, sent to Mereton Hall."

Mr. Ancroft laughed; he seemed well pleased with himself.

"There was, indeed, but it has not yet been written. I take it that it should not be, at least until after we have dealt with Kelsby?"

Jeremy drew a deep breath of satisfaction.

"That it shouldn't, sir," he agreed heartily. "Squire Tedburn'll learn who Gallant is, I promise you, but it's got to be done in a way as won't harm Polly and Japhet. You leave it to me, Mr. Ancroft!"

Stephen nodded, and withdrew, and Jeremy resumed his seat on the bucket, smiling grimly to himself. For perhaps half an hour he waited, and then Reuben came back into the barn with the letter in his hand.

"Here it be, Jerry," he said gloomily. "I showed it to Titus, him being able to read, and he says it seems honest enough." He watched the other man stow the paper safely away, and shook his head with an air of deep foreboding. "Seems a daft scheme to me, when all's said and done. D'ye suppose it will happen like you says?"

Jeremy had turned away to saddle the mare, but he paused to glance over his shoulder at his pessimistic relative.

"It must, Reuben lad," he said grimly, "or there's more than one of us'll be wearing the hempen cravat. I've told young Ancroft a deal more than is safe, to lead him into this trap. 'Tis up to the three of us to see as he don't walk out of it again."

18

Broken Fetters

Mr. Walter Kelsby was an exceedingly worried man. His troubles had begun with the stopping of his coach by Captain Gallant, while Helen Westlake's letter informing him of the highwayman's identity had increased rather than allayed his dismay. He had no doubt of the accuracy of her guess, and would have liked nothing better than to see Captain Clare under arrest, but for a variety of reasons he had refrained from passing on her information to the authorities.

Chief among these was his uncertainty concerning the present whereabouts of Edmund Westlake's confession. Gallant had taken it from him, so it was either still in his possession, or else he had handed it over to Christina. If he were captured by Mr. Kelsby's contriving, she would be more than likely to publish it at once, and he would find it extremely difficult to explain why it had been suppressed for more than twenty years. Unless and until that incriminating document could be recovered, his hands were tied.

So he burned Helen's letter and waited apprehensively to see what would befall. He knew that soldiers were scouring the country around Coombe Royal in search of the elusive highwayman, and was torn between hope and fear that they would be successful. Helen, too, was a constant source of danger. Mr. Kelsby had seen Sir Deryk Mandeville at Coombe Royal on the occasion of his last visit there, and had no doubt that this gentleman figured largely in Mrs. Westlake's future plans, but first, no doubt, she would have to find some way of ridding herself of Captain Clare. If Mr. Kelsby made no move in the matter, she would probably do so herself. Her interests must be served, no matter who else suffered in the process.

He was still in a miserable state of anxiety and indecision when, on the second evening after his misadventure, Stephen Ancroft's letter was brought to him. He opened it dejectedly, but one swift glance at its contents was sufficient to send his spirits soaring. Then, hard upon the heels of relief, suspicion came pelting. He glared at the servant who had brought the message.

"How came this letter here?" he demanded.

"A young lad brought it, sir," the man replied woodenly. "An ill-favoured urchin I have never seen before. He is waiting below-stairs for your answer."

Mr. Kelsby looked again at the letter.

"Let him wait," he said. "I must consider this matter, and will ring for you when my answer is ready."

The servant withdrew, and Mr. Kelsby heaved himself up out of his chair and began to move restlessly about the room, wondering uneasily what lay behind this overture from Gallant. It must be a trick of some kind. The fellow could have no need to bargain with him, when the rich prize of Coombe Royal was under his hand, as it must surely be by now. Had not Helen Westlake hinted in her letter that she had disturbed a very pretty little love-scene at the inn on the day following the robbery?

The thought of Helen brought him up with a jerk, and a sudden resurrection of hope. Her arrival must have done much to spoil the effect of Captain Clare's romantic declarations, and Mr. Kelsby was sufficiently well acquainted with the lady to be certain that injured vanity would have added extra venom to her tongue. Christina Westlake had pride—she would not be her father's daughter if she had not—and it might be that she had refused the proposal of Helen's discarded lover.

If that were the case, and he had already handed over to her the paper signed by Edmund Westlake, he would have no means of compelling her. What, then, was more likely than that he should try to bargain with Mr. Kelsby for something no longer in his possession? It was the kind of trickery which Kelsby himself had been practising all his life.

He looked again at the letter. Oliver's Mill at eight in the evening—even a summer's evening—would be a desolate and lonely place, and he would be a fool to venture himself there without some precaution, some hostage for his safety. He pondered the problem, and presently a gleam of satisfaction crept into his pale eyes. Fetching pen and paper, he wrote a brief note agreeing to the proposed rendezvous, and despatched it by the hand of his servant. Then he locked himself into his study, and spent a great deal of time on the cleaning, priming and loading of a small but deadly pistol.

It was on the afternoon of the following day, while Mr. Kelsby was still engaged upon the final preparations for his trial of strength with Captain Gallant, that Helen Westlake's patience and temper alike became exhausted. For two days she had waited with growing impatience for Kelsby to make some move, and for the news of Gallant's arrest to spread through the countryside, but nothing of the kind had occurred. Even the soldiers who had been searching so assiduously for him appeared to have given up the quest, and presently her two personal servants brought her word that Gallant had made a series of daring robberies on the very outskirts of Bath, and that the search for him had been transferred to that area. Helen smiled scornfully when she heard this. It was obvious that Adrian was determined to draw the pursuit well away from the inn which was his headquarters, and that the authorities had been completely duped by his sudden change of tactics.

His triumph, however, should be short-lived, and if Kelsby would do nothing to put an end to his career, then she would do it herself. A letter to Mr. Tedburn at Mereton Hall would be sufficient, and when next Adrian returned to the Merry Month of May, he would find that he had walked into a trap from which there was no escape.

With this amiable intention in mind Helen seated herself at the writing-desk in her boudoir, where the portrait of Godfrey Westlake looked down from the wall, and that of his younger brother lay on the table beneath, between the candles and the bowls of flowers. With great deliberation she drew towards her a piece of paper, and selected and trimmed a pen, but the letter was barely begun when the door behind her opened to admit her husband.

Helen looked round, mild surprise mingling with the irritation she felt at his return. If Kelsby had acted promptly on the information sent to him, Adrian would have been arrested and she away to London with Sir Deryk, before Marcus's return from whatever business had been engaging him for the past two days. What this was she neither knew nor cared, but it would have suited her better had it been less promptly completed.

"I find you occupied, madam," he greeted her sardonically. "Should I ask your pardon for disturbing you?"

"You should, but I have ceased to look for civility from you," she retorted waspishly. "I did not even know that you had returned."

"I have been in the house for close upon two hours," he informed her with a sneer, "but just as you have ceased to expect civility, I have ceased to expect any interest on your part in my comings and goings. You were in the garden with Mandeville when I arrived, and now I find you engaged with your correspondence." He had crossed the room to her side as he spoke, and now, with a suddenness that made her jump, his hand came heavily down upon her wrist, causing the pen to splutter a trail of blots across the page. His tone changed from sarcasm to one of harsh command. "Leave that, and attend to me! I have something of importance to say to you!"

For a moment, sheer surprise held her mute, and then she wrenched her hand away and came to her feet in one swift, graceful movement, magnificent in her anger.

"I will not be spoken to in such a tone," she said furiously. "Have you taken leave of your senses?"

"No, madam, I have come to them!" A heavy hand on her shoulder thrust her back into her chair. "Be still, and listen to me. I have borne with your insolence long enough."

Helen gaped at him. If the portrait on the wall had suddenly opened its lips to rebuke her, she could not have been more astonished, and she obeyed him simply because the unexpectedness of the attack had numbed her wits and her temper alike. Westlake let go her shoulder and folded his arms, eyeing her grimly.

"When I married you, Helen," he said harshly, "I did so with the full knowledge that only my wealth induced you to accept me, and that as a man you looked on me with complete indifference. I knew it, and I accepted it, because I desired you more than any woman I had ever known. I was even fool enough to believe that we might be happy together." He laughed, a sound bitter with self-mockery. "It was not long, was it, before you taught me how barren that hope was? Your greed was insatiable, but no matter how much gold I squandered on your senseless demands, you still hated and resented the claims I had upon you. Then, five years ago, you discovered how I had come by my inheritance."

He paused, but his sombre regard never shifted from her face, and the brooding gaze of the deep-set hazel eyes held her against her will, making her incapable of any retort. This was Marcus as she had never before seen him, not the besotted lover of the early days of their marriage, or the bitter, baffled dupe of more recent years, but a man strong and confident, with a look of vengeful triumph in his eyes which filled her with vague misgiving.

"Five years!" he repeated slowly. "So short a time, measured in months and days, but measured in jealousy and humiliation and dishonour it is an eternity! Kelsby has shared my secret for twenty years and more, battening upon me like some infernal vampire, using me to crawl up from the gutter in which I found him, but that was the price I had to pay for Coombe Royal. A heavy price, but not intolerable until you also learned the truth. There have been times since then when I almost wished it were possible to turn back time, and restore to my brother the birthright I had stole from him."

His gaze left her face at last, and turned towards the portrait. He moved away from her and stood before that travesty of a shrine, looking up at the pictured face, while Helen watched him uneasily and furtively rubbed her wrist, where the marks of his fingers still lingered.

"How delighted you were with this piece of petty cruelty," Marcus resumed at length, "and how it amused Kelsby the first time he saw it. You were so pleased with yourselves, the pair of you, so proud of the wits which had brought you each the things you most desired, while I was the poor dupe to be mocked and flouted, utterly at your mercy, bound hand and foot by the fear of all that betrayal of my secret would mean." He swung round again towards her, and she saw that his heavy face was inflamed with triumph, the vengeful triumph of a hard and unscrupulous nature. "But those days are over, Helen! The fetters are broken!"

"Broken?" The word came in a voice little louder than a whisper, as her eyes widened with an alarm as yet undefined. "What do you mean? What nonsense is this?"

"Do you need to ask? Can those sharp wits not find the answer?" he asked her with fierce mockery. "What is the threat which has been held over me by Kelsby and by you?" He strode across and leaned his hands on the desk, towering over her. "Answer me, woman! What had I most to fear?"

Helen put a hand to her head. This scene was beginning to have the mad, horrible quality of a nightmare.

"Fear of betrayal, of course," she said uncertainly. "Fear that the truth would become known and that you would lose everything."

"But I have lost everything," he pointed out mockingly. "Kelsby saw to that when he proved my niece's claim, and you made certainty more certain with your scheme to elope with Mandeville." He saw the first faint flicker of dismayed comprehension beginning to creep into her eyes, and laughed savagely. "Did you suppose that I would surrender it all, and leave you both in possession of your own dishonest gains? That I would fall without dragging you down with me? No, Helen! I have too much to avenge."

"What do you mean?" she asked again, but now there

was panic in her voice. She clutched at his sleeve, making no attempt to dissemble her fear. "My God, Marcus! what have you done?"

"I have confessed the truth," he said with brutal deliberation. "I have set down in every detail, not once, but twice, the whole truth of Giles Carew's death, the manner in which Godfrey shielded Edmund, and how when Edmund signed a death-bed confession of his guilt, I conspired with Kelsby to cheat Godfrey of his rights. One copy of that confession I have sent to George Tedburn, the other to old Beauchamp, who, so I am told, is sufficiently recovered to deal with business again. By nightfall they will both know the whole story."

Helen sank back in her chair, her grip on his sleeve slackening, her eyes wide and dark with horror in a whitening face. Marcus had not moved; he still leaned above her with his clenched fists resting on the desk, watching her with gloating triumph, and there was that in his eyes which struck sudden terror to her heart. She had shown him no mercy; what hope had she of finding mercy now?

"I had no hand in that," she cried in a voice shrill with alarm. "I was still in the nursery when you and Kelsby plotted to steal Coombe Royal!" She jumped up, the movement so swift and sudden that her chair toppled and crashed over backwards. "I will not stay! If you are mad enough to destroy yourself for the sake of revenge, I will not stay to be implicated in your wicked folly."

"You are implicated already!" Westlake's voice was mocking, halting her even in the act of flight. "Do you suppose I would destroy him and let you go free? You have known the truth for five years! Why did you not invoke the law against me, and make some effort to discover what I had never sought to learn—whether Godfrey was alive or dead? You cannot plead loyalty to me, or fear of what I might do to you. Your light conduct during those five years has shown the world how little you care for either."

Her head came up; triumph flashed in her eyes.

"Sir Deryk——"

"Has gone," her husband broke in ruthlessly. "For a brief spell I am once again master in this house, and the first person tó feel the truth of that was your present favourite. Would to God I might have dealt in the same way with all his predecessors." He saw her glance stray towards the bell-rope, and laughed. "Your servants, too! Your creatures who obeyed your lightest wish, and sneered at me with their sly grins and mock respect. I have waited a long while to mete out to them the punishment they merited. No, Helen, there is no one left for you to turn to now. The others are all my servants, and will remain so until my niece comes to take my place, and not one of them would lift a finger to help you. You have made yourself too thoroughly hated by them all."

She recognized the truth of his words, and despair rushed upon her. Deserted by Sir Deryk, deprived even of her servants, she found herself utterly alone, for what Marcus had said of the other servants could with equal truth be applied to the whole neighbourhood. Deliberately and contemptuously she had flouted them all, and now in her hour of need she knew what it was to be completely friendless. Marcus, watching her, could read her thoughts in the hunted glances she cast about her, in the desperate indecision of her attitude, and laughed again with cruel satisfaction.

"No, there is no one," he taunted her. "No one save myself. I am not the fool you choose to think me, and I did not despatch those confessions until I was certain of a way of escape. These two days past I have spent in Bristol, where I was lucky enough to find a ship whose captain will give us passage. She sails on the morning tide."

Hope flared in her eyes as she swung to face him, and a scornful triumph which she hastily concealed. So she had despaired too soon! Marcus was still enslaved by her beauty, and she had only to bear with him for a while, to feign humility and gratitude while he carried her out of danger, and then when safety was reached she could cast him off for good. In France, or Italy, or wherever they were bound, she would soon find a new protector to take Sir Deryk's place. She ran to her husband and caught his hand between her own.

"So you intended all the time to take me with you!" she exclaimed. "Oh, Marcus, it is more than I deserve! I have treated you shamefully, but it will be different now, I swear it!"

"Yes, it will be different," he agreed, but his voice had lost none of its grimness. It would not be easy, she reflected, to bring him again into suitable subjection. "There will be no more dalliance, no more gay gallants!"

"Never, I promise you," she said fervently, and caught his hand to her lips before releasing it. "I will go now to make ready for the journey. If you have dismissed my woman, one of the chambermaids must help me."

"I have already given order for that." Marcus caught her by the arm as she turned away. "Such things as you need will have been packed by now, and in a few minutes the coach will be at the door."

"But that is impossible! My dear, you do not realize the extent of my wardrobe, and it would be senseless extravagance to leave any of it behind." She tried fruitlessly to break free. "Let me go, and I will make the greatest speed I can."

He shook his head.

"You will have no need henceforth of ball-gowns or of jewels," he said harshly. "We are bound for America, for the port of Boston in Massachusetts, but it is my intention to travel on and settle in one of the small communities inland. The loss of Coombe Royal leaves me a poor man, Helen! We shall be able to live, but there will be no luxury, and very little comfort." He laughed as dismay flooded her face again, and it was not a pleasant sound. "You must forget gaiety and extravagance, and study instead to acquire virtues you do not possess. Virtues such as frugality, and constancy, and obedience."

"You are mad!" she exclaimed. "I will not go with you! You cannot make me!"

"You have no choice," he pointed out mockingly. "I have enmeshed you so deep in the plot to cheat my brother that if you stay in England nothing can save you

from arrest. Kelsby will be taken, and he is not of the
nature to suffer alone. If I escape him, he will turn the
more viciously upon you. Can you face imprisonment,
Helen? There will be no rich protectors there, no silken
boudoirs or costly trinkets, but dirt and degradation and
ultimate destruction. Will you risk that, or will you come
to New England with me?"

She glared at him, fury in her eyes, a baffled, impotent
fury such as he had suffered himself on so many occasions.
Remembrance of that suffering was vivid in both their
minds, breeding a savage triumph in him, and planting in
her heart a cold dread of the future. She was trapped,
and she knew it; two roads confronted her, and both led
to the end of life as she knew and valued it.

"I will come," she said in a low, vicious tone, "but as
God is my witness, Marcus, I will make you regret the
thing you do to me today. Somehow I will make you pay
for it!"

"You will make me pay?" He was still holding her by
the arm, and now he dragged her close to him, his fingers
digging into her flesh with a brutality that wrenched a
gasp of pain from her lips. He held her so, looking down
into her eyes, and now at last she knew terror, complete
and absolute. She had flouted him for years, reckless
of the hatred her conduct bred, deeming herself safe behind the barriers of his fear. Now those barriers were
down, and the devil she had so carelessly raised was
loosed against her.

"You will make me pay?" he repeated savagely. "No,
Helen, the debt is yours, not mine! You have given me
five years in hell, set me up as a laughing-stock in the
eyes of the world, made a cuckold of me a dozen times
over. I have sounded the depths of the corruption your
beauty hides, and I have learned to hate you as I hate
no other living being, but I will never let you go. No,
by God, I will not! I will have payment in full for all
that you have made me suffer."

A hesitant tapping on the door interrupted him. He
glanced up at the gilded French clock above the fireplace.

"The coach is waiting," he said curtly. "Come!"

Still gripping her arm, he thrust her before him out of the room and along the wide corridor to the hall, where a frightened maidservant was waiting with her mistress's cloak. Marcus took it from her and cast it round Helen's shoulders, and then thrust her before him out of the house.

A light travelling-coach, the same which he had used in his desperate bid to kill Christina, was waiting, with the same team of spirited horses harnessed to it, and attended by servants whose wooden-faced stolidity masked excitement and a burning curiosity. Helen looked despairingly about her, but saw only blank countenances, and eyes gleaming with triumph at the disaster which had befallen her. Sobbing with apprehension and self-pity, she preceded her husband into the coach. A whip cracked, the grooms sprang away from the horses' heads, and the vehicle lurched forward across the wide sweep of gravel and entered the long, straight avenue of trees leading to the road.

In the white-panelled boudoir a chair lay overturned upon the floor, the unfinished letter of betrayal on the desk, while from the portrait the grey eyes of Godfrey Westlake gazed serenely across the deserted room. Justice had been done at last, and Coombe Royal awaited its rightful mistress.

19

Oliver's Mill

Towards evening of that same day, Adrian returned to the Merry Month of May. He came openly this time, unmasked and riding his grey horse, for Captain Gallant had been left behind at the cottage in the woods, where Jeremy Brigg had been waiting in a fever of impatience, dismayed at seeing his whole elaborate scheme imperilled by the Captain's continued absence.

In other quarters, however, that absence had had the desired effect, and the painstaking efforts of the military to capture the elusive highwayman were no longer centred perilously on the country around the inn. As Helen had surmised, that had been the purpose behind Gallant's spectacular activities around Bath during the past two days, for while the soldiers might at any time descend upon the house where Christina was, Adrian could know not a moment's peace of mind.

It was to Christina that he came riding homewards now, but the meeting brought him a crushing sense of disappointment. For two days he had cherished the memory of their last brief meeting when he brought Ned Sparrow to safety, but in the aloof young woman who greeted him he could see nothing of the anxious girl who had bidden him God-speed that night. He could not know that this outward self-possession was masking a tumult of emotion, or how desperately she longed to pour out to him all the doubts and fears that still tormented her.

Before long, Japhet came into the parlour on some pretext, and contrived to whisper to Adrian that Ned Sparrow was asking to see him. He was still feverish as a result of his injuries, and almost beside himself with worry on behalf of his wife and family. Adrian nodded, and after a few minutes made an excuse to withdraw, hoping that later, when he had set Ned's mind at rest, he would have an opportunity to talk to Christina without the handicap of her mother's presence.

It took some time, however, to reassure the sick man, and Adrian was still with him when Titus came to him with the information that an urgent message had been brought from Mr. Tedburn, requesting the Captain's presence at Mereton Hall without delay. Adrian stared at him.

"What the devil can Tedburn want with me?" he demanded in astonishment. "We have scarcely spoken to each other except when common civility demanded it."

"As to that, sir, I cannot say," Titus replied imperturbably. "The servant who brought word to me knew no more than that your presence is required. It is imperative, the message ran, that you should be at the Hall before eight o'clock."

Adrian frowned.

"It seems a devilish odd affair," he remarked, "but if it is of such vital importance, I suppose I had better do as Tedburn asks. What time is it now?"

"It lacks a few minutes to seven, sir."

"Then I will go at once. Ask someone to saddle my horse." He rose, but paused to lay his hand on Sparrow's sound shoulder. "Be easy, Ned! You may trust me to see that all is well with your family until you are whole again."

It was Clem who brought the Captain's horse to the door some ten minutes later. Titus was nowhere to be seen, and Adrian was informed, when he inquired for his servant, that he had ridden out with Reuben Barnby a few minutes before.

"Uncle Reuben were a-waiting wi' the horses saddled," Clem explained stolidly, "and as soon as Mr. Titus came up from the cellar, they were off and away. I don't know where they be gone."

Adrian was faintly surprised, but he knew Titus well enough to suppose that there was good reason for this odd behaviour, and dismissed it from his mind. Swinging up into the saddle, he said to Clem:

"I am going to Mereton Hall, but I shall return as soon as may be. If Miss Westlake should ask for me, you may give her that message."

He rode briskly away, and urged his horse to a canter along the grass bordering the road. With perplexity and faint misgiving he wondered what lay behind this extraordinary summons from a man with whom he was barely acquainted, but before long his thoughts drifted away from that problem and returned to Christina. He had hoped that after a lapse of two days Helen's taunts would have begun to lose their sting, but nothing in her attitude this afternoon encouraged the hope. She seemed to have withdrawn from him, and even the confidence of their earlier friendship was missing.

When he reached Mereton Hall he thought that the butler who admitted him looked a trifle surprised when he heard that Mr. Tedburn was expecting the Captain, but he begged him courteously to be seated, and went away. Returning after a few minutes, he led Adrian across the wide hall and ushered him into a room where George Tedburn was standing by the window, frowning over some closely-written sheets of paper. He looked up as Adrian was announced, and came forward to greet him.

"This is an unlooked-for pleasure, Captain Clare," he said civilly. "In what way may I be of service to you?"

Adrian's brows lifted.

"I was about to ask you the same question, sir," he replied frankly. "I was given to understand that you desired to see me upon a matter of urgency."

Tedburn shook his head.

"There is some misunderstanding," he said in a puzzled voice. "I sent you no such message, but none the less I am extremely glad that you have come. You cannot fail to know how matters stand between the two branches of the Westlake family, and I should like your opinion of this extraordinary document. It was brought to me not half an hour ago."

Adrian took the papers held out to him and began to read, but the opening words were sufficient to cause him to direct a startled glance at his host. Tedburn signed to him to continue, and while he did so began to pace to and fro across the room, hands clasped behind him and his brow creased in thought. When Adrian came to the end of Marcus Westlake's confession, and stood silent, staring down at the scrawled signature, Tedburn said impatiently:

"Well?"

Adrian looked up.

"Soon after our first meeting," he said quietly, "Miss Westlake and her mother told me their version of what happened twenty-odd years ago. This document confirms it in every detail."

"So Kelsby's was the brain behind it all," Tedburn

replied reflectively. "Small wonder he has prospered so greatly. How Westlake must have come to hate him!"

Adrian nodded, and moved to place the papers on the table.

"He has revenged himself very thoroughly," he remarked. "Kelsby should have realized that in depriving him of Coombe Royal he was destroying his own only safeguard. Strange how a man can plot so deeply, yet still overlook the obvious." He glanced at Tedburn. "Well, sir, what next? Are they to be arrested?"

The other man shrugged.

"Kelsby will be taken. I have already taken steps to insure that, but Marcus Westlake is a different matter. He would not have sent me that confession and stayed for me to act on it. I dare swear he is halfway to the coast by now."

"He might be overtaken."

"Perhaps. All I desire to know is whether or not Miss Westlake would wish that. He is, after all, her father's brother."

"He showed her father no mercy, and less than a week ago he tried to kill Miss Westlake herself," Adrian said slowly. "In spite of that, Mr. Tedburn, I venture to predict that she will seek no further vengeance upon him. That her father's innocence is finally established will be enough. However, I do not ask you to take my word for that. She is at the inn. Ride back with me now, and hear it from her own lips."

Mr. Tedburn nodded. He had been careful to avoid all mention of Helen, and Captain Clare had done the same, but both were wondering what vengeance Marcus Westlake had chosen to exact from his faithless wife. Had he left her to face the Law's retribution, as he had left Kelsby, or had some other punishment been singled out for her?

"I will do that, Captain Clare," he said with sudden decision, "and then I believe it will be best to ride on to Coombe Royal. Something of Westlake's intentions can surely be discovered there."

He moved towards the bell-rope, but before he reached

it the butler came into the room and looked apologetically from one to the other.

"One of the lads from the Merry Month of May is here, sir," he informed his master. "He says it is necessary for him to see Captain Clare at once."

Adrian looked up quickly, misgiving clutching at his heart. What could have happened at the inn in the short time since he had left it?

"I will see him," he said sharply, and glanced at Tedburn. "With your permission, sir!"

"Of course, of course! Bring the boy here at once."

The butler withdrew, and within a very few moments Clem came hastily into the room. He touched his forehead to Tedburn, but addressed himself breathlessly to Adrian.

"It be Miss Westlake, Captain," he said urgently. "Not five minutes after you rode away, Mr. Kelsby drove up to the door. He talked to the ladies for ten minutes or so, and then Miss got into his coach with him and they drove away. Mrs. Westlake told Mother as he'd taken Miss to Coombe Royal, but Diccon followed the coach— being mindful o' what you'd told us, sir, about keeping watch over her—and it didn't take the Coombe Royal road at all. It went down the lane to the ford. So Mother sent me after you, sir, to tell you."

Adrian went white, and his glance turned involuntarily to the sheaf of papers on the table. Tedburn, guessing the trend of his thoughts, said in a shaken voice:

"Could he possibly have known?"

"God knows!" Adrian replied curtly. "Whatever his motive, he has carried her off by a trick, and if he has harmed her——" he broke off, and swung round again to Clem. "You have done very well. Now bid them fetch me my horse."

"I will come with you!" Tedburn said hastily. The young man was looking appallingly grim, and he would not stake much upon Kelsby's chances of survival if Captain Clare alone came up with him and his prisoner. "If we cut across country we can strike that road on the other side of the woods."

Adrian nodded, only half aware of what the other man had said. He was thinking of Christina, alone and defenceless in the power of the man she so greatly feared. What fresh scheme had burgeoned in that cunning brain to prompt this unlooked-for move? Had Kelsby, having lost the document which had purchased Christina's consent to their marriage, resorted to methods more direct and brutal to achieve his purpose? Where was he taking her, and why?

Those same questions were echoing in Christina's mind as she sat pressed into the corner of the coach, as far away from her companion as the narrow confines of the vehicle permitted her to go. She had not wanted to go with him, but his tale had been very plausible, her mother overwhelmingly insistent, and there had been no one to whom she could turn for advice. Adrian had left the inn again, Stephen had ridden out some time earlier, and even Titus was nowhere to be found. In the end, and against her better judgment, she had allowed herself to be persuaded, only to learn, within ten minutes of leaving the inn, how well founded her suspicions were.

They had certainly set out in the direction of Coombe Royal, but at the fork in the road the coach had taken the right-hand lane, plunging down that steep hillside which was so familiar to her. In alarm and dismay she had swung round to face Kelsby.

"This is not the way to Coombe Royal! Where are you taking me?"

The cold, pale eyes returned her gaze indifferently.

"We are going to keep an assignation with a close friend of yours. With Captain Gallant."

She stared blankly at him, certain that he was lying yet wondering what purpose lay behind so palpable a falsehood. Perhaps he was trying to trick her into betraying some knowledge of Gallant's identity.

"You make game of me, I think," she said coldly. "I know no more of Captain Gallant than is to be learned from common report. I repeat, where are you taking me?"

"And I repeat, Miss Westlake, to meet Captain Gallant.

Or Captain Clare, if you prefer to call him by his real name. You cannot play fast and loose with me, my girl! I am too old a hand to be deceived for long."

Still she would admit nothing. She masked fear and bewilderment with cool disdain, and answered him as coldly as before.

"I wish that what you say were true, Mr. Kelsby. Captain Clare is a gentleman, and even Captain Gallant, so I have heard, uses all women with respect. Neither of them would hesitate to deliver me from you."

She turned her head away and looked from the window beside her, but words and gesture alike had no effect at all on the composure of the man beside her. He made no reply, and when she stole a glance at him he was not even looking in her direction, but staring straight before him with prominent, glass-pale eyes, his repulsive, pallid face devoid of all expression.

She shivered, and shrank farther into the corner, forcing down the panic rising within her. If only she knew what lay ahead, she could summon all her resources to avert it, or, if escape proved impossible, to endure it with such courage as she could command, but the unknown end of this fantastic journey loomed hideously in her imagination, filled with possibilities from which her mind recoiled in horror.

Beyond the ford the country was unfamiliar to her, but she saw that the road they followed was a lonely one, devoid of all habitation. The sun was setting in a stormy sky, so that the landscape was alternately flooded with sultry light and plunged into premature twilight Mr Kelsby took out his watch and consulted it, and then apparently satisfied with the message it conveyed, returned it to his pocket and folded his hands once more across his swollen body.

Their pace slackened as they climbed a hill, and increased again as they began the descent. The road curved here, and Christina caught a glimpse of a little shadowed valley, where the ruin of a derelict mill lifted its crumbling mossy walls and rotting wheel beside a lazy stream. It was a desolate scene, and a little shiver shook her as she looked upon it.

Then, as they reached the foot of the hill, Kelsby moved again, with a suddenness that took her unawares. He reached out a pudgy hand that was yet unexpectedly strong, and gripped her by the arm, pulling her close beside him. Her flesh crept beneath his touch, and then his other hand moved also, and she saw to her horror that it grasped a silver-mounted pistol.

He had lowered the window on his side of the coach, and she found herself looking past him, away from the mill and up a steep slope to a thick clump of trees which still caught the light of the sinking sun. The place had seemed utterly deserted, but suddenly the silence was broken by a ringing shout and a swift thunder of hoof-beats, and she caught one flashing glimpse of a tall, masked rider on a black horse before her view was blocked by Kelsby's great bulk.

He was leaning forward, peering from the window, but he still retained his hold on her arm while with his other hand he thrust the pistol against her side. She was crushed into the corner of the coach, unable to see, scarcely even to breathe, but she heard the approaching hoofbeats draw near and cease, and an instant later a pistol-shot crashed out close at hand. Kelsby gave a queer, convulsive jerk and his grip on her arm relaxed, his own weapon dropping to the seat beside her. He lurched forward against the door, which gave way beneath his great weight so that he fell headlong to the ground below.

Christina crouched still in a paralysis of terror, and saw, framed in the opening left by the swinging door, the highwayman wheel his horse about and spur up the slope again towards the trees. Through a rent in the storm-clouds the westering sun poured a sudden lurid light across his fleeing figure, and then there was the crack of a second shot, and he flung up his hands and pitched from the saddle, to be dragged for some yards by the maddened horse before his foot worked free of the stirrup in which it had been entangled.

Christina's piercing scream shattered the silence anew,

and she started up, conscious only of the need to reach his huddled figure. She tried to jump down from the coach, but the horses were rearing and backing and she lost her balance, falling helplessly on to the inert body of Walter Kelsby. The force of her fall was broken, but the horror of contact with that gross corpse was too great to be borne. She tried to rise, but the whole scene spun madly before her eyes for an instant in a dazzle of light and shadow, and then everything was overwhelmed by merciful darkness.

20

The Hour of Honesty

She came to herself with the spicy scent of bracken in her nostrils, and the coolness of grass beneath her hand. She was lying on the ground and someone was holding her, supporting her against a bent knee, but before she could open her eyes to look about her, horror rushed upon her again with the sight which seemed to have branded itself indelibly on her memory. The black horse careering up the slope, and Captain Gallant, shot from the saddle by an unknown hand, dragged in its wake and then left to lie huddled upon the ground. She moved her head as though trying to escape the hideous recollection, and a little moan broke from her lips.

"Adrian!"

It was a murmur of anguish, of utter desolation, and then, incredibly, his voice answered her, very gentle and very close at hand.

"I am here, my love. You are safe now, and there is no more to fear."

In wonder and terror, half afraid still that she was the victim of some cruel hallucination, she opened her eyes and looked up into the beloved face bent above her.

It was no delusion; he was alive and unhurt, and his were the arms that held her now. Relief brought swift reaction, and turning her face against his shoulder she began to weep with violent, shattering sobs. He held her tightly, murmuring reassurance and comfort until she grew quieter, and lifted her face again towards his.

"But what happened?" she asked piteously. "I do not understand."

For a moment Adrian did not reply. He raised his head and looked past her to the little group of men clustered about something which lay on the ground half-way up the slope, and though when he answered her his voice was gentle as before, she saw that his expression was very stern.

"No more do I, sweetheart," he said quietly. "No more do I."

Mr. Tedburn detached himself from the group and came slowly down the slope towards them. He looked white and shocked.

"This is a terrible business, Clare," he said in a low voice, and looked at Christina. "I can make no sense of it at all. Perhaps, if Miss Westlake is sufficiently recovered——" he paused inquiringly.

"She is in no fit state to answer questions at present," Adrian replied firmly. "Good God, man, she has just seen two men killed! I am going to take her back to the inn." His voice softened as he looked down again at Christina. "Do you think you can stand, my dear, or shall I carry you to the coach?"

"I can walk," she said faintly, and let them help her to her feet. Leaning against Adrian, supported by his arm around her, she looked fearfully in the direction of the road where Kelsby's body lay, decently shrouded in a coat. A violent shudder shook her, and she turned her head away. "What happened to—the other?"

"Clare's servant shot him," Mr. Tedburn explained gravely. "He and Reuben Barnby rode over the hill to-gether just as Captain Gallant killed Kelsby, and not two minutes before Clare and I arrived on the scene." He paused to cast a dubious glance at Adrian. "I fear that this will come as a great shock to you, Miss Westlake, but you will have to know the truth. Young Ancroft was Captain Gallant."

"Stephen?" she whispered incredulously. "Oh, no!"

"Believe me, I am as shocked as you are to discover it, but there can be no doubt at all," he assured her solemnly. "We are all witnesses to that."

Titus descended the slope to join them. Reuben had mounted again and ridden away, Kelsby's coachman had returned to his team, the groom stood nearby holding the bridles of the horses, including Captain Gallant's famous black, which Barnby had ridden after and caught. Titus bowed gravely to Christina, but addressed himself to Tedburn.

"Reuben has gone to procure a cart from the nearest farm, sir," he said, "and I have desired Mr. Kelsby's man to turn the coach and make ready to convey Miss Westlake back to the inn."

Mr. Tedburn nodded, and glanced at Adrian.

"That is very well. Clare, will you escort Miss Westlake? I will attend to matters here."

The coach was turned, and brought to a halt again close by, and Adrian led Christina across to it. Mr. Tedburn accompanied them, and Titus made haste to open the door and let down the steps. Christina was helped inside, and Tedburn said quietly to Adrian:

"I shall come to the inn as soon as I have settled matters here. We must try to discover what lies behind this business."

"I shall be there," Adrian assured him, and turned to his servant. "Give Mr. Tedburn any assistance you can," he said with a hint of sternness, "and then bring my horse back to the inn. I am curious to know what brought you to this place tonight."

He followed Christina into the coach and the vehicle lumbered away. Titus stood looking after it as it climbed the hill; he rubbed his chin, and there was a slightly rueful expression in his eyes. The plot which he and Jeremy Brigg had hatched together had been overwhelmingly successful and he regretted none of it, but it might not be altogether easy to persuade the Captain to regard it in the same complacent way.

This suspicion was confirmed when he returned to the Merry Month of May. Adrian was waiting for him in his bedchamber, his countenance set in an expression which Titus knew well. He eyed his servant grimly, and said, with a decided edge to his voice:

"So there you are! Now perhaps you will be good enough to tell me what trickery you and Jerry Brigg have been indulging in behind my back. I say nothing of Reuben, for I have no doubt he was merely a tool in your hands, but Jerry most certainly had a finger in this pie. Ancroft could never have got possession of my horse and clothes without his aid."

"Now, Captain, there's no call to lose your temper," Titus replied placatingly. "Kelsby was a fat toad who's no loss to anyone, and young Mr. Ancroft had learned your secret and was threatening Miss Westlake. He'd have been a danger to you, and to everyone under this roof, as long as he lived. We meant it all for the best."

"And Miss Westlake? Did you mean it for the best that she should be thrust in Kelsby's clutches and frightened half to death?" His hand shot out and fastened upon the front of the servant's coat. He was white with anger, and his voice cut like a lash. "By God, Titus! if I thought that you had deliberately planned that ordeal for her, to further your own damned, twisted schemes——"

"Sir, is that likely?" Titus broke in, indignant reproach in his voice. "I swear to you that Miss Westlake was at the mill through no plan of mine. Why Kelsby brought her there I cannot tell, but it was for his own purpose, and not to further ours."

There was no mistaking the sincerity in his voice. Some of the anger died out of Adrian's eyes, and he said more mildly:

"If that is so, I make you my apologies, but it does not explain the rest of the affair. Come, Titus, I want the whole story, and I want it now!"

"Very well, sir," Titus said resignedly, and embarked at once on an account of Stephen's discovery of the truth, and all that had stemmed from it. Adrian listened with no relenting of his expression, and when the tale was told he said sternly:

"So tonight two men lie dead by your contriving. You tricked Ancroft into murdering Kelsby, and then shot him down in cold blood. And you say you meant it for the best."

Titus spread out his hands in a helpless gesture.

"It's not a deed I can take pride in, Captain, I grant you that, but there are times when only harsh measures will serve. We both know that Kelsby deserved no better, for his share in cheating Miss Westlake's father if for nothing else. He'd have been arrested for that before morning in any event, so I heard Mr. Tedburn say. As for Ancroft, he'd not have rested till he'd bled Coombe Royal white as the price of his silence, and he was willing enough to do murder when he thought he could lay the blame on you. When Jerry put the plot to him, he fair jumped at the chance."

He paused, but Adrian made no reply. Titus sighed, and, lifting his hands, let them drop again to his sides.

"If you mean to turn me off for this, Captain, I can't prevent you. I won't say I'm sorry for what I did, because it'd be a lie. You're safe now, and so's the young lady, and that's good enough for me."

Adrian got up from his chair. He set a hand on his servant's shoulder and gripped it hard, giving it a little shake. There was a reluctant grin tugging at the corners of his mouth.

"Confound you, Titus, you know damned well I would never turn you off! You have solved some devilish awkward problems for me, and if I cannot approve of the means you used, there is nothing I can do now to alter them. We'll say no more of it, and you can tell that rogue Jerry so when next you see him. All that remains now is to satisfy Mr. Tedburn's curiosity."

This proved to be easier than he had dared to hope. When Tedburn arrived at the inn, he brought with him the letter which Stephen, in the guise of Captain Gallant, had sent to Walter Kelsby. Holding it out to Adrian, he said grimly:

"We found this in Kelsby's pocket. It explains a good deal, I think. The confession referred to there must have been stolen from him when Ancroft held up his coach for the first time, and he hoped to recover it tonight."

Adrian read the letter and handed it back. They were alone in the parlour, for Mrs. Westlake had been thrown into strong hysterics by the news of the double tragedy at Oliver's Mill, and Christina, from sheer force of habit, had set aside the effects of her own ordeal in order to minister to her. Polly had taken them both upstairs, and returned presently to inform the Captain that they had retired for the night.

"If that were so," Adrian said slowly in reply to Tedburn, "why did Ancroft kill Kelsby?"

"Because that letter was no more than the bait in a trap. He had no intention of handing over Edmund Westlake's confession, for we did not find it on him. No doubt it is somewhere among his effects. The Constable is searching his room now."

This was a less welcome piece of information. Adrian said easily:

"He may have hidden it elsewhere."

"Perhaps. It will probably come to light in time. Let us return to the motives behind Ancroft's actions tonight." It was plain that Mr. Tedburn had evolved some theory, and was extremely proud of it. Adrian bowed politely and assumed an expression of respectful interest, hoping that his companion's suppositions would be sufficiently feasible to fit in with the known facts.

"It is my belief," Mr. Tedburn resumed impressively, "that Ancroft meant to play the same game as Kelsby, and bribe Miss Westlake into marrying him by offering to make known her father's innocence. We know from Marcus Westlake's confession that that was Kelsby's intention. But to do that he had to silence Kelsby, who was the only person who knew that the paper had been stolen by Captain Gallant. Kelsby, I fancy, had begun to suspect Gallant's identity, and he certainly doubted his honesty. Therefore he tricked Miss Westlake into accompanying him to the rendezvous so that he might use her as a hostage."

He leaned back in his chair and looked smugly at the Captain, who was eyeing him, he thought, with considerable respect. He could not know that this was assumed to mask a leaping elation.

"I am sure that you are right," Adrian agreed. "Miss Westlake told me that when they reached the mill, Kelsby threatened her with a pistol. That would seem to bear out your theory."

Tedburn nodded.

"Did you tell her of her uncle's confession?"

"I did. My prophecy was correct, and she does not wish him to be pursued, if he has indeed taken refuge in flight."

"He has gone," Tedburn said laconically. "I visited Coombe Royal on my way here, and Westlake and his wife left very hurriedly this afternoon. The servants were of the opinion that Mrs. Westlake went with him against her will."

This information did not appear to inspire Captain Clare with any desire to hasten to Helen's rescue, and Mr. Tedburn concluded that he had by this time discovered the lady's true character. Any comment which he might have made, however, was forestalled by the arrival of the Constable. He laid a handful of papers before the magistrate, saying as he did so:

"Those be all I can find, sir. Maybe the one as you want is among 'em."

Tedburn glanced swiftly through the papers and uttered an exclamation of satisfaction. Drawing one out from the rest, he held it so that Adrian could see the signature. It was Edmund Westlake's confession.

"This would appear to clinch the matter," he said pleasedly. "I thought I could not be mistaken. Well, well, there is still a deal to be done, and I must be about it without further delay! We will discuss this matter at greater length another time, Captain."

He declined Adrian's invitation to drink a glass of

wine, and hurried away, very full of his own importance. Left alone, Captain Clare remained for a while lost in thought. The reappearance of the confession had puzzled as much as it had surprised him, but upon reflection he realized that only Christina could have been responsible for it. Incredible as it seemed after the ordeal she had undergone, she must have realized that it ought to be found among the possessions of the supposed Captain Gallant, and hidden it in Ancroft's room before the arrival of Mr. Tedburn and the Constable.

She admitted as much next morning, when she and Adrian met in the otherwise deserted parlour, and seemed surprised that he should think her action in any way remarkable. She dismissed it as a matter of little importance, and said anxiously:

"Adrian, will you do something for me?"

He smiled lovingly down at her.

"Anything you wish, sweetheart."

"Then will you take me to Coombe Royal—now, this morning? Mamma has such grand plans for our homecoming, with all the village there to greet us, but that is not how I wish to see it for the first time. I should like to go there quietly, with you."

So, a short while later, they rode away from the inn together, Adrian on his spirited grey, Christina riding the docile mare that Ruth and Betsy sometimes used. She was unaccustomed to the saddle, but her mount was quiet enough, and Adrian at her side was ready with hand and voice if anything should go amiss. They came without incident to the gates of Coombe Royal, and passed through them, and so to the crest of the rise where the house first came into view.

They halted there, and for several minutes Christina gazed in silence at the mellow old mansion rising from its flower-filled gardens, with the soft greens of the wooded hill like a gentle tapestry behind it. When at last she turned her face towards Adrian, he saw that her eyes were filled with tears.

"Father described it to me so often," she said in a low voice, "but not even he could tell me how beautiful it is.

I feel closer to him now than at any time since he died."

They rode on down the hill and dismounted before the house, to which they were admitted by servants too well-trained to betray the surprise they felt at seeing Captain Clare escorting the new mistress of Coombe Royal. He paid no heed to them, but, knowing instinctively the one thing above all others which Christina would most wish to see, led her straight to the room which had been Helen's boudoir.

It was exactly as its previous occupant had left it, the chair lying on its side before the desk, the flowers already fading on the table below Godfrey Westlake's portrait. Christina paid no heed to this. She limped across the room and stood looking up at the pictured face so like her own, stood there so long and in such deep absorption that Adrian, respecting that rapt communion with memory, moved softly away and, scarcely thinking what he was doing, picked up the fallen chair and set it again in its place at the desk.

"I have kept faith with him," Christina said quietly at last. "Soon everyone will know the sacrifice he made, and how deeply he was wronged."

Adrian made no reply, and after a moment she turned to look at him. He was standing by the desk, his hands still grasping the back of the chair, staring down at something on the table before him with a look in his face which took her swiftly to his side. The thing which seemed to mesmerize him was the beginning of a letter, and as she read it in her turn, horror rushed upon her.

To George Tedburn Esquire, J.P.
at Mereton Hall in the County of Wiltshire.
Sir,
   It has come to my knowledge that the highwayman known as Captain Gallant is in fact Captain Adrian Clare, who, as you are aware, is at present. . . .

The letter ended there in a great flurry of blots, as though the pen had dropped suddenly from the writer's hand, but the few lines already written were deadly enough. With a gasp Christina snatched it up, crumpling it between her hands, and turned a horrified glance upon Adrian.

"Can anyone else have seen it, do you think?"

He shook his head. He was very pale, and there was a gleam of sweat on his brow.

"No, I think not. If any of the servants had been in here the room would have been set to rights and the letter taken, but if we had not come here today——"

He left the sentence unfinished, for they both knew, without putting it into words, how nearly he had been betrayed. Christina caught her breath and cast herself into his arms, clinging tightly to him as though the danger still threatened.

"She would have sent you to your death," she whispered. "Oh, she is cruel, and wicked! Whatever punishment befalls her, it will be no more than she deserves."

Adrian did not immediately reply. He was remembering the first time he had come into this room, and seen Helen there like a tall statue of rose and ivory and gold, and how he had believed then that she was all that he desired on earth or in heaven. How many men had believed it before him, and how many would believe it in the future? Wherever she went, there would be those who were blinded by her beauty, on whom she would smile for a little time, and who would learn, as he had learned, the evil the beauty hid. He looked down at Christina, and a vast and humble thankfulness flooded his whole being. Helen's gifts were death and ultimate damnation, but here in his arms was the salvation which had so miraculously been granted to him.

He took the letter she was still clutching, and from the crumpled page the boldly-written words seemed to taunt him with an echo of Helen's lazy, mocking laughter. "The highwayman known as Captain Gallant". Seeing it thus set down in black-and-white seemed suddenly to strip away the aura of devil-may-care romance and show him the past three months in all their stark and ugly truth. He had taken to the High Toby in a spirit of gay adventure, and he had kept his hands as clean as might be, yet what was he, after all, but a common thief?

He lifted his eyes to the portrait, and studied the fine, sensitive face of the man who had sacrificed and suffered so much, while shame swept over him like a sickening wave. By the mercy of providence the secret of Captain Gallant's identity could still be kept, but what of Adrian Clare? Everyone knew that he had been Helen's lover, and he was sufficiently well acquainted with the world to foresee the reaction which would be aroused if it were made known that he was now to marry Christina. He would be shown in a singularly unfavourable light, and the knowledge troubled him, not for his own sake but for hers.

She was quick to sense his change of mood, and stood looking up at him, her hands resting lightly against his chest, her grey eyes anxiously searching his face. He met the grave, inquiring gaze, and, thrusting the letter into his pocket, covered the slender fingers with his own.

"I am not worthy of you, Christina," he said bitterly. "Do you imagine that if your father were alive he would permit you to marry such a man as I, a thief, a spendthrift, a besotted fool who was for years a willing victim in the toils of such a woman as Helen? You said just now that you had kept faith with him. How can you continue to do so if I come here to take his place?"

For a moment or two she continued to regard him without speaking, and then she, too, turned her eyes towards the portrait.

"How can I keep faith with him if you do not?" she asked quietly. "He taught me all I know of good and evil, of life and of people, and his teaching has never failed me yet. These things you despise in yourself are not important now. It is the future that matters to us, not the past."

His fingers tightened upon hers.

"You make me feel very humble," he said in a low voice. "God knows I ask only to share that future with you, and to make of it something that will atone for the past, but I think you do not realize what difficulties lie ahead. There will be talk and to spare if we marry, and gossip can be a vicious and destructive thing."

"I know," she agreed calmly. "It will be said that you amused yourself with Helen, but paid court to me because of my inheritance; that I accepted you on those terms because I could hope for no others. Do you think I do not know that, and have not already faced it?" She was looking up into his eyes again, and her voice was very earnest. "But it does not matter, Adrian, do you not see that? We two know the truth, and idle chatter cannot harm us as long as we keep faith with each other."

She paused, and for several moments there was silence as he realized slowly the truth of what she said. It would not be easy. For years, perhaps, the events of the past few months would be remembered; hated or loved, Helen would not be readily forgotten, and here in this house memory would linger longest of all. Yet she would be vanquished in the end. With the passing of time the bright, cruel ghost would fade, and meanwhile, as Christina in this hour of honesty had been given the wisdom to perceive, the truth and the love they shared had forged a bond between them that neither memory nor malice could ever touch.

"I will keep faith, my love," he said softly at length. "With all my heart, every day of my life."

He bent his head, and their lips met in a kiss which was a pledge of that faith, and then he let go her hands and crossed the room again to lift down her father's portrait from the wall.

"This was placed here as a mockery and a cruel jest," he said quietly, "and it is not fitting that it should stay here now." He held out his free hand to Christina. "Come, sweetheart, we will find a setting for it more worthy of a gallant gentleman."

In the hall Adrian paused and looked about him. Opposite to the door through which anyone entering the house must pass rose the broad, shallow staircase, and where it divided, two flights rising at right angles to the first to serve the gallery, a landscape similar in size to the painting he held graced the panelled wall. He glanced questioningly at Christina, who smiled and nodded. Adrian beckoned the butler forward and pointed to the landscape.

"Have that taken down, and put this in its place," he commanded, and handed him the portrait.

In silence they watched it done, and when the exchange had been effected, and Godfrey Westlake's likeness gazed down again on the hall where he had once been master, Adrian looked at Christina, and smiled, and once more held out his hand to her. She slipped hers into it, and in an understanding too deep and perfect to have need of words, they turned and went out together into the sunshine.